CW00375994

NO PLAIN

F. C. D. Hansen

ARTHUR H. STOCKWELL LTD.
Torrs Park   Ilfracombe   Devon
Established 1898
www.ahstockwell.co.uk

© F.C.D. Hansen, 2003
First published in Great Britain, 2003
All rights reserved.
No part of this publication may be reproduced
or transmitted in any form or by any means,
electronic or mechanical, including photocopy,
recording, or any information storage and
retrieval system, without permission
in writing from the copyright holder.

British Library Cataloguing-in-Publication Data.
A catalogue record for this book is available
from the British Library.

These are entirely fictional stories,
and no conscious attempt has been made
to accurately record or recreate
any real-life events.

ISBN 0 7223 3553-9
Printed in Great Britain by
Arthur H. Stockwell Ltd.
Torrs Park   Ilfracombe
Devon

Contents

No Plain Sailing

Chapter 1

Brief Ecounters

Jeff Cavanagh drove his car into the garage, got out and closed the garage doors. He looked at his detached four bedroomed house and gave a little sigh. After an exhilarating afternoon on his sailing boat he was loth to go indoors on such a lovely day. He went to the front door, inserted his key and entered. "It's me Ruby" he called to his wife.

"I'm in the dining room."

The door opened and a plump elderly woman appeared. Jeff greeted her with "Oh hello Mrs Richings, everything all right?"

"Yes Mr Cavanagh, I'm just finishing getting the meal ready."

"Right." He went into the dining room. It was a large, long room with doors opening on to a terrace at the rear.

By the doors was a wheelchair and in it a pleasant looking woman of about forty. She moved the chair forward. "Did you have a nice sail Jeff?" she enquired.

Jeff looked at her slightly wan face. He could still feel the glow from the sea breeze on his own cheeks. "It's a good day for sailing, today. I wish you could have been there." He was thinking of the days they both went sailing when they were first married, and he and Ruby spent most of their spare time in the summer sailing the Channel.

There was a lull in their activity when Ruby became pregnant, but when the baby Eleanor was a year old they all went together. The child was a good sailor and was never any trouble. By the time she was six she was like an extra hand on the boat.

Then disaster fell. Ruby contracted sclerosis. Gradual at first, the symptoms left her feeling weak and tired. Over the next few years each attack left her a bit weaker but now it appeared to have stabilised, so although she was unable to move about freely, she could use her arms and brain. She was not able to stand for any length of time so they had decided to get someone in to prepare the evening meal, and in Mrs Richings they had found the ideal person. She lived only five or ten minutes' walk away so there was no problem with travelling.

Mrs Richings re-entered the room. "Dinner will be ready in about ten minutes Mr Cavanagh."

"Right, I'll nip upstairs and tidy up."

When he came down he asked after Eleanor, their seventeen-year-old daughter.

"She's out with her friends. They're having a meal then going to the theatre in Chichester" said Ruby. "It's funny she's become such a landlubber. How she used to like sailing with us, or with you particularly. Then suddenly she didn't want to go any more. She was about twelve wasn't she?"

Jeff thought back to the time when Eleanor last went out with him. It was about two years after Ruby had first fallen ill. He had brought the boat in and tied up. As they did so a man hurried up to Jeff, they spoke a few words and then went down into the tiny cabin. The man left after a few minutes and Jeff took Eleanor home. On the way back Jeff told Eleanor that she could not go with him the next week as that man was going with him instead. Eleanor seemed to lose interest and she never asked to go again, and Jeff never pressed her. "Yes, twelve or thirteen" Jeff answered. "Most children change at that age, get other interests. Perhaps she didn't want to develop muscles" he added jokingly.

'No it wasn't that' thought Ruby, 'it was that man Jeff had taken on the boat. She had taken an instant dislike to him and thought he was evil. And Jeff's attitude has changed too,' she mused. 'He has not slept with me for all these years. In the same room, yes, but he does not seem to want me physically any more.' She sighed, 'Our lives are finished, romantically that is. I wonder what Jeff really feels?'

Over on the other side of town, in a house in a slightly more affluent suburb, two people glared at each other. They were Lionel and Priscilla Bulmer. They had been bickering ever since Lionel had returned from his car showroom. He was not staying in for dinner, and so Priscilla was feeling decidedly put out.

"Where are you going, and who with?" she almost yelled at him.

"I'm going with friends, that's all you need to know."

"But what if I need you urgently? Where will you be?"

"You don't ever need me urgently so that's irrelevant" he said sarcastically.

Priscilla sank into a chair. She knew what he was referring to. Their first years of marriage had been as good as anyone could expect, but it was later, when they were more familiar with each other that Lionel had begun to make demands on her which she found went against her natural inclinations. He had tried to change their lovemaking into something bordering on the sadistic and he became intolerably rough, so that when he came near her she only felt repugnance. Lionel had become unsatisfied. Priscilla was non-cooperative, so it was not long before he began to seek another more willing partner. He gave Priscilla no indication of what he was doing, to her he was just "going out".

She felt she needed some fresh air so she picked up her handbag and a jacket, went out to her car and drove down to the marina. She parked the car and then walked along the quayside, watching the boats coming in as evening approached.

Jeff Cavanagh dropped the sail and stowed it. He started the engine and edged the boat gently towards his berth in the marina. He could almost do it blindfolded now, and within a few minutes he had secured the boat. He looked up when he felt he was being watched and spotted Priscilla strolling along the quayside. She was almost opposite him now. He called "Hello Mrs Bulmer, nice evening."

"Hello Mr Cavanagh, haven't seen you for a while."

Jeff looked at her admiringly. He knew her husband Lionel from having given him the order for his new fleet of taxis a couple of years previously. He had thought Lionel was hard but he had got a fair deal from him in the end, and it was good to keep the trade in the town.

Priscilla stopped opposite the boat and watched Jeff stowing things away. "How often do you sail?" she asked, just for something to say.

"Every week throughout the summer if I can" he answered.

"Rather you than me" said Priscilla, "I'm the world's worst sailor. I even get queasy on the Isle of Wight ferry."

"That's a bit of a drawback, I know, but for anyone who gets their sea-legs quickly there is nothing to compare with being under sail in a stiff breeze."

"I'll take your word for it, I'll stick to my car."

Jeff looked at his watch. "Six o'clock, a bit too early for a drink" he said "but how about a cup of tea over at the cafe?"

Priscilla hesitated, then said "Well yes, I'd like one."

They crossed the road and strolled down the street to the corner where there was a small restaurant. They found a table and sat down. Jeff ordered a pot of tea.

They chatted for a while and then, because their common point of interest was Lionel, Jeff asked "And how is Lionel these days? I haven't seen him for months."

"Oh he's fine, keeping pretty busy, so I don't see much of him." She bit her lip. She realised that saying that was unnecessary.

Jeff had noted her slight air of frustration as she spoke, but he did not pursue that line of conversation.

"Do you always sail alone?" asked Priscilla.

"Yes, I do now" Jeff replied, "my wife used to be my sailmate but I'm afraid she can't manage it any more, not since she became poorly."

Priscilla sympathised. "I have heard about her. How is she by the way?"

"Well, she has her off days and on days, but generally she is only partly mobile although in herself she is as bright as she ever was. Eleanor, my daughter, helps of course, but she is busy growing up and finishing her education so we do not expect her to be a home help all the time."

As he spoke Jeff was studying Priscilla's face. He liked what he saw, she was near his age and was quite attractive. He wondered how her marriage was working out. She had seemed rueful when talking of Lionel, but there was nothing about her to suggest that she was unhappy. All the same, if Lionel was not there, meaning at home, perhaps there was something not quite right. It had been a long time since he and Ruby had — he sighed, he found himself having thoughts about Priscilla.

Priscilla said "I must go now, thanks for the tea."

"Oh it was nothing, but I really enjoyed your company."

"Yes so did I."

She waited, and that was Jeff's cue to say "If you should be by the marina next Saturday I shall most likely be around, so if you feel like a cup of tea and some conversation I'll look out for you."

"You're on" she laughed.

Then Jeff said "My name's Jeff, and most people, except my bank manager, call me that."

"Thank you Jeff, I'm Priscilla and it is not shortened."

They parted at the door. Jeff walked back to the marina car park, found his car and unlocked it.

As he was about to get in a man in a dark blue reefer jacket came up to him. "Jeff, where's the stuff? You should have got it last week."

"I told you not to come here. Get in the car quick, out of sight." He got in and Jeff said, "I'm doing the best I can. I can't help it if they don't show up. If the weather is bad we have to wait. I shall try again tomorrow, if they don't come leave it till next week."

"Just you remember, don't double-cross me or you'll regret it, and I'm not kidding" said the man.

"You're taking a risk being seen here, now go!"

The man left and Jeff sped away as quickly as he could.

Monday morning came, Priscilla got up and went down to prepare breakfast. She used the kitchen as a breakfast room because the builders were completing an extension to their house and it had necessitated stripping the dining room. At eight o'clock Lionel came down, grabbed a quick breakfast of toast and marmalade and tea, and by half-past he was off to the showroom.

Neither of them were particularly talkative in the mornings so their conversation was mainly about their breakfast requirements.

"Tea?"

"Yes please."

"Toast?"

"No thanks."

After he had gone there was the sound of another vehicle in the drive. It was the young builder Bill Hopkins. Only twenty-five, Bill had built up a small business by virtue of his thorough work and pleasant nature. He had been recommended to them by a car mechanic who serviced Lionel's used cars. Priscilla went out to the dining room and unlocked the patio doors.

"Morning Mrs Bulmer, nice morning again." Bill Hopkins was dressed in his brown overalls ready to start.

"Good morning Bill" said Priscilla. "What's the score then, have you got a final date yet?"

"Well that's always difficult" answered Bill. "Right now we have about three days' work before the plasterers come in. Give them a week or so providing they come on time. After that we come back to do skirtings and doors and things like that, and then the final decorating, that's if you have chosen the wallpapers. Say four weeks, give or take a bit, but that's not a promise, there's many a slip you know" he laughed. He was like a breath of fresh air, but then he was hardly more than a boy, and probably had not had many downs compared to the ups.

"Well, I promise I'll not delay you over the wallpaper" said Priscilla.

She left him and returned to the kitchen. Nothing much to do that day; Tuesday and Thursday there was the charity shop, Wednesday she was stand-by driver for meals on wheels, Friday was her main shopping day and that was that. She would have liked to have something more demanding to do but she was not trained for anything. She could have helped Lionel with the car sales business but he said her place was there, he would be the earner. She could not complain, they were fairly well off and never wanted for anything. They always went abroad for two weeks every year, usually with two or three other couples who were connected with the car business. On these occasions Lionel was almost his old self and would make love to her as he used to, but she felt that he expected more and this inhibited her somewhat.

The week dragged on, she found herself thinking about Jeff Cavanagh. She wondered about his poor wife Ruby. 'She is probably just as frustrated as I am,' thought Priscilla.

Saturday afternoon Priscilla made a special effort and groomed herself until she felt confident enough for anything. Lionel would not be back till after six, this was his busy day. She went out to the car and drove into town. Avoiding the marina she went further out to the cinema car park and then strolled back towards the quayside, looking out to sea and half watching the sailing boats bobbing around out there.

It was well after six when she spotted Jeff's boat making for the marina. Suddenly she felt nervous, almost guilty about being there, but this feeling disappeared when she saw Jeff chug into his berth and tie up.

He looked up, saw Priscilla and gave her a big grin. 'This is nice' he thought, 'having someone to welcome me in.'

Priscilla approached the boat. "Hello Jeff, thought I'd get some sea air. How was your trip?"

"Trip? Not a trip, more of a haphazard manoeuvring about for three hours, but it certainly blows the cobwebs away." He jumped on to the quayside and joined her. "How about a nice cup of tea, or would you like something a bit stronger?"

"Oh no, tea will be fine" said Priscilla, "I'm driving anyway so it will not be wise to have anything stronger."

"I'll tell you what" said Jeff, "you wait here, I'll get my car and we'll go out to Arundel and have some tea there, then no one will be any the wiser." He looked at Priscilla, saw her slight frown and said "I mean, I don't want to compromise you, you know, both being married and all that."

"Yes" said Priscilla slowly, "perhaps it would be as well."

Jeff picked up his gear, hurried over the road to the car park and brought the car round to the quay. Priscilla jumped in and they sped away on the road to Arundel. As they drove through the Sussex countryside they found they were content to be in each other's company.

'This is how Lionel and I should be,' she thought, 'enjoying life and sharing the moment.'

Jeff drove well; with years of driving experience behind him handling a car was second nature to him. Priscilla stole a glance at him as he drove expertly along the ring road.

He was looking straight ahead, never taking his eyes off the road, yet he felt he was being watched. He spoke, "Everything all right?"

"Oh yes" replied Priscilla, "I'm fine, and enjoying the ride."

They soon arrived in Arundel. Jeff found the car park and they walked to the cafe.

Outside the cafe Priscilla suddenly said "I'm not bothered about tea, let's stroll around."

"A good idea" answered Jeff.

They walked up the hill and round the castle walls. As they wandered along, chatting about nothing in particular, it felt natural that Jeff should take her arm. For the next ten minutes Priscilla found herself walking with a much lighter step. She was happy and relaxed, her husband was forgotten and she was a young vibrant woman again in the company of a pleasant young man. Jeff felt that Priscilla was happy. He looked at her and saw the radiance in her sparkling eyes and slightly flushed cheeks. They walked right round the town and eventually arrived at the car park.

"I'm afraid I'll have to get back now" said Jeff. "I try not to — ."

"I know" broke in Priscilla. "You have your obligations and I wouldn't want to prevent you from fulfilling them. Let's go then."

They were silent on the drive back. Something had happened, they were changed from the two people who had set out earlier. They reached the marina and Priscilla reminded him that her car was by the cinema, so Jeff drove down into the car park. He applied the handbrake then turned to Priscilla and said "I would like it very much if we could spend some more time together. What do you like doing?"

"I'm fond of music and good plays. I'm too old for discos but I like dancing, and I like the open air."

Jeff thought this meant 'yes' to his first question. "I can get away most weekday afternoons, as I don't need to be there all the time" said Jeff, "so if afternoons would suit you I'll leave the choice of day to you."

"Afternoons are fine, I suppose" said Priscilla, "but that doesn't give one much choice of entertainment as most shows and concerts are in the evening."

"We could go to Brighton and play bingo on the pier" said Jeff, laughing out loud, "or go on the roller coaster at Littlehampton." He quietened down and then said "You are quite right, afternoons are not the best time for adult entertainment, so what do you suggest?"

Priscilla felt deflated. Their pleasant early evening jaunt was now tinged with guilt, and any future meetings would be just the same. "Leave it till next Saturday after your sailing" said Priscilla suddenly. "We need time to think about it."

Jeff was subdued. "I think you are right" he said, "but one afternoon wouldn't hurt anyone, would it?"

Priscilla remembered her obligations at home; the builders were still there so she couldn't leave the house unattended during the daytime. She explained this to Jeff who could see the reason in it, so they agreed to meet the following Saturday at the quay.

Priscilla said goodbye and went to her car. Jeff watched her leave then drove home to Ruby.

Bill Hopkins was in the bar at the Royal Oak. He was with his mates as usual on a Friday, having a few beers before going to the disco. He was really over the age for discos but how else could he meet girls? He looked at his friends, three chaps of similar age to his, all single and in a bit of a rut.

"Let's skip the disco" said Bill on an impulse. "What say we go to the Eversleigh. They've got a great group playing and singing there this weekend." The others agreed. "OK then, drink up and we'll get down there."

They left the pub and walked down the street. They came to a row of Victorian houses and started to cross the road. A car drew into the kerb near them as they waited. A woman who had been waiting at the door of one of the houses ran out to the car. The man had got out and opened the passenger door. The woman got in, the driver returned to his seat and they drove away.

"Did you see that?" Bill called to his mates.

"What? See what?" one of them answered.

"Those two. That was that Lionel Bulmer, the bloke I'm doing some work for."

"What about it then?" asked one of them.

"He was with that old tart Wendy Truman. Fancy leaving his wife at home for that old banger. I'll bet she doesn't know what's going on." He looked back at the house and made a mental note of the number, '56 Prospect Road. Poor Mrs Bulmer,' he thought.

The weeks passed. Priscilla had not been to the quay again as she had been obliged to stay at home as much as possible. The builders had finished and she was busy putting everything straight, getting new curtains and making the place more like home.

In his office Bill Hopkins struggled with the paperwork and finally finished the account for the work at Lionel Bulmer's house. He put it in the post that night.

Three days later he received a telephone call from Lionel asking him to be at the house that evening.

'Well well' thought Bill, 'I wouldn't have thought he would be ready to pay up as quickly as this.'

He was right. When he arrived at the Bulmers' house and went into the sitting room Lionel blurted out quite suddenly, "I'm not paying this. For a start it's much more than the estimate, and for another thing your vehicles have messed up my drive, so I want that done."

Bill was taken aback but he kept cool and said "Of course it's more than the estimate, there was a lot of rotten timber that only came to light when we started cutting out for the extension. I told you all about it at the time, and as far as I'm concerned you agreed to it. As for the drive, well perhaps we did slightly damage the surface, so I'll regravel the parts that are affected and roll it in."

"I'm not paying all that extra" shouted Lionel.

"We'll have to see" said Bill, and he left the house.

Later that week Bill sent some men and a lorry with the gravel and they did all the patches as he had promised. He then resubmitted the account and waited. He also phoned his solicitor and told him what had transpired. Bill was advised to wait for Bulmer's reaction.

This came about ten days later. Bulmer phoned Bill and told him to come round when he would pay the amount of the contract but not the extras. Again Bill went to the house.

Priscilla showed him in, whispering quickly "I'm sorry about this but there's nothing I can do."

"It's all right Mrs Bulmer, don't you worry." He went in.

Lionel was sitting at the side table. He got up and came across to Bill. In his hand he had a cheque. "This is for £2,500, the final amount left on the contract. That's all you are getting. You can write on the bill 'In full and final settlement of the account'."

"Mr Bulmer, I am entitled to be paid for the extra work I have carried out, £3,000, plus the £2,500 balance from the main contract, that's £5,500, as it says on the account. If I don't get it I shall ask my solicitor to take action."

"Don't you threaten me with solicitors, I know more about them than you do." Lionel put the cheque back on the table.

Bill felt his temper rising. He took a deep breath and looked at Bulmer. "I wonder what Mrs Bulmer would say if she knew her husband was going with a tart in town?"

"Are you threatening me? Well I don't care if she knows, so you go ahead and tell her, I shall deny it anyway."

There was nothing Bill could say so he just walked out.

The next day Bill told his solicitor of his second meeting with Bulmer. He was advised to wait a month before taking action.

Later that day Bill phoned Mrs Bulmer. He knew that Lionel was at the showroom so he arranged to go over to see her straightaway.

When he arrived Priscilla let him in. "Now" she said, "what's all this important information?"

"Your husband refused to pay me the balance of my account and I said suppose I tell you about his goings on, and he said he didn't care, so as I didn't like the idea of you being two-timed here I am." Bill stopped, slightly embarrassed.

"You'd better tell me then, if I haven't guessed already."

Bill told her as calmly as he could about seeing Lionel with that

13

woman and how sorry he felt for Priscilla.

"Thank you Bill" said Priscilla when he had finished. "I half suspected something might be going on, but now that I know, it has made everything clearer for me. I can't do anything about your money, but if you do need backing up in any legal action I shall be pleased to help you."

Bill left the house feeling very sorry for Priscilla. 'How could that Bulmer prefer a tart to his lovely wife? He's an absolute rotter.' He found himself seething with hatred of Bulmer.

Back in the house Priscilla slumped into a chair and heaved a big sigh. 'So it has come to this has it!' she thought. 'He's not only unfaithful but with a woman who is nothing more than a prostitute!' It was too much. The thought of Lionel coming near her was now unbearable, but she knew what she had to do. She went to the phone, looked up a firm of solicitors and tapped in the number. "I wish to start proceedings for a divorce" she said. Then she went upstairs and packed.

Jeff sat in his office at his hire car and taxi business centre. The phone rang, Jeff lifted the receiver. "Hello" he said.

"Jeff, it's Tim here." Tim Freshman was his foreman who ran the taxi side of the business like clockwork. "There's a Mrs Arundel on the line, wants to speak to you personally."

"OK put her through. Yes, hello."

"Is that Jeff Cavanagh?"

"Yes, speaking."

"This is Priscilla."

Now Jeff recognised the voice. "Priscilla" he said with obvious pleasure, "I was wondering what had happened to you."

"Listen Jeff" Priscilla said slightly breathlessly, "I have left Lionel and I am at my mother's. I am starting proceedings for a divorce. The reason I am ringing is to ask you not to try and see me as it might be seen as an act of unfaithfulness and could jeopardise my petition." She waited.

Jeff thought for a moment. "May I ask what are your grounds for a divorce?"

"Lionel has been unfaithful. I know who it was, or is, and I don't want you involved."

"Of course, I quite understand. I shall keep out of your way until it's all over. I shall want to see you then."

"Thank you Jeff. I won't give you my mother's address or phone number, so you must wait to hear from me. It may be a long time."

"Whatever you say is all right with me" said Jeff, "take care."

"Thanks, I will. Bye for now." Priscilla rang off.

The prison recreation room was almost empty. In one of the armchairs sat Bandy Truman, nearing the end of a four year sentence for robbery with violence. His wife Wendy had not come to see him because it would be only another week before his release. He looked up as he heard the others coming back from the visitors' room. His mate Albert French came over to him and sat down. "Hello Frenchy, anything new?"

Albert French always had titbits of news and today was no exception. "You're not going to like this Bandy, but my missus says your missus is having it off with some well-off bloke."

"'Ere, 'ow does she know what my missus is doing, eh? Answer me that." Bandy was clearly rattled.

"She says she's seen 'em going off in the car together."

"That don't mean nothin'" retorted Bandy. "Who was it then?"

"Bloke called Lionel Bulmer. Has that car showroom in Crantock Road. He's married, lives a bit out of the town."

"If that's true I'll kill 'im, and 'er as well perhaps."

"Steady on Bandy, nobody's worth that, give 'er a good hiding and show 'er who's boss, that should do it."

"We'll see what she has to say about it next Wednesday when I get out."

The following morning Bandy was putting away his towel and soap when in came one of the warders. "Right Truman, jacket on quickly, the governor wants to see you."

"What's it all about then?" asked Bandy.

"No idea, you'll find out soon enough."

They reached the governor's office, the officer knocked, a voice said "Enter", the officer opened the door and marched Bandy in.

"Ah Truman." The governor didn't seem unfriendly. "I expect you are wondering why I have sent for you, eh?" He looked up at Bandy, saying "You're due out on Wednesday next, right?"

"Yes sir" said Bandy.

"Well, there's a change of plan. We need space here next week, so your release date has been brought forward to this Friday, the day after tomorrow. So tomorrow you will prepare for your release by handing in library books, collecting outstanding laundry and not sending any new laundry. Your pay and other legal entitlements will be dealt with on Friday. You may have one free phone call to inform your wife of your change of date. Any questions?"

"No sir, thank you sir. I'll not phone the wife, I think I'll surprise her instead."

"Right then Truman, that's up to you. Good luck."

They marched out and back to the cell. Alone again, he thought over this turn of events and started to plan how he would surprise

Wendy.

That Thursday evening , as Wendy Truman was getting ready to wash her hair the phone rang. She answered "Hello."

"Is that you Wendy? This is Lionel."

"Oh Lionel, nothing up, is there?"

"No, far from it. My wife has gone off so there's no one at my house. I need some comforting."

"Well, you know I can help you there, but this time it will have to be something special, you see —" she hesitated, "— my husband George is coming home next week. You know, he's been away on a trades mission somewhere or other."

"Oh blast! Well, there's only one thing for it — you come to my place for the whole weekend. We'll have champagne and anything that comes after —."

"That sounds delightful. darling. What time will you pick me up?"

"Around six o'clock tomorrow evening. I'll come round straight from the showroom."

"I'll be ready and waiting. Bye." She rang off. 'A last fling,' she thought.

On the bus from Southsea to Chichester Bandy Truman had time to think out how he would confront Wendy. He would like to surprise them together, that would give him the excuse he needed to give Bulmer a real bashing. He did not know when the two of them would be meeting, but he guessed that it would be that night or more likely the next day — Saturday. The bus sped on towards Chichester.

When the bus reached the terminal Bandy picked up his holdall and went over to a call box. He put in a coin, dialled his home number and waited. He recognised Wendy's voice as she gave her number. He hung up immediately, retrieved his coin and went into the tea bar. Over a cup of tea he thought very carefully about his next move. His wife was at home and he wanted to keep an eye on her to catch her with Bulmer. What he needed was a car that he could sit in near his home. He had a credit card, a current driving licence and a home address so he would be able to get a hire car for a couple of days. He could stay at a bed and breakfast place for a night or perhaps two.

He finished his tea, got up and went outside to a phone box. There were no phone books in there but on the wall were several business cards for taxis and hire cars. He noted two of them and set off to find them. There was no problem with getting a small car for two days, and the transaction was soon completed.Whilst in the office he asked to see their phone book for the area. He found the name Bulmer and noted the address. He knew the road. What he did not know was where and when the two would be meeting again. He could not keep watch for twenty-four hours, he needed information about Wendy.

Suddenly he brightened up. 'Albert French's missis,' he thought. 'She if anyone, will know about Wendy.'

He drove to the street next to his own, parked the car and walked to the end of his street. The end house but one was Albert French's and that was where Bandy went. He banged on the door.

After a minute the door opened and Mrs French peered out. When she saw him she gasped, "Bandy! I thought you were in — ."

Bandy pushed his way into the hall and closed the door behind him. "Listen!" Bandy had assumed a threatening attitude. "I don't want anyone knowing I'm here, right?"

Mrs French nodded, she knew Bandy could be rough.

"Now, what do you know about my missis? What's she doing this weekend?"

"All I know is her bloke is taking her out tonight. She might not be back tonight she told me."

"Who is he?" Bandy needed confirmation.

"He's Mr Bulmer from the showroom."

"Right. I shall stay here till about six o'clock, then I shall bring my car round to your front door. I shall sit there and wait to see if he turns up. You keep away from that phone, do you hear?"

"All right Bandy." Mrs French was frightened.

Lionel Bulmer whistled as he closed the drawer of his desk. He was always last to leave. He locked the drawer, left the office and locked the door. He went through the showroom where the head salesman was waiting to lock the outer doors. When all was secure they went to their respective cars.

"Good night Mr Bulmer, see you in the morning."

"Yes. Good night."

Bulmer got into his sleek red car and drove off. When he got to Prospect Road Wendy Truman was waiting just inside the door. She saw him pull in, grabbed her overnight bag and went out, locking the door behind her. She ran round to the passenger door and got in.

At the end of the street Bandy sitting in his hire car saw everything. He got out and went into Frenchy's house. "I'll just check up." He lifted the phone and tapped the number, there was no reply. "Right. I'll kill that bitch, and him. Don't you go phoning anybody or you'll regret it." He left quickly and went out to the car.

Bulmer drove straight to his home with Wendy Truman. They went into the front hall.

"Mmm, this is nice, isn't it" said Wendy, "It's very posh."

"Yes, it has only recently been finished. Come upstairs and I will show you where you can tidy up if you need to." He carried her case up to the large bedroom that was his and Priscilla's. "Come down when you are ready and we'll have a drink."

He went into the kitchen and selected some ingredients for a quick meal. He was not entirely useless when it came to rustling up something quickly, and he soon had things organised.

He heard Wendy come down. He went through to the sitting room and over to the drinks cabinet. "What would you like? The champagne comes later."

"Gin and tonic please, with ice if you've got it."

"Of course we've got it. Never without it." He wondered why he had said that, it was a kind of a 'put down'. He finished pouring the drinks and they sat down. "I've got a couple of things ready in the kitchen, so when we've had these perhaps you could come and give me a hand with the microwave."

"I'm not too sure about the microwave" said Wendy, "but I can manage the electric cooker or gas."

Lionel left her to carry on while he went into the dining room. He placed mats and cutlery for two, looked at the two candles on the table and decided against lighting them. He took a bottle of hock from the sideboard and removed the cork. 'Take too long to cool it, and this isn't a proper dinner anyway' he thought.

He returned to the kitchen where Wendy was already serving up the meal on two plates. Lionel put them on a tray and carried them into the dining room. Wendy followed, bringing two dishes of fruit and cream which she put on the sideboard.

As they sat there Wendy looked around the room, taking note of the furnishings and the polished furniture, then down to the expensive rug. "I must say it's really lovely the way you've done it."

"Well it wasn't really me, my wife chose the colour schemes and fabrics."

"I'd give my eye teeth for a place like this" she prattled on.

She was beginning to irritate him a bit. He thought how graceful Priscilla had looked when at the dining room table, whereas Wendy — he dismissed the thought from his mind. It was only a few days since Priscilla had gone, but already he was feeling guilty about Wendy being there at their table. "Have some more wine Wendy."

"I don't mind if I do, and why don't you, you're not driving anywhere tonight."

They finished their wine then went through to the sitting room. Lionel poured two liqueurs and brought them to the small table. They sat on the settee together sipping the liqueur.

"You'll get me tiddly with all this stuff. I'll bet you're doing it on purpose so that you can have your way with me." She laughed out loud. "Not that you haven't already before now" she giggled.

Lionel was silent. He was struggling inwardly to recreate the lustful feeling Wendy engendered when they had been in a different environment. It seemed that being there any sexual activity would be a violation. He had been going to take Wendy into his and Priscilla's room but as these irritating doubts flitted through his mind he decided that the spare room was good enough for her. After all, she was really only a tart, but she did have a way of satisfying him that Priscilla couldn't or wouldn't take part in. "Have you finished your liqueur?"he asked.

Wendy put her glass down. "Yes" she said, "now I'm ready for anything." She laughed again.

"Right then, let's —." Lionel never finished what he was going to say. As he was speaking there was a terrific crash as the front door was flung open and crashed into the coat and hat stand behind it. "What the hell was that?" shouted Lionel.

He started for the door, but at that moment Bandy Truman burst through from the hall and into the sitting room. "George!" screamed Wendy, "what are you doing here?"

Lionel looked from one to the other."George? George who?" he shouted.

"George bloody Truman, and that's my missis!" Bandy had obviously put a few whiskies away before setting out for the Bulmers' house. He lurched towards Lionel, looking very menacing, and without any warning he swung his left clenched fist in a backward arc. The back of the fist caught Lionel full in the face and he fell back on to the settee.

Wendy screamed "Don't hit him George!"

"Get out of my way woman." Bandy grabbed her arm and dragged her towards the door. "Get out and don't interfere! I'll get to you later." He turned towards Lionel who was struggling up from the settee.

"You get out of my house and take her with you!" yelled Lionel. He moved towards Bandy as if to strike him.

Bandy stood stock still. "I know how to deal with your sort" he growled. Whilst moving forward his right hand had slipped into his jacket pocket. When he pulled it out he was holding a wicked-looking short-bladed dagger. When Lionel saw the knife he rushed toward Bandy intending to hit him before he could wield it, but Bandy was experienced in violence as his record proved. His right arm came up and down as Lionel rushed him. The knife penetrated Lionel's chest. Lionel stopped dead, a look of disbelief on his face, but before he could say or do anything Bandy pulled the knife out, plunged it once more into Lionel's chest and left it there.

Wendy was screaming "George! George! Come off him! You'll

19

kill him."

"And bloody good riddance too!" Bandy pushed her once more towards the door. "Get outside!" he shouted, "I'm going to get my knife." He turned back towards Lionel.

Wendy stood by the door watching the drama unfold but she was horrified by what she witnessed next. Lionel was kneeling on the floor tugging at the knife. His face was ashen and it was clear he was weakening. Bandy moved towards him. As he bent down to get his knife, Lionel pulled the knife free and with one mighty circular stroke he slashed the blade across Bandy's neck. It cut right through the jugular. Bandy was still reaching for the knife as he fell almost alongside the sitting Lionel who was swaying. He looked down at the knife in his hand then threw it to one side. He sank gently backwards against the settee, took a deep breath and expired.

Wendy had seen more than she could bear. She ran wildly out into the driveway and down the road where a passer-by managed to calm her long enough to get the gist of what had happened in the Bulmers' house.

Jeff Cavanagh's boat was gently rocking at anchor some fifteen miles out in the Channel. He'd been waiting over an hour and had spent the time stretched out on a bunk. He liked to be back in the marina well before the sun went down, so he was fidgeting about in his impatience.

"Ahoy there!" the voice cut through his reverie.

He jumped up and went up top. Coming in close was a yacht of similar size to his but the port of origin was in France.

As the yacht was steered almost alongside a man called out to him. "Do you want some water mate?"

"Yes, I could do with some."

The man went below then reappeared with a two-gallon water container. He tied a line to the handle and with a deft swing deposited the container on Jeff's boat. Jeff quickly untied the line, retied it to an identical container and tossed it towards the man who then hauled in the line. It was all over in less than two minutes, and the other boat was soon under way and out to sea.

Jeff took the container below. He poured some water from it into a mug, sniffed it then tasted it. "That'll do" he said to himself. He then emptied the container of its small amount of water into the sink and replaced the large screw cap.

He hauled up the anchor and set sail for home. It was almost two hours later that he drifted into his berth in the marina. He had had to use the engine most of the way because the wind had dropped and he was barely moving. He secured the boat then went below to collect his belongings.

Two men in uniform approached the boat. "Ahoy Mr Cavanagh! Can we come aboard?" They were the two customs officials who periodically checked.

"Yes. Come down below, nothing to declare," he laughed.

They looked around, checked the heads and bilges and all the odd little corners and cubbyholes found on yachts.

"Seems all clear sir. Did you have a nice trip?"

"It was all right outward but the wind dropped and I had to motor most of the way home."

"Well thanks a lot. Cheerio." They left.

Jeff packed up his things. He took a quick look outside and saw the retreating backs of the customs men. Then he dived back down and picked up the water container, then he came up, closed the hatch and was just about to lock it when a voice behind him said, "Excuse me sir, but could I trouble you to leave the hatch open, I would like to check." There were two different officials standing on the side.

"Certainly" said Jeff affably, "but I've just had a visit from the two regular officers."

"Yes, we know. We have to double check occasionally."

"OK go ahead."

One of them went below, the other stayed next to Jeff.

After a short while the official reappeared from below saying "All seems to be OK down there. Now if you don't mind I'd like to look at your water container."

Jeff blanched. "Certainly officer." He handed it over.

The officer took the container, unscrewed the cap and sniffed the inside. He then tipped it up as if to empty it then peered into the neck. He shook it a couple of times then said to Jeff, "Could you come over to the office and bring your belongings. Lock the hatch. I'll take the water container."

When they got to the office the officer put the water container on the table, tapped it all over and put it on the floor. "I'm sorry sir, but I'll have to trouble you to submit to a search. If all is satisfactory you will be on your way home in twenty minutes."

They went into an adjoining room. One of the officers took Jeff's jacket and said, "While I am looking at this could you please undress down to your underpants."

Jeff slowly removed his shirt and shoes. Then with an air of resignation he undid his zip, lowered his trousers and stepped out of them.

The senior of the two officers said politely "Would you please sit on this chair."

Jeff complied, then sat in embarrassed silence as the officer slowly undid the plastic packages taped to Jeff's legs below the knees and placed them on the table.

"Right, you may dress now. Please remain here while I fetch my colleague."

In a moment he returned with a man carrying some instruments. He put them on the table. took one of the packages and slit it open. He poured some of the contents into a small crucible and proceeded to carry out a test on the powder. He did this with each of the four packages, then he spoke briefly to the officer and then left the room.

The officer then turned to Jeff who had said nothing while all this was going on. "I am going to reseal these packets and label them. We believe them to contain cocaine. So Jeffrey Cavanagh, I am arresting you for being in possession of a narcotic substance and must warn you that —" he went on to complete the warning.

Jeff heard the caution as if from far away. He was caught. He had got away with it for four years and had put away a tidy sum of money, but now it was over. He had been doing it for Ruby. She would need full medical attention as the sclerosis worsened, and he was aiming to give her the best chance he could. The money had been put into a trust fund for Ruby, to be used for her treatment if the need arose. He wondered if they could confiscate it.

"You may telephone your solicitor."

Jeff came to with a start. "Yes, right, I'll phone now. What about my wife? She's a semi-invalid and needs someone there. My daughter's only seventeen, she can't be responsible for her mother all the time."

"Tell your solicitor and he'll arrange it. "You'll see the magistrate on Monday and then you'll know about bail."

Jeff went to the phone.

Priscilla's mother was resting quietly on the settee. It was Saturday afternoon and they had just had a light lunch.

Priscilla was in her room when the phone rang. "I'll get it" she called to her mother. She went into the hall. "Hello, Brighton 07843."

"I wish to speak to Mrs Bulmer, is she there?"

"I am Mrs Bulmer. Who is calling?"

"This is the East Sussex Police. Can I ask you to remain there for the next half-hour. You will be having a visit from one of our officers."

"Why, what's it about?"

"The officer will give you the details when she comes. Thank you madam, goodbye."

Less than fifteen minutes later there was a ring at the door. Priscilla answered and in reply to the WPC's enquiry said "Yes, I'm Priscilla Bulmer. Please come in."

When they were sitting down the WPC said "I'm afraid I have

some bad news for you."

"Is it my husband?"

"Yes, I'm afraid it is." The WPC went on to give Priscilla the outline of what they had found at the house. "So, Mrs Bulmer, when you feel up to it we would like you to come and identify the body."

While the WPC had been talking Priscilla had been trying to imagine the whole ghastly scene. Two people killed in their home, one of them Lionel, her husband. If she had not walked out on him perhaps this would never have happened. "Who was the other man?" she asked.

"We have not as yet had the positive identification but we believe it to be a Mr Truman. The woman with your husband at the time was Mrs Truman. I'm sorry, Mrs Bulmer."

Priscilla composed herself. "What happens now?" she asked.

"First the identification, then later on there will be the inquest. We don't know how long we shall have to wait for that, it may be weeks."

"Thank you. I'd like to get the identification over, please. I'll just tell my mother, she's in the next room. Will you be taking me or do I come on my own?"

"Oh no, we'll take you there and back. Take your time, when you are ready we'll go."

Priscilla went into her mother and told her the whole story. She then found that in the retelling she was overwhelmed with genuine sorrow and the tears streamed down her cheeks.

With all his faults Lionel had not deserved such a tragic and ignominious end.

She went into her bedroom and tidied her face and then went out to where the WPC was waiting.

The identification was a lot easier than she had imagined it would be. Lionel looked serene, but he had a large discoloration under his left eye. "That's my husband, Lionel Bulmer." She was very calm. After being asked a few more questions she was taken back to her mother's flat in Brighton. It was all over.

It was then that she began to realise that she was alone. She now had no husband, no commitments, the divorce had been eclipsed, and even the house had become a burden after recent events. Priscilla's life was now unfettered. She was free to pursue any activity she chose in order to realise her true potential, but how to do it?

On Sunday afternoon Priscilla and her mother were sitting quietly after lunch. The phone rang, Priscilla answered it.

"Hello, is that Mrs Bulmer?"

"Yes. Who are you?"

"I'm James Clark, head salesman at the showroom. I've only just found out about Lionel and I don't know what to do."

Priscilla was nonplussed, but after a bit of thought she said, "I think you'd better carry on with your usual work, but don't take any big decisions. I can't get into the house as the police have it shut up while they investigate, but I'll tell you what I think I can do. I'll phone the bank manager to see how the business stands with them. They may wish to close it temporarily. After that I'll come to the showroom. We may have to contact the main car distributor's manager."

"Oh, right, thank you Mrs Bulmer. I hope you are feeling all right, are you?"

"Oh yes, Mr Clark, I'm quite recovered from the shock, thank you."

"Right then. We'll see you tomorrow, goodbye."

Priscilla sat for a moment. She had amazed herself by her immediate responses and consequently began to feel a new confidence.

The following day Priscilla phoned the bank manager and told him what had happened and of the salesman's anxieties. The manager was sympathetic and suggested a meeting for later that day.

After lunch she drove over to Chichester. She went to the bank and was soon in the manager's office. "Well Mrs Bulmer" he said after he had expressed his sorrow at the loss of her husband. "You have to realise that our arrangements about the business are all founded on Mr Bulmer's expertise in running a successful enterprise. Somebody else taking over may well result in a reduction of the trading figures. So what I intend to do is put someone in the office there to go over the current situation and assess the immediate potential. If the trend is satisfactory we may, I stress *may* allow the business to continue to the end of the present financial year. Of course the probate office may have something to say about that, but for the time being you and your Mr Clark had better continue. As I say, our man will be there in a couple of days to keep an eye on the cash."

"What about money to live on?" She was quivering as she spoke.

The bank manager sensed her worry. "You have your personal account, Mrs Bulmer, about four thousand I believe."

"Yes, but what about the joint housekeeping account?"

"You can use that up, but there will not be any more. Also, you cannot touch any of your husband's account until probate has been granted."

"And when will that be?"

"A month, maybe two or even three. It depends on the police to a large extent."

"Thank you."

Priscilla left the bank and went straight to the showroom and gave James Clark the plan for the immediate future. They discussed a few areas where she thought she might help.

Then James Clark said "Have you seen the papers yet?"

"No, I haven't" said Priscilla.

"Well, perhaps you'd like to look at this one then." James pushed a copy of the morning paper towards her.

The headline "*Double Killing in Suburbia*" with a picture of their house underneath it gave her a hollow feeling. She felt sick. She started to fold the paper, then stopped suddenly and unfolded it again. Lower down the page was a smaller headline. It read, "*Chichester Man held on Drugs Charge*". There followed a brief account of the arrest of Jeff Cavanagh on his return from a sailing trip in the Channel. Priscilla was shocked. "Oh my God, what next! Poor Ruby!"

"I'll get you a cup of tea" said James, and went into the small kitchen at the back of the showroom.

At the back of her mind Priscilla had always felt that Jeff Cavanagh would perhaps be someone whom she could turn to for help or comfort. Now he too was eliminated. Was there no one except her mother? It seemed not.

When she had finished her tea she took up the phone and rang the police. She asked for DI Ryecroft.

"Hello Mrs Bulmer, we were going to contact you today. There is nothing for you to do at present. The investigation is just about complete and it seems that no one else is involved."

"What about the woman?"

"No. She witnessed the whole episode and she does not appear to have been involved in the violence. The postmortems are being carried out today and the inquest is fixed for Thursday this week. We shall send a car for you to your mother's flat in Brighton. Is that where you are now?"

"No. I'm at the showroom, my husb — my late husband's car sales showroom."

"Yes, I know it. How are you? Do you need anyone to be with you?"

"No, I'm fine thank you. Goodbye." She got up to leave. James came across and asked if she needed anything. "No thanks Mr Clark — James. I shall go back to my mother's now, so if you want me that's where I shall be."

She went out on to the forecourt and made her way to the side where her car was parked. As she reached her car a van turned in and pulled up near her. The door opened and out got a young man. "Hello Mrs Bulmer. I thought I recognised your car so I came in to say hello. I was sorry to hear about Mr Bulmer —."

"Why, it's Bill, how nice to see you."

It was Bill Hopkins the young builder who was still waiting for his account to be settled.

"I know Lionel owed you that money but —."

"Don't worry Mrs Bulmer. I know I shall get it one day, but when I saw you I thought I would ask if I could be of any help during this time. You must have lots of things to do or to worry about."

"Yes Bill, I do. But things are gradually being sorted out. The worst part is that I have no home to go to, as the police have it all sealed up, not that I'd want to go there anyway." She found herself gabbling on. "It wouldn't be the same now after — you know — even with your new extension, so I don't know what I shall be doing after all this is settled. I suppose I shall stay with my —."

"Mrs Bulmer!" Bill's voice was firm. "You are not to worry. If you want me to I can drive you to Brighton and back, or fetch you when you have to come into Chichester. I should be happy to help." He looked at her earnestly. 'God, she's lovely,' he thought.

"Oh Bill, you really are kind. I promise to let you know if I need anything. Thursday will be the worst day I think, you know — the inquest. The police are fetching my mother and me so we should be all right."

"I'll come to the inquest. I'll be there if you want me."

"Thanks Bill. It is nice to know one has real friends." She went to her car and drove off.

Bill got into his van. He felt glad that that rotten Lionel Bulmer was not there any more.

As she drove back to Brighton Priscilla's mind was overrun with conflicting thoughts about Lionel, the bank, the showroom, Jeff Cavanagh's arrest, the inquest and — with some relief — Bill Hopkins. She also thought about Ruby, Jeff's wife. She almost felt guilty about Jeff. She had fancied him, but had that feeling changed, or gone? Yes, she was sorry for Ruby who was unable to enjoy the love of her husband, and if not him — no one. 'We're both without our men, but at least I'm mobile,' she thought. 'I wonder who's looking after her, or Jeff's taxi business?' She and Ruby were in similar circumstances, but how would they overcome the upheavals they were both suffering. At present she could see no further ahead than Thursday — the inquest.

It had been a long day. She was glad to get back to her mother's flat and rest.

On Thursday the police called for her and took her and her mother to Chichester.

Wendy Truman was the only witness to the actual event, so it was on her story that the verdicts were given. Lionel died of two knife wounds inflicted by one George Truman. George Truman died of loss of blood from a single knife wound inflicted in self-defence by

26

one Lionel Bulmer.

When it was over, Priscilla's solicitor took her and her mother to the funeral director's office where she arranged that the following Tuesday would be the day for cremation and burial.

Bill Hopkins had gone to the inquest but had kept out of the way.

Tuesday came and went. Priscilla had remained perfectly calm throughout. It was as if Lionel had been a stranger. Gone was the memory of the man she had married, the past had died with him. She was alone.

Her solicitor had read the will, everything was left to her. Probate had been applied for.

The next few weeks seemed to fly by. She made visits to the showroom, but the business was in a kind of limbo, trade was continuing but on a reduced scale.

Finally, one day the solicitor rang her to say that everything was cleared and she owned the home and the business. She now knew exactly what she was going to do. She rang Bill. "Ah, Bill. Can you meet me at my old home sometime? Yes, I want some work done and I'd like to discuss it. This afternoon? Fine, I'll see you there at two. Goodbye."

That afternoon she drove down to Chichester and with a heavily beating heart she turned into their old drive. Bill's van was there already.

"Hello Mrs Bulmer —."

"Priscilla, if you don't mind."

"Oh, right, Priscilla. You are looking very well."

"I am very well" she replied "and I know why. It's because I am certain of what I am going to do."

"Good for you. So where do I come in?"

"Well, I'm going to sell this place and I want you to go over it top to bottom and give it a new clean appearance. You will have an empty house because I am selling all the contents first."

"Phew! You really are having a clean sweep."

"And that's not all. I am reverting to my maiden name, so I shall be Mrs Priscilla Thurston from now on, and one more thing — here's your cheque for the amount that was owing to you."

"I don't know what to say, but I feel as though the rain had just stopped and the sun come out."

They went through the house, Priscilla pointed out where the main decorating would be needed and left the rest to him.

"All I want is a perfectly presentable property that will fetch its right price."

"Mrs — er — Priscilla, I'm overwhelmed, I could hug you."

"Well not here if you don't mind, I've finished with this place."

"When can I start the work?"

"The house will be empty within a week. You ring me when you know which day you can start and I'll come down and give you a key."

"Right, that suits me. I should be able to make an early start."

They parted. Bill was whistling as he went to his van.

Priscilla drove straight to an estate agent's office.

"Good afternoon madam, how can we help you?"

"Good afternoon. I have a house to sell and I wish to buy another, so let's see what's available."

There was one other piece of business for Priscilla to attend to, the car sales business.

She went to the showroom and into James Clark's office. "James, I've decided that it would be in everyone's interest if I sold the business. I am not really the right person to run this sort of concern, it needs an experienced person. I shall get the Crossfire rep to come here for a discussion and then put it on the market. I shall try to make all your jobs secure."

"I'm sorry to hear this, Mrs Bulmer —."

"Er, I'm Mrs Thurston now."

"Oh, sorry. Is there no chance of you changing your mind?"

"I don't think so. I shall go in for something I can cope with quickly, and I shall be out of the shadow of Mr Bulmer's activities."

"I think I understand. So what do we do now?"

"Carry on as before. I'll let you know when the rep is coming down and we'll take it from there."

Within a few days the Crossfire rep came down to the showroom and he decided that any new buyer would have their agency for one year after the sale, to be reviewed after that. With this proviso the business was put on the market immediately.

Ruby Cavanagh woke early. She had not slept at all well anyway, her mind full of thoughts about today's events. Jeff would be on trial for drug running. She still could hardly believe it. She could understand his concern for her and her illness, but they were not short of money, and there was always treatment available on the health service. So why did he do it?

She thought back to that day when she was first diagnosed as having sclerosis. Jeff had seemed to shut himself off from her mentally. Oh yes, he was very concerned for her physical comfort and nothing was too much trouble, but how she longed for the close contact and loving embraces that they used to share. Jeff just did not realise that she still had needs, or if he did he was not willing to participate any more. Perhaps getting lots of money was Jeff's way of easing his conscience about his lack of sexual interest in her. 'Well, he is not likely to change now. He has made a mess of his life, but I am not going under,' she thought. 'I am going to survive without him.'

The trial went on for three days. The defence made the most of Jeff's reasons for his alleged offences, that Ruby was in need of special attention and treatment, but in the end he was found guilty and sentenced to seven years in gaol.

Ruby was in her wheelchair being pushed by Eleanor. They made their way out of the courtroom.

Outside, the defence lawyer approached them. "You can have a few minutes with Jeff in the anteroom, if you wish."

"Yes, I'd like to see him."

They went along the corridor and into a small room. Two officers were with Jeff. They remained while Ruby was there, Eleanor waited outside.

"Ruby, I'm sorry, I —."

Jeff moved towards her but the officer said "No contact, please."

Jeff was unable to say more, he was overcome with shame and guilt. He rallied. "Sell the business. Get yourself a permanent help. There will be enough for that."

"We'll see" said Ruby. It was uncomfortable trying to find something to say in front of all these onlookers. "Keep your spirits up" she said. "I'll manage."

She looked at the lawyer. He motioned to the two officers and they took Jeff outside and away to start his sentence.

Eleanor watched her father disappear down the corridor, then she went in to collect her mother in the wheelchair.

When Priscilla read the report of Jeff's trial she was shocked at the sentence he had been given, but was logical in seeing that any sign of leniency would give the green light to other would-be get-rich-quick aspirants. She wondered what Ruby would do now. She would probably have to dispose of the business, she couldn't possibly manage to run it by herself. 'Ah, but two of us could.' She suddenly had a feeling of excitement. Supposing she could buy in to the business and help run it, that would be an outlet for her latent energy.

When she went to bed that night, her mind was racing ahead through all the possibilities of such a move.

A few weeks later Ruby was sitting in the office of the taxi yard. Opposite her was Tim Freshman the foreman who had been keeping the business going since Jeff's arrest. He was looking very serious. "There has been a marked decline in work since last month." He avoided saying 'since Jeff's trial'. "As I see it, you have no option but to sell it while it is a going concern or you may end up with a big liability. A new name would help revive the custom, something that was unconnected with Cavanagh's Taxis."

"I take your point, Tim, but I would like to remain a part of the firm. It's all we've known and I couldn't bear just to get rid of it and stay at home doing nothing. Maybe I could sell half the business, or get a partner."

"Well, whatever you decide, please don't delay much longer or we shall all be in trouble."

Chapter 2

A Partnership

There were two letters for Priscilla that morning. One was the account from Bill Hopkins for the work on the Bulmers' old house. Very reasonable, she thought. The other was from the estate agents who had received an offer for the house and was this acceptable. That too was very reasonable, so she phoned right away and told them to go ahead and accept. Then she sat down to write out a cheque for Bill Hopkins.

She had been hoping to hear about her late husband's showroom disposal. There were two firms interested but nothing definite from either of them. The agents were going to fix a final date for offers.

A few days later she received a phone call from Bill Hopkins to thank her for the cheque.

"You did a good job, Bill, and I'm really grateful."

"Thank you" said Bill, "there was something else I wanted to ask you. Because I appreciate your handling of my accounts and all that, I'd like to take you to dinner somewhere, that is if you are not too busy or anything —" he faltered.

"Oh Bill, that is nice of you. I'd like to go with you. I haven't much to do these days, I can fit almost any evening you like."

"Oh, right. Well how about this Thursday then?"

"Fine. Do you want me to drive somewhere to meet you?"

"Oh no. I'll pick you up at your mother's flat at seven-thirty and we'll be dining in Brighton so you won't be far from home."

"Lovely Bill. I'll look forward to Thursday then. Goodbye."

On Thursday Bill was tying his tie. Its bluish background went well with his medium grey suit, in fact he thought he looked pretty smart for a builder.

He had booked a table at one of Brighton's large hotels and he was determined to show Priscilla that he was not just a hick. Also he was not going to be caught out by any snobbish waiter, so he had a wallet containing three hundred pounds as well as his credit card.

Priscilla was choosing a pair of earrings to wear with her simple black shift-like dress relieved only by a large opal brooch on the left shoulder strap. She settled for a pair of small gold filigree leaves, fixed them in, patted her hair and was satisfied.

She wondered why she was taking so much trouble, after all he was only — she stopped herself thinking like that. No, he was a bit more than just her builder, he had been quite instrumental in her seeing through Lionel, and he had been so solid dealing with the house and — he always appreciated her as a good-looking woman. But he was only twenty-five or six, so what was his interest in her? Perhaps he had ideas of a closer relationship.

The door bell rang. It was Bill. She slipped on her matching jacket and they went out to Bill's car. A short drive to the hotel, the attendant parked the car below, they went in.

If Bill was not used to dining out in such luxurious surroundings he did not show it. Everything went right, even the menu posed no difficulties; stick to what you know and leave the experimenting to the more unself-conscious types was his maxim, and it worked well.

While they were eating the sweet five men in dinner jackets came in and took their places on a small dais at one end. They were the group who were to play for dancing, for which there was a large area of polished floor in front of the dais. The restaurant was quite full, and it was not long before there were three or four couples dancing to the slow beat dreamy music.

Bill saw that Priscilla was appreciative of the tunes they were playing. "Would you like to dance a bit? I can manage the slow stuff but I am more at home with rock, I'm afraid."

"Oh yes, these tunes are from my childhood really, but they are very easy listening."

As they got to the floor the band's medley of songs went on to "Slow Boat to China". Priscilla hummed as they shuffled round the floor, then, remembering the words she sang softly, "I'd like to get you on a slow boat to China, All to myself alone —." Do you know it Bill?"

"No, I'm afraid not. Bit before my time I suppose." He realised he had made a gaffe and mumbled "I didn't mean —."

"It's all right Bill, I'm not offended. Let's go back to our table."

When they had seated themselves and Priscilla had helped them to the coffee, she looked steadily at him and said, "Bill, it was extremely nice of you to ask me out this evening and I have enjoyed the evening so far. I know you admire me because you have said so on at least two occasions. But this is a one-off date. There is almost a whole generation between us, so I think I am better qualified to say that much as I like you this is as far as it goes."

Bill was silent. He found it difficult to look her in the eye, but when at last he did, he said, "I'll be quite honest with you. When I asked you out I had a hope that perhaps it might develop. But when we were dancing and you were singing I felt that I was out of my depth. This was something I couldn't relate to, you were someone I could never have common interests with. So in a way we have both made up our minds."

Priscilla looked at him, then laughed.

Bill laughed with her and said "Come on, let's dance a bit more."

If anything, that evening Priscilla had learned more about herself than about Bill. She realised now that her life was becoming empty. As a couple, she and Lionel had never wanted for friends, mostly other couples. But now those friends found it difficult to entertain single people so she was more or less on her own. It had been nice going out with Bill. He had shown her that she was an attractive woman, but at forty she did not want the inexperience of a younger man, she needed the attention of someone who knew how to match her mental as well as her physical needs. She began wondering who could fit that description. He would be very unlike her late husband, perhaps someone like — suddenly she remembered the rep from Crossfire Cars whom she had met at the showroom. 'What was his name? Mr Eldon, that was it, Michael Eldon. I wonder if he will be coming down here again.' If he did she would probably not see him, the showroom being in Chichester and she still with her mother in Brighton.

She picked up the phone and rang the estate agents. "Have you got anything new in yet?"

"Just a moment madam, I'll check your file." She hung on, then after a moment, "Hello. We have sent you details of all the current places of the type you require, but we have two just in that we have not finished the paperwork for. If you can come in you may see whether they have possibilities, if not we'll send you the details in a few days."

"I'll come in, thank you." She hung up.

With time hanging heavily on her hands she welcomed the chance of a run into Chichester. That afternoon Priscilla drove over to the city, parked and then walked round to the estate agent's. There were two other estate agents in that same street, and as she was passing one of them she glanced in the window. Her eye caught a picture of a property. She stopped and read the details. It sounded just what she had been looking for but it did not mention the locality. She went in and enquired. The assistant brought out all the details of the property that was situated on the edge of the town at the opposite end from where she and Lionel had lived. Apparently the elderly lady had died and the property was vacant, only the curtains and carpets remaining.

"When may I see it?" she asked.

"As there is no one there, we have to take you. I don't know if we have anyone here who can do that."

"I've got my car, so I could take someone if you like."

"Ah, Miss Somers is available, if you would just wait a moment. Can I have your particulars please?"

Priscilla obliged, and a few moments later Miss Somers came out with a bunch of keys and details of the property. They drove out to the suburbs, turned down a small lane and there at the end was the house. Priscilla liked the area and the look of the house, and when they went in she was taken at once by its feeling of comfort and cosiness, yet it was quite spacious.

"It needs a bit of decorating here and there but it is quite a sound property" said Miss Somers.

They spent a good half-hour inspecting the inside and the outside, and at the end of it all Priscilla said she was interested and could she arrange for a survey. Miss Somers said that they could arrange for Priscilla's surveyor to have a key for this purpose.

Back at the flat she waited until evening and then rang Bill Hopkins. She told him about the house and asked him if he could go to the house to survey it and look for any problems. He was glad to do so, he said. Priscilla asked him to arrange with the agents about getting access to the property.

Next day she rang the agents to give them Bill's details

It was a week before Bill rang to say that he had done a survey, that it was in good condition and that his full report was in the post. If she liked the house, he said she should make an offer as it was a very good property.

When Bill's report arrived Priscilla read it then went straight down to the agent's and made an offer based on their 'offers over' figure.

Only a day or two later they rang her to say that her offer had been accepted, and subject to contract the property would be hers.

Almost a month later the contracts were exchanged, Priscilla paid the full amount and she became the owner of 'Normington House'. By then, Priscilla had received the money from the sale of their old house, so she was left with a few thousands over that would more than cover any work there was to be done.

Priscilla had planned to spend a week or two living in the house before deciding what to do about decorating or alterations so she chose the minimum of furniture to enable her to live in reasonable comfort, a bed and dressing table, an easy chair, an occasional table and two table lamps. The curtains and carpets were already there and would do for now.

When she had been installed for a couple of weeks she rang Bill to make an appointment for him to come and estimate for the work she had planned.

Bill arrived at Priscilla's new home after lunch. She took him round the ground floor and showed him the various things she wanted altered, kitchen cupboards, decorations and some electrical points. They went upstairs. Priscilla pointed out the rooms for redecorating and then the bathroom where a new suite was to be installed.

Finally they moved into Priscilla's bedroom, sparsely furnished but having carpet and curtains. Priscilla went over to the window and looked out. "I love the view from here" she said.

Bill, who had been making notes and measurements came over to her side and looked out. He had not said much as they walked round. As he came close to her and looked out of the window he was very much aware of her presence. "This is a really nice outlook" he said. He could smell her perfume now and suddenly had difficulty swallowing. "Look" he said, "you can just see Jackson's Folly."

"Where?" Priscilla pushed towards him to see where he was pointing. Bill put his arm out and rested it on her shoulder.

It was as though a current of electricity had passed up his arm, and he was breathing heavily. As his arm brushed her hair Priscilla was transfixed and every thought left her head. She felt a little dizzy and swayed. "Oh Bill" she said.

In a moment his arm went round her shoulders. He pulled her towards him, Priscilla went soft in his arms. She slowly raised her head and their lips met in a soft but passionate kiss.

Bill realised he was still holding his notebook and pencil. He threw them on to the windowsill then clasped her to him once more with almost uncontrollable passion.

As if by mutual consent they moved towards the bed and sat down, still tightly embraced. Bill's hands started to move over her body under her summer dress. She kicked off her shoes and lay back. Bill's hands explored her body frantically. She felt him wrestling with his own clothes and when all her senses seemed to have left her she felt his naked body roll over on top of her.

She spread her legs wide and with a gasp she felt Bill's deep penetration, with a feeling so intense she was transported into a world of complete abandon. She put her hands on his buttocks and held him tightly. With such intensity it seemed only seconds before they reached a simultaneous climax followed by a deep sense of togetherness.

They lay quietly for a few minutes then Priscilla slipped out of bed and went into the bathroom. When she returned she was wearing a gossamer neglige. She paused at the end of the bed. "Bill."

He looked at her dreamily. "What is it?" Bill was holding the bedclothes by his chest.

"I want to look at you." She sat on the edge of the bed, reached over and pulled the bedclothes slowly downwards. She stood up and continued pulling the clothes off until Bill's lithe body was fully uncovered. Her eyes travelled down his body, over his chest across his stomach to the pubic hair. She saw his strong thighs and legs. As he felt her gaze taking in all of him Bill reacted in the usual masculine way, he erected again.

Priscilla shed her neglige and threw herself on top of him. She felt the firmness of Bill's erection pressing against her stomach. She raised herself slowly and edged up higher then she gently eased herself down on to him. She felt him enter and once again experienced that intense sensation that had wracked her body the first time. Bill's hands on her thighs pulled her down. Their passion flared up again and Priscilla found herself moving and pulsating in a way that she never would have believed herself capable. Her inhibitions vanished, and she revelled in this freedom of expression as she moved in unison with Bill.

All too soon it was over and they lay together for a while. Bill made a move to get up. "I'll just go in to the bathroom and then I must get on with my work."

When he reappeared dressed and refreshed Priscilla was still on the bed.

He sat down by her side and took her hand. "We may not be of the same generation" he said, "but we have something in common."

Priscilla looked at him. "Mmm, I know" she said, "but let's not plan anything, no dates or anything. If we happen to be together and — er — well, let's leave it to chance, it's more exciting."

"Right" said Bill. "Goodbye, I'll phone when my lads are coming."

A week later Bill phoned Priscilla to let her know that his men would be there the following week. Priscilla arranged that she would be there on the day agreed. Meanwhile she also decided that she would stay at her mother's flat while her own house was being decorated.

On the Monday she opened the door to Bill. "Hello Bill. You'll have a free hand here. I'm off to stay with Mother, so here are the keys. I shall come over each Friday morning to see how your chaps are getting on, or any other time if there is anything urgent to discuss or decide. All right?"

"Oh fine, fine" said Bill. "I shall be working elsewhere I expect, but we shall need about three weeks."

Priscilla got into her car and left. Bill stared after her and then took the men in to the house.

"Not a bad bit of crumpet that" said one of them.

"No. Not bad at all" said Bill.

"Yes, we have a potential buyer for this business of yours. We are vetting him to see if we can safely transfer the Crossfire agency to him." It was Michael Eldon talking to Priscilla who had come down to the showroom at his request.

Priscilla felt that a great weight was being lifted from her shoulders. When this transaction was over she would at last be free of the past completely.

Although Michael Eldon was not conducting the sale of the business, it was his decision about the suitability of the buyer as their agent which would influence the sale.

They were sitting in the sales office where Lionel used to spend most of his time. Priscilla glanced around and tried to exclude her late husband from the scenario. "What's this buyer like? Is he a good risk, do you think?" Priscilla hoped the sale would go through and was anxious to know how near it was.

"I think this one will be all right. Apparently he owned a similar business nearer to London, but the site became very valuable as a development area. So, he has the money, but he has a manager with considerable trade experience so it's really him we are vetting. It should be OK."

Priscilla felt better after hearing that. She got up from her chair. "I think I should be going. It was nice seeing you again." She moved towards the door. Michael Eldon came round the table and stood by the door. "I shall be going to lunch shortly, how would you like to join me?"

Priscilla thought for a while. She looked at him steadily, then said, "I would like to but —" she paused. "Well, at this stage of your negotiations I would not like to be seen as perhaps er influencing the outcome, if you see what I mean."

"Yes I do see what you mean, but I assure you that —."

"I only meant that it's the look of the thing, you know, people put two and two together. I suggest that if and when this sale is over we have a celebratory lunch."

"You are absolutely right of course. I shall look forward to a possible lunch soon, but no promises."

He opened the door and Priscilla left.

A phone call from Bill Hopkins reminded Priscilla that she had other responsibilities. "We shall finish on Thursday and on Friday we shall be clearing out our equipment, so if you could come over on Friday morning and inspect it. then if there is anything not quite right we can rectify it."

"Certainly. Bill. I'll be there at eleven. Bye."

On the Friday morning Priscilla helped her mother in to the car and together they set off to see her newly-decorated house.

On arrival they were met by Bill and taken inside. His men were busy loading things in to a lorry.

"Oh. Bill." Priscilla called, "I've brought some fresh milk and coffee. Would you please make some coffee while I go round with my mother and we'll meet you back here in the kitchen that looks absolutely lovely."

"Thanks. OK I'll wait here."

Priscilla and her mother went on a tour of the house. Bill's men had made a magnificent job of everything, and the house had a much brighter appearance than when Priscilla had first acquired it.

As they stood by her bedroom window looking out, Priscilla glanced over her shoulder to where the bed was, still covered by a dust sheet. "Well Mother, what do you think of it?"

"I think it's lovely. They've done a good job."

"I agree. I'm lucky. There aren't many so-called builders and decorators that one can trust to do a good job these days. Come on, let's go and see how good he is at coffee making."

They returned to the kitchen where Bill was waiting. "Well, tell me the worst" said Bill.

"There's no 'worst', it's all 'best'. We both think that it just couldn't be better. So thank you very much indeed."

"It was mostly my two blokes" said Bill.

"Oh no" broke in Priscilla, "those two blokes are good because they have a good boss, so don't be so modest."

"All right then. Thank you very much. Now, here's your coffee."

The whole of the next week was spent on an enormous shopping spree. Some new curtains, rugs for the dining and sitting rooms. Practically a whole new lot of furniture, easy chairs, dining room table and chairs and bedroom furniture. There was nothing to remind her of her former life. This was a completely new start. When it was all installed she flopped in to a chair. 'Now' she thought 'where do we go from here?'

The phone rang. Priscilla lifted the receiver. "Hello?"

"Hello Mrs Thurston, this is Michael Eldon."

"Oh yes Mr Eldon, it seems ages since we spoke."

"Yes, it's over three weeks. Well, I thought I'd let you know that I have OK'd the people who are buying the showroom, and they are going ahead with the purchase. You should be hearing from your solicitor shortly."

"Oh thank you. I'm so glad. You don't know what a relief this is."

"I think I do. But don't get too excited, remember the sale isn't complete yet."

"No, I won't, but I think we'll be having that lunch fairly soon."

"I shall look forward to that. Bye for the present."

It was the next day that her solicitor phoned. He had received a deposit on the sale price and anticipated that it would be a month before the final completion.

She asked him what the final sale price was, he gave her a figure. Priscilla gasped. "I had no idea values had increased so much. I shall be well off."

"If you need any advice on handling your money we can offer you quite a good service."

"Thanks, I'll remember that." Priscilla rang off.

A few days later her solicitor rang again. "Mrs Thurston? Yes, Smith and Burt here. We have heard of something that might interest you, something to use some of your money on and also occupy you fully. Yes, if you could come down sometime I'll give you all the details. Right, Wednesday then, two o'clock."

On Wednesday Priscilla duly presented herself at the solicitor's office.

"Come in Mrs Thurston. Tea? No, righto."

When she was settled the solicitor gave her the details of what his colleague in Ruby Cavanagh's solicitor's firm had told him.

"It seems that Mrs Cavanagh has been overseeing her husband's taxi business, well hers really, and with the adverse publicity there has been a marked falling off of customers. She feels that the firm needs new life pumped into it, plus a bit of cash to replace the fleet of cars."

Priscilla was extremely surprised. So much had been happening in her own life that she had almost forgotten about Ruby and Jeff. Jeff would be out of circulation for years, and Ruby being a semi-invalid must be finding it very hard.

The solicitor was talking again. "I am not involved with this professionally yet," he said. "All I can do at present is put you in touch with Mrs Cavanagh's solicitor and he will arrange a meeting with Mrs Cavanagh."

Priscilla was silent for a while then said "I'll need time to mull this over. Look, I'll ring you when I've thought it through."

She left and drove back to her house.

When she got home her mind was assailed with all sorts of ideas, plans and possibilities. After Lionel had died she had thought of running the showroom and car sales, and she had never felt that she would not succeed. This proposed venture was not as complicated as the car business was, so why not? It wouldn't hurt to discuss it with Ruby Cavanagh. She decided she would go ahead with the meeting and next day she phoned her solicitor.

On the morning of the appointment to meet Ruby and her solicitor Priscilla was going over the probable scenario in her mind. Ostensibly she would be joining with Ruby to run a taxi business — taking Jeff's place, she mused. What would she herself do? She had no intention of being a sleeping partner in any business, she wanted to be in the running of it. She felt a thrill of latent ambition, she wanted to achieve something. Was there enough in this business to satisfy her? What did she know about taxi hire, taxi maintenance or customer relations? That was one area everyone had an opinion on — customer relations, so why not start right now, this very morning.

She went to the phone. "Hello, I would like a taxi at eleven-fifteen this morning please. Yes, just to go into town. I have an appointment at eleven-thirty so it must be here at eleven-fifteen. Mrs Thurston."

She gave the address then went upstairs to get ready. Promptly at eleven-thirteen the taxi arrived at the front door. Priscilla took her bag and went out, locked the door and turned towards the taxi. The driver was already standing by the car and when Priscilla came out he went to the rear door and opened it.

"Thank you" said Priscilla as she got in and sat down.

When the driver was in his seat he said "Where to, madam?"

Priscilla gave him the name of a street quite near to the taxi depot. It was not a long journey and at eleven-twenty-five they were in the street she had mentioned.

"Any particular part of the street madam?"

"Yes, the far end please." She would then only have to walk round the corner to the depot.

The car stopped, the driver got out and went round to open the door.

"How much please?" asked Priscilla.

"Two-forty madam."

She gave him a five pound note.

"Thank you madam, two-sixty change."

Priscilla took the change and gave the sixty pence back to the driver. "Thank you."

"Thank you madam." He got back in to the car and drove off.

Priscilla walked round the corner and found the yard where the office was. She knocked and walked in. This was the front office where Tim Freshman the foreman more or less ran the business.

He got up as Priscilla entered. "You must be Mrs Thurston."

"Yes I am. Is Mrs Cavanagh here?"

"They're in the main office. Go right through please." He returned to his seat to continue with his work.

Priscilla went over to the other door, knocked and walked in. A man rose from his chair. "I'm John Alderney, acting for Mrs Cavanagh."

"How do you do," said Priscilla.

"And this is Mrs Cavanagh."

Priscilla looked at the person seated by the large table. She saw a forty-five-year-old motherly woman, tidily if not smartly dressed.

"Forgive me for not getting up" she said. "Nice to see you, Mrs Thurston." They shook hands.

"Take a seat Mrs Thurston," said Mr Alderney, " and I'll try to put you in the picture."

"Just a moment" said Ruby, "I think it might be as well if I explained a little about how the business was started by my husband Jeff."

Mr Alderney gestured to say Ruby had the floor.

"When we were married," Ruby went on, "Jeff had one car and a few regular runs, the rest were casual pick-ups. Nothing was too much trouble for Jeff and people got to know him and to like him."

'So did I,' thought Priscilla.

Ruby continued, saying how the business had escalated so that soon Jeff had to get another car and driver, then another and another. They had found this yard and had bought it for a very reasonable price.

"It is now worth at least one hundred and fifty thousand" said Mr Alderney.

Ruby went on with her story up to when she became incapacitated by the sclerosis. "Jeff changed then" she said. "He didn't neglect the business, but he always had other things to do. I felt that I was of no further use to him. He started to spend more time sailing on his own, and finally, as you know, came this disaster. People now associate the name Cavanagh with other less savoury things, and I'm afraid it's affecting business."

Mr Alderney then began to outline the financial position of the business which was fairly sound, but what was needed was a new image, not without some urgency.

Priscilla then stated her position. She told them that she would not know her own financial state for at least another month, but she felt that this could be the opportunity she had been looking for, to do something that would be satisfying to her personally as well as perhaps financially rewarding. She turned to Ruby. "Mrs Cavanagh, I —."

"Please call me Ruby."

"All right, Ruby, I'd like to have chat with you at your home if you like, in about a week, when I've had time to consider it."

"I'd like that" said Ruby, "give me a ring when you are ready."

During the next week Priscilla gave a lot of thought to the business that she was expecting to be having a hand with, and soon was devising all sorts of plans for making it a thriving business. She jotted down everything she thought was worth pursuing, and as she did so she felt her enthusiasm for the project increasing. So it was with an almost contented attitude that she phoned Ruby. They agreed that Priscilla should go to Ruby's house next week.

On the day, Priscilla took all the notes and drove over to Ruby's.

On arrival, the door was opened by a pretty seventeen-year-old girl. "You must be —."

"Eleanor Cavanagh. Come in, Mum's in the sitting room." She closed the front door and led the way. "Mum, Mrs Thurston's here."

"I think I'm young enough and you are old enough to call me Priscilla."

"Right you are then."

Priscilla went into the room where Ruby was ensconced in an easy chair. "Come in, come in. Eleanor will make us some tea, then she's off for a driving lesson."

They chatted for a while about the weather and Priscilla's house. Eleanor brought the tea and put it on the table. "I'm off now, Mum, see you about five. Cheerio."

"Well now, Priscilla, what do you think?" said Ruby.

Priscilla needed no second bidding. With her notes to guide her she launched in to a programme that would have been approved by any logistics department of the military. "As I see it, to change the image there are three main things to do. First, remove the name Cavanagh completely by calling it 'Ruby's Cars' for example. Second, consolidate that image by changing the present cars for a new fleet of ruby-coloured saloons with white tops. And thirdly, advertise everywhere, papers, pubs, hotels, telephone kiosks, the station, the nearest airfield, theatres and other places of entertainment. Also, draw up a set of simple rules for the drivers so that customer appreciation is always prevalent. Provide a few safeguards for them and for you by insisting on having a name and a phone number from any inquiry so that in the event of being unable to get a car to a pick up they can be informed. This could also help to reduce false call-outs. Now, I know that probably a lot of the these last items are already part of your regular routine, but people — drivers — do get stale and apathetic, so a reminder won't hurt."

She paused for breath, so Ruby, who had listened intently said "How

42

much money shall we need to do all that?"

"Well, I don't know. But I do know that when the new owner takes over the showroom, he'll be more than pleased to get an order for a ten car fleet in the first month, and we'd get a generous discount, I'll bet."

Ruby laughed at that. "I notice you said 'We', almost as if you had already made up your mind, have you?"

"Not quite," answered Priscilla, "a bird in the hand you know. But if all goes well with the sale of the showroom I think I can safely say 'yes'."

"Well I suppose we shall survive," said Ruby, "but I am not sure that I can cope by myself."

Up till now Ruby had not mentioned Jeff, so it was with some trepidation that Priscilla brought his name up. "How does Jeff fit into all this?" she asked.

"Only as adviser. He has nothing, owns nothing. I own this house and the business, and that's it. If it fails we go bust, and from then on it's all downhill."

"What will happen when Jeff comes home?"

"God only knows. He'll probably have to keep clear of the business. People do remember. He will be different anyway, I imagine. I might not be here either, unless I can keep this disease under control."

"You mustn't talk like that" said Priscilla. "You are not much older than me, and you have a strong constitution."

"That's true, but sometimes I get so tired that I feel that I shall never be any better."

"I'm sure you will cope with any situation, but if I do decide to join you in the business you can rest assured that I shall be very active. I need to be doing something."

"I for one shall look forward to having you around so I'm going to pray that your sale goes through all right."

Priscilla got up to leave. "Goodbye, Ruby, I've enjoyed our little chat. I think we shall be seeing more of each other."

She went out to her car, and as she drove home she compared their lives, hers and Ruby's. They were in similar circumstances, both having been deprived of their husbands and left on their own to run businesses. She, Priscilla, was better off financially and also had her health and strength, whereas Ruby was only half mobile and was owner of a declining business. She felt pity for Ruby. Was this pity encouraging her to rescue the taxi business? No, she remembered thinking about this possibility weeks ago and now it was more than a possiblity. She wanted to take part in this project because she felt she needed to be really active but without the ties of having a husband looking over her shoulder. She knew she could do it, and when the money became available that is what she intended to do.

So, she was very light-hearted when some three weeks later she went along to her solicitor in response to his request to come and sign the contracts for the sale of the showroom.

"There we are Mrs — ah — Thurston, that seems to be all in order. When everything is settled up and death duties etc., are paid I think you will have almost a quarter of a million. Have you given any more thought to your future?"

"Oh yes, I certainly have. I shall go in with Mrs Cavanagh and I shall take an active part in the business."

"Well that sounds very enterprising. I would like to make a suggestion, if I may."

"Go ahead" said Priscilla, "I'm quite receptive to new ideas."

"When you put your money in we shall of course prepare a legal agreement for you, but you should also employ a new accountant to oversee your money. No, not your husband's accountants or Mrs Cavanagh's, but someone new. That way you should have a double safeguard of your interests."

"Have you any firm in mind?" asked Priscilla.

"Yes, we know several small firms of accountants. I'll give you some names, then you can select one."

With the address of one of them in her wallet Priscilla left to embark on her new career.

The next few weeks were one long round of meetings. First with Ruby and her solicitor, then with the accountants and solicitors, then more of the same until all the legal aspects were covered and agreed. Only then did Ruby and Priscilla get together to start planning the new set-up.

Most of the meetings took place at the taxi office where Ruby had a spare wheelchair. She had been brought each time by taxi and then it was an easy matter to transfer to the wheelchair. On her good days she managed to walk the few steps into the office, but always she was alert and seemingly unaffected by the sclerosis.

Together she and Priscilla took decisions on the suggestions put forward by Priscilla. The new cars were ordered and a date agreed upon for the launch of 'Ruby's Taxis'. Once again Bill Hopkins was contacted and given the job of renovating the offices and yard, and providing signs proclaiming the new title.

Priscilla spent hours each day in the office checking their publicity arrangements. She had handbills, cards and small posters printed for distribution throughout the area. She had got to know the drivers personally.

They were not too enthusiastic about having a new woman boss, but Priscilla soon became popular, so during the week before the launch she got them together and gave them a pep talk. "This is our chance to get a good slice of the hire business available in our city. It depends almost entirely on how the public sees us. New cars are not enough by themselves. There has to be a good relationship with the public, or most of them, that is. These days there are an increasing number of muggers. Fortunately up till now any trouble has usually been from drunks. So if you are engaged to take a drunk home, see if he can be accompanied by a more sober friend. You can refuse to take him, or her, of course. But remember that if a drunk is in your car he is not driving himself and posing a danger to everybody. Your image will be reflected in the amount of business we do. Even if you've got toothache, keep smiling. We are one big team working together to make money, and in doing so you are ensured of good employment and well-maintained vehicles. Use them carefully and keep on the right side of the law."

There were a few 'thank yous' from the drivers, then they went off to their work.

Bill Hopkins' men had done the usual good job of renovation at the offices and yard. It was not until the Friday before Monday's launch that Priscilla saw Bill and was able to discuss the work.

"How are you enjoying your new role, Priscilla?" Bill was almost formal even though he was appreciative of her as a woman. She had a new sparkle about her.

"I'm revelling in it" she answered. "I'm so busy I don't seem to have any spare time at all."

"It must suit you" said Bill, "you don't look tired or harassed."

"I may not be harassed but my brain is working overtime dealing with a thousand decisions a day!" She laughed at her exaggeration.

"If you do get any spare time I could —." said Bill tentatively.

"No Bill. Remember what I said. If we should bump into one another and if —."

"If nothing" said Bill, "I want to make love to you again."

"Send me your account, Bill, I'll see you are paid." She turned away, then came back. "I do like you, Bill, and maybe I want you to make love to me, but please not by arrangement. Bye!" She went into the office.

Bill went towards his van and as he was opening the door a small car drove into the yard and stopped. It was partially blocking the way for Bill to reverse, so he walked over to the driver to ask him to move.

The door of the car opened and Bill saw that the driver was a very young lady. "Excuse me" he said, "but I'm just leaving, so would you mind moving your car over a bit so I can reverse?"

Eleanor looked at Bill from her seat in the car. "I'll move it" she said, "but as I haven't long passed my test I may be a bit longer manoeuvring it over." She closed her door, then opened the window. "Where would be a good place to put it?" she asked.

"If you go straight back for five yards or so, then come forward right hand down hard, that should do it."

Bill waited until Eleanor had completed his instructions then went over to her side of the car. "That wasn't too bad" he said. "I don't know what you were worrying about."

"Well, you know what it's like when someone's watching you."

"Yes, I did once," answered Bill. He liked the look of this young lady. "I'm Bill Hopkins, are you connected with this place?"

"In a way" said Eleanor, "my mum's one of the proprietors, I'm Eleanor Cavanagh." She got out of the car, shut and locked the door and moved towards the office.

Bill wanted to continue the conversation. "I've been doing the work here, well, my blokes have, but I haven't seen you here before."

"I don't come here that often, in fact this is the first time for weeks. I spend a lot of time with my mum, you know she's —."

"Yes, I've seen her. I'm sorry for her."

"Oh, she's very cheerful but needs a bit of help now and then." She turned to go to the office. "Well, cheerio, see you."

"Yes. See you," said Bill. He had wanted to say 'how about seeing you soon' but somehow he was unable to voice the words. He knew why. She was very young, about eighteen he thought. He was twenty-six and probably looked it. She was barely out of school but she was quite mature in her manner. He sighed and went to his van.

Ruby and Priscilla spent the whole of that weekend in the final preparations for the launch of their new firm. Priscilla drove for miles to see hotel proprietors and clubs where she left cards and notices for display. Printed in eye-catching colour they stood out from those from other firms, vital when toting for the custom of people in a hurry. She was optimistic about her and Ruby's venture. They had become good friends over the last few weeks, and Jeff Cavanagh seemed to have been completely forgotten.

Ruby visited him regularly in prison but she never spoke about him to Priscilla, and Priscilla had never mentioned that she had met Jeff before. That feeling of rapport she had had when with him was fading. Also, she was sorry for Ruby who had endured two blows to her very existence. They worked well together and both were confident of the future.

Priscilla had arranged to spend every morning at the office whilst Ruby attended during the afternoon. They were responsible mainly for administration work, the allocation of the taxis being the job of the foreman Tim Freshman. He was the linchpin of the firm. He had a second-in-command who relieved him on a shift basis, and one of the two office girls was able to stand in for either of the two men when necessary.

On the Monday all the new cars took to the road. Calls were average, but gradually as the week progressed there seemed to be a small increase in business. All the drivers were enthusiastic about the new cars and everything pointed to them being successful.

Ruby was driven to the office most afternoons by one of the firm's drivers, and occasionally by Eleanor who was now trying to decide her future — college or commerce.

One afternoon as she was driving her mother to the office she suddenly said "Mum, how would you feel if I went to college?"

"I was wondering when you were going to decide about that, but I would never stand in your way, ever."

"What about the house, and what about if you don't improve, how would you cope?" Eleanor was worried.

"Look, I've got Mrs Richings who comes every day. I know she wouldn't mind doing a bit extra now and then, and I'm not exactly immobile, am I?"

They reached the taxi yard and Eleanor drove up to the office door. She went round to the passenger door and helped her mother out of the car. "Do you want the wheelchair?" she asked.

"Oh no, I can manage." She edged her way round to the office door. Eleanor waited as she got to the door.

"I've applied to Reading and Hull for a place in September, so perhaps you could speak to Mrs Richings, just in case."

"Stop worrying. I shall sort it out if and when it happens, and anyway, I've felt a lot better since we started this new business. I'll be all right."

"OK Mum. I'll be off then, see you at half past four." She got into her car and drove off.

When Ruby got into the office she phoned Priscilla. "Hello Priscilla. No, there's nothing wrong, it's just that I shall not be in tomorrow as I am going to the hospital."

"Oh Ruby —."

"No!" Ruby broke in, "it's only a routine check to monitor the progress of the treatment I'm having. I'm quite all right, even better than I used to be, I think."

"What about a car, can I take you?"

"No thanks, Eleanor is around so she will take me. I'll be in as usual the day after tomorrow." She hung up.

47

There was a rap on the door, the door opened and Tim Freshman the foreman poked his head in. "There's a Mr Eldon here to see Mrs Thurston."

"Ask him in here" said Ruby. She had met Mr Eldon during the negotiations for the supply of the taxi fleet. "Hello Mr Eldon, nice to see you again."

"Hello Mrs Cavanagh, how are you and how's business?"

"I'm fine and we're coming along nicely thanks."

"I really came to see Mrs Thurston, Priscilla. I thought she might be here."

"No, Priscilla comes here mornings and I come afternoons, that gives us time for other household things."

"Sounds like a good arrangement to me," said Eldon. "This though is really a social call. I was down here for the day and I thought I would look in and say hello."

"If you like I'll call her and tell her you are here, or would you rather call her yourself?"

"Yes, all right." He took the phone and tapped the number. He heard her answer. "Hello Mrs Thurston, this is Michael Eldon."

"Oh, Mr Eldon, how nice to hear from you." She sounded pleased.

"I was in town so I thought I'd look you up. You know, we've never had that lunch we promised."

"That's right, we haven't. Look, if you have the afternoon free why not come round and have some tea. You know where I am, don't you?"

"Yes, I have a pretty good idea."

Priscilla gave him a few directions and then said "I'll see you in about fifteen minutes then, goodbye."

Eldon put the receiver down then stood up. "I'll be off then," he said. "Going round to Priscilla's for a cup of tea. See you again sometime. Cheerio." He left.

Priscilla ran upstairs to tidy herself up and put on some fresh lipstick. She was trying to analyse her feelings about Michael Eldon. She knew so little about him. Was he married? If so, what was he doing seeking her out?

She looked at her reflection in the mirror. 'Why are you trying to make yourself more presentable?' she thought. She gave her hair a pat and went downstairs.

A few moments later she heard a car on the drive. She waited until he rang the bell. Priscilla went slowly to the front door and opened it.

"Hello Mrs Thurston."

"Hello Mr Eldon, come in."

They had never been alone together before, and Priscilla could sense that they were both a little apprehensive at this close contact. They went into the sitting room.

48

"This is quite a nice house and a nice location" said Eldon.

"Yes" said Priscilla, "it was a bit of luck that it became available just as I was looking for somewhere. I liked it the first time I saw it."

"Is it a four-bedroomed house?" Eldon asked.

"It was once, but the fourth bedroom was made into an extra bathroom."

"Oh yes, I see."

They were both stilted in their conversation. Priscilla felt that she — they — needed more space. "It's fairly warm today. Let's go on to the terrace at the back, then I'll get some tea."

Priscilla led the way through the dining room and out on to the wide patio where there was a set of white chairs and table.

She went back in for the cushions and put them in place. "There" she said, "make yourself comfortable and I'll put the kettle on."

"I'll just wander down the garden for a while." Eldon strolled away from the house. He started to wonder about what Priscilla thought of him. He was a few years older than Priscilla. He had the sort of features one would associate with a rugged outdoor type, slightly muscular build, wavy brown hair brushed straight back from the forehead. He used to have a moustache, but that had made him look older and unapproachable so he had been told, so he quickly got rid of it. He was dressed semi-formally in a two-piece single-breasted greyish suit, pale blue shirt and a darker blue tie.

It was getting warmer as he meandered round the garden so he slipped his jacket off and put it over his arm. He thought he heard the rattle of crockery so he turned and ambled up to the terrace.

As he reached the steps Priscilla called to him. "How do you like your tea Mr Eldon?"

He went up the steps towards her and said, "Well, first of all I wish you would call me Mike or Michael."

"All right Mike, it suits you. I'm just Priscilla."

"Right. I like my tea with one and a half spoonfuls of sugar, or three sugar knobs, and a little milk."

"It's Earl Grey tea" said Priscilla.

"Same for all tea, whatever blend" answered Mike.

Priscilla looked at him as she served the tea. He seemed more human, she thought, than when they were dealing with the motor business. She still knew nothing of his private life and was not sure if she should be too inquiring. "What kind of a house have you got?" Priscilla thought that this was a good way to find out something of the way he lived.

"We used to have a Victorian semi in North London, but now I have a flat in Ealing."

"You live alone then?" asked Priscilla.

"Yes, for about four years" said Mike.

Now that she could see his face closer to than when they had met on other occasions she saw a trace of sorrow or hardship in his eyes. She wondered about him, was he separated, divorced or even a widower? She was not anxious to pursue a relationship with anyone she knew nothing about, and one could not expect him to bare his soul at their first social meeting.

"I couldn't live in London" said Priscilla. "It's getting crowded everywhere of course, but we do have a bit more room in Hampshire and Sussex."

"If you want to survive commercially you have to be where the people are" Mike said seriously. "After all, they are the ones who provide the trade that balances the economy, and when you are in business you have to be prepared to work hard and suffer the ups and downs if you are to make a go of it. That's really why my wife left me." He paused. "She couldn't stand me being away all day and every day, and being late in the evenings." He paused again. "There doesn't seem to be any answer to it. If you relax for a moment someone is there ready to take your place or filch your business. It really is a hard life. Oh, I'm sorry, I didn't mean to bore you with my life story."

Priscilla was silent for a while as she absorbed what he had told her. "You have given me something to think about" she said. "I am beginning to understand why so many marriages fail. If couples do not get time to themselves they can become as strangers. So what is the answer? Stifle your ambitions and work only nine till five always? I don't know, but since I have been in the taxi business I am beginning to realise how the pressure is on you to keep forging ahead."

"Yes, that's it exactly, and in the end it's the people out there who can make or break you. It's all a continuous challenge. Not today though. I've done my call for today and so there will be no more challenging until tomorrow. What are your plans for today?"

"Oh, nothing special, I was just going to potter around."

"If you would like to do anything or go anywhere I am at your service."

"Well" said Priscilla, "I could do with a good dose of fresh air and the best place for that would be on the downs, half an hour's drive. Do you mind doing more driving?"

"No, of course not, anywhere you like."

"Right. Give me a couple of minutes and I'll be ready." She picked up the tray and they went inside.

"The cloakroom is through there." She pointed to the hall. "I'll be down soon."

Some ten minutes later they went out of the front door, Priscilla carefully locked up and they got into Mike's car, a two litre coupe, royal blue in colour.

As they drove off Priscilla said "If you take the A285 for about ten or twelve miles then turn off left, that will bring you to a small village where we can park and then walk."

"OK. Anything you say."

The sun was out and the afternoon had warmed up nicely. Priscilla leaned back in her seat and let her mind go blank. She closed her eyes and as she did so she suddenly felt she was in Jeff's car again on the way to Arundel. How long ago that seemed.

She opened her eyes quickly. "Next road on the left."

When they arrived at the village Mike parked the car. They found a narrow road that wound up out of the village on to the rising ground of the downs. As they strolled along Priscilla hummed a little tune to herself.

"Enjoying yourself?" Mike asked.

"Oh yes, I love walking, especially when you can see a long way."

They were now high enough to see over to the Goodwood racecourse. The downs rolled away to the west.

"What were you humming? It sounded familiar" said Mike.

"It was 'Slow Boat to China'. Do you know it?"

"Yes I do. But after that came one of my favourites, 'Cara Mia Mine' by —."

"David Whitfield! Yes, I loved that too." Priscilla was enthusiastic, and they both went on to recall other favourites of that era as they walked gently to the top of the next rise that gave them a panoramic view for several miles. "This is lovely" said Priscilla softly, "one can forget one's troubles here."

"You surely have no troubles now, have you?"

"No, not really, but I sometimes wonder what the future has in store for me."

"Don't we all" said Mike. "What's more to the point is what about the immediate future, like this evening for instance."

"This evening? It's evening now, it's almost six."

"I thought that if you can bear my company a bit longer we might drive along to somewhere or other and have a bar meal, then I could drop you off at your house later."

"Don't be so self-deprecating! I've quite enjoyed our time here today, and yes, I would like a bar meal. We don't have to dress up for that, so no problem."

They started to stroll down to the village. On the way they discussed their tastes in music, TV, cinema and politics, and were pleasantly surprised to find that they had similar tastes.

When they got to the car Mike asked if she had any suggestions as to where she would like to go.

"I think Bognor would be all right. They have several choices of bars where you can get a nice meal, also it would be handy for getting me back to Chichester and you to London."

"Very well then, Bognor it is" said Mike.

When they arrived in Bognor Mike found a car park. They then walked to the sea front and found a likely looking place. They went in, found a table then ordered at the bar. They sat down and waited.

"You know, I have really enjoyed myself today" said Mike.

"I've already said that" broke in Priscilla.

"I know. But what I mean is, if we enjoy each other's company why shouldn't we do it again?"

Priscilla looked thoughtful. "If you have commitments that keep you busy, I don't see how you are going to have time to come down here, and I have no intention of going up to London."

"I didn't mean I would come down a lot, just now and then until we got to know each other better."

"Well, I'll think about it. Meanwhile tell me more about your company. How long have you been with them?"

Mike started to recount the history of the company. The meals were ready so Mike fetched them from the bar. Throughout the meal he talked about his rise within the company. He was now chief rep with them and as such was virtually his own boss, but still very much accountable to the board.

They chatted comfortably for an hour, finished their meal and left. They drove back to Chichester and out to Priscilla's house.

When they arrived there Mike made as if to get out of the car, but Priscilla restrained him. "I don't think I ought to ask you in."

"I wasn't coming in" Mike said quickly, "but I was going to check that you hadn't had a break-in while you were out."

"Oh thank you Mike." She got out.

Mike took her key, went to the front door, unlocked it and threw it open. "It looks all right" he said.

They stood in the hall. Priscilla said "Thanks for a lovely time even if it was short."

"Short and sweet." Mike winced as he came out with this cliche. He always became tongue-tied when he was feeling embarrassed. He would have liked to have kissed her but this wasn't the time, he thought.

Priscilla sensed his discomfort. "Give me a ring sometime when you have some more free time" she said. "If I'm free too we might get together again."

"Right, I will. Well, goodbye Priscilla. Take care." He turned and left.

Priscilla watched as he got into his car then she closed the door.

Chapter 3

Back to Square One

Bill Hopkins was out with three of his friends. They had all been to an 'Over 25' disco and samba competition, and at 2 a.m. were walking round to where Bill's car was parked.

"There's one of my jobs" he said, pointing to where the Ruby's Taxis' premises were.

They came to the gateway and one of the chaps said "That looks like smoke coming from that door."

As they all peered there was a sudden noise of someone running. They saw a figure rush from the yard and head down the street.

"After him!" called out Bill as he and two of his friends set off in pursuit.

They were much younger and fitter than the man they were chasing and within the length of the street they had overtaken him and forced him to the ground. Meanwhile the other member of their party had found a phone and had called the fire brigade.

Bill and his mates frogmarched the man back to the yard. Bill was horrified at what he saw. Within those ten minutes the whole of the taxi stores and garage, as well as the offices were well and truly ablaze.

People were now congregating. Within minutes the first of three fire engines arrived and commenced hosing the buildings. Then a police car came.

Bill told the other two not to let their captive go, then walked over to the police car.

"Keep back sir, please" the officer said to Bill.

"Officer, we saw a man running from the place so we caught him and have him over there." He pointed.

"Right. Let's go and see what he has to say."

They went over to where Bill's two friends were holding the rough-looking character.

"Name?" said the officer.

"I ain't saying nothing" said the man.

"Right. Can you blokes bring him over to the car and I'll send for someone to take him in. You'll be needed for the statements as well."

They took the man to the car and put him in the back. As they did so the officer still in the car said "Cor, what a whiff of paraffin or something. Is that coming from him?" He nodded towards the suspect. The others started sniffing. They all agreed that the smell was coming from the man.

Bill turned to the officer. "I've got my car near. I'll bring it down to the station and we'll make statements there."

"Right" the officer replied.

By this time the flames had engulfed the garage and had spread to the offices which were now well alight.

Bill looked shattered. 'Poor Priscilla and Mrs Cavanagh' he thought, 'what the hell will they do now?' He watched for a few minutes more then left to get his car.

On the way he started to wonder whether anyone had told them about the fire. There was a phone box near the car park.

Bill called Priscilla's number. A sleepy voice said "Hello."

"Hello Priscilla, this is Bill."

"Bill! What on earth are you ringing about at —."

He cut her off with "Listen Priscilla. The taxi yard is on fire. It doesn't look as if they will save anything. There are three fire engines there doing their best but it looks hopeless."

"I hope this isn't a joke Bill."

"Joke nothing! This is serious. We caught a bloke running away and he's on his way to the police station, and I'm going down there now. You go and see for yourself and then come down to the police station."

"What about Ruby — Mrs Cavanagh?"

"I don't know. You could call her when you have seen the fire, unless the police have contacted her already."

"Right Bill. See you later." She replaced the phone, sat for a second on the edge of the bed, then she hurriedly dressed, grabbed her bag and rushed out to her car.

She had to stop a couple of streets away from the yard. She ran all the way to the fire, the glow from which was lighting the night sky. The sight that met her eyes as she turned the corner made her heart sink. The whole of the range of buildings including the garage where all the taxis were kept at night was burning fiercely. Occasionally there was an explosion as another petrol tank ignited. The fire engines were pouring thousands of gallons of water on to the fire but now all they could do was to try to prevent it spreading to the adjoining premises.

Priscilla turned away. She saw a police car with an officer standing beside it. She went over to him. "Excuse me, I am Mrs Thurston, part owner of this place with Mrs Cavanagh. Has she been contacted, do you know?"

"Just a minute madam." He called his station and after a moment said "Yes, madam, she has been told. They have been trying to locate you so I told them you were here."

"Thank you." She took one more look at the burning pile of what was her and Ruby's enterprise then went to her car.

At the police station the officer at the desk took her particulars and then asked her to wait.

After about ten minutes an un-uniformed officer appeared. "Sorry to keep you waiting Mrs Thurston. If you will come with me I have to ask a few questions."

"Oh? What about? I'm a victim not a perpetrator."

"We just have to establish a few facts." They went into a vacant room and were followed in by a uniformed officer.

"Now, Mrs Thurston, can you tell me where you were from midnight onwards?"

"In bed."

"How did you come to be at the fire?"

"I received a phone call from Mr Hopkins. He's a builder who worked on the premises."

"What time did you arrive at the fire?"

"I don't know. You'll have to ask the officer at the scene. I told him who I was and he called his station."

It was all over quite quickly and at the end the officer said "This will be typed out and I'il get you to sign it, then we shall not keep you any longer."

"I believe Mr Hopkins is here. Can I see him?"

"When he has given his statement he will be free to go, so you can see him then. It shouldn't be long."

In fact it was a further twenty minutes before Bill and his mates appeared from the corridor. Bill went straight towards Priscilla. He turned to his friends, gave one of them the car keys and said "Sit yourselves in the car, I'll be a couple of minutes." He looked at Priscilla. "How do you feel now? Will you be all right?" he asked.

"I'm OK but it has been a bit of a shock. I really need to be home now, perhaps in the morning it will look better."

"It's four-thirty now. Why don't you get some rest and don't do anything until the afternoon at least."

"I want to hear all about the man you caught."

"Time enough for that later. I'll tell you what — you go back to bed. Phone me when you are up and about, then we'll go to Mrs Cavanagh's and I'll tell you both all the details."

"I'll do that" said Priscilla. "Good night Bill." She left. Bill followed her and went to his car and friends.

Ruby Cavanagh woke about ten o'clock. She had dozed fitfully since last night. There had been a phone call at about two-thirty. The police were asking her to receive a visit from an officer shortly. Eleanor helped her to dress and together they waited for the police. When they arrived they went into the sitting room. They told Ruby about the fire and asked her the usual questions. where was she that evening, how was business and so on. They took a short statement from each of them, then left, saying that the detective inspector would see them later.

Eleanor was still asleep this morning, so Ruby just lay there thinking over the devastating news of last night. She had to go and see it for herself. She called Eleanor.

When Eleanor came in Ruby said "Let's have some breakfast, then I want to go and see the damage."

They were about ready to leave when the phone rang. Eleanor answered, it was Priscilla. "Can I speak to your mother please?"

Ruby took the phone.

"Hello Ruby, it's me, Priscilla. Are you feeling all right?"

"Yes, not too bad. It's been a terrible shock though."

"Look will it be all right if I come over this afternoon? Oh good. Well, I'd like to bring Bill Hopkins as well, he has something to tell you about last night."

That fixed, Priscilla rang Bill and they agreed to meet at Ruby's at two.

Ruby and Eleanor reached the taxi yard and stopped near the entrance. There was one small fire tender in case of a flare up but there was not much left to burn now. They could see the burnt out wrecks of all their new taxis. In a group in the yard were some of the drivers and Tim the foreman. Ruby got out of the car and took a few steps towards the men.

Tim Freshman approached her. "This is a disaster Mrs Cavanagh. How on earth could this have happened?"

"Heaven knows. Have the police interviewed you yet?"

"Yes, they have asked all of us lots of questions but no one knows anything."

Ruby looked over to the ruins and saw two fire investigators poking about the debris. "Have they said anything yet?" Ruby asked, pointing to the officers.

"No, and I don't suppose they'd tell us anyway" said Tim.

"Is there anything left in the offices, records or anything?" she asked.

"Not a thing. It'll take some sorting out." He looked gloomy.

"There is one thing we may be able to do" said Ruby. "Can you remember if there are any orders for hire cars for weddings or other functions?"

"There are two or three I think. If I could get together with Angie we might remember between us" said Tim.

"Could you do that please. Here's a tenner. Get two phone cards, contact those clients you remember and tell them what has happened. We shall not be able to fulfil those orders so they will have to go elsewhere."

"Right Mrs Cavanagh."

Ruby turned away. She knew that this was the end of their attempt to build up a fresh business. She sighed and went back to the car.

Priscilla arrived at Ruby's at two-thirty. Bill's car was already outside the house but Bill had waited for Priscilla to arrive. He got out of the car and went to meet Priscilla. "How do you feel now?" he asked.

"Completely shattered. It all seems so pointless."

"At least there was no loss of life, so that's a blessing I suppose."

"Trust you to look on the bright side, but you are quite right."

They reached the door, Bill rang the bell and stood back.

Eleanor opened the door. "Hello Priscilla, come in."

"This is Bill Hopkins" said Priscilla, turning.

"We've met, at the office. Come in."

Ruby was in the sitting room waiting for them. "Well, this is a pretty kettle of fish, isn't it" said Ruby. "I thought we'd had all our allocation of troubles, but it looks as though someone up there, or down here has got it in for us." She gave a little laugh.

Bill broke in with "I'll tell you about last night, then you can judge whether someone has got it in for you." He went on to tell them the whole story and at the end he said "The bloke wouldn't give his name so I can't tell you any more."

"Who would want to ruin us?" queried Ruby.

"The only person who could possibly feel anything against me" said Priscilla, "would be the wife of the man who killed Lionel, but I really think that is unlikely."

"What about Dad's clique?" asked Eleanor.

"We don't know who they are, the police never got one, even," said Ruby. "I don't know" she sighed.

The phone rang, Eleanor answered. "Yes, she's here, and Mrs Thurston." She turned to the others. "It's a Detective Inspector Ryecroft, wants to know if you will be in for the next half hour."

"Of course. Tell him it's all right."

Eleanor gave him the message and replaced the phone.

"I wonder what he wants?" said Priscilla.

"Well, if it does turn out to be arson there will be a pretty thorough investigation, especially of the proprietors" put in Bill.

"That's only if the business was failing" said Priscilla, "and ours certainly was not."

They continued discussing the possibilities until they saw the car pull up outside. There was a ring at the door and Eleanor went to let them in.

Detective Inspector Ryecroft and his sergeant came into the room. "Good afternoon Mrs Cavanagh, Mrs Thurston" he said.

"My name is Hopkins" said Bill. "I caught the suspect last night."

"Oh yes, my sergeant told me. I'd like you to stay, if you will."

Bill returned to his chair.

"First of all let me say how sorry I am that you have had this misfortune. I suppose you were properly insured, but that's only compensation for the material loss. The business and goodwill are gone completely. However, my main reason for coming round concerns the suspect. Do any of you know a man called Hughes, Edwin Hughes?" They all shook their heads. Ryecroft put his hand in his pocket and brought out an envelope and from this he produced a photograph. He handed it to Ruby. "Do you know him?" The photograph had been taken that morning and was now in circulation among the police.

"No I don't" said Ruby. "Sorry."

He took the photograph and handed it to Priscilla. "How about you Mrs Thurston?"

"Never seen him before" said Priscilla.

He turned to Bill. "This is the man you caught last night. Do you think this is a good likeness?"

Bill took the photograph. "Yes, that's him all right. Wouldn't trust him far."

Ryecroft took the photo back. "How about you miss" he said to Eleanor, "would you have seen him before?"

Eleanor took the photograph and looked at it closely. Her face must have given her away.

"What's up Eleanor?" said Ruby, "What is it?"

Eleanor found it hard to speak. Finally she said "I think I've seen him with Dad, on the boat a few years ago." Inside, she knew it was the same man.

Ryecroft went closer to Eleanor. "Are you sure, miss?" he asked.

After another pause Eleanor said "Yes I'm sure."

"Mrs Cavanagh," said the inspector, "I shall have to ask Eleanor a few more questions, but not here. If I could take her down to the station I'll bring her back as soon as it is over."

58

"Do you want me to come with her?"

"No, not if she's over eighteen."

"She is" said Ruby.

"If you like I'll go with you" said Priscilla.

"Thanks" said Eleanor. "Perhaps it would be as well."

The four of them left. Bill was still hovering, unsure what to do now.

"I fancy a cup of tea Mr Hopkins, how about you?"

"I could do with one, but please call me Bill."

After the questioning Eleanor was taken home, Priscilla went in her own car.

In the station Detective Inspector Ryecroft realised that they might have something other than arson on their hands. "So now we know someone who was connected with Cavanagh. Was Cavanagh supplying Hughes or what? We'll get a warrant to search Hughes' place, only now we shall be looking not only for traces of paraffin and fuel oil but for narcotics. Pity Cavanagh kept silent during his trial or we could have nabbed this fellow, maybe."

Ryecroft got things moving, and the next day he set up a search of Hughes' place. They took Hughes along so that if anything should be found then he could see that it had not been planted. The forensic lab had identified the fuel that had been on Hughes' clothes and which the police officers had smelt when Hughes was taken into custody. They needed a bit of luck now to find enough evidence to charge him.

Hughes lived in a bungalow outside the town in a normal residential area. His wife was in when they arrived to do the search, and a policewoman sat with her while the search was going on. All the rooms were thoroughly searched and finally they all stood in the hall.

"There's just the loft now sir" said one of the officers. He looked up at the ceiling where the trap door was. "This is one of them with a ladder that comes down with the trap door." He looked around and soon found the short pole used to spring the latch and pull the door down. He soon had the ladder in place and quickly went up and disappeared.

A second officer went up the ladder and remained with his head through the opening so that he could see. The man who was searching had not found anything. He turned to come back to the trap door.

"Have you looked in the water tanks?" asked the one on the ladder.

"Yes, nothing there."

"What about under the tanks then?"

"There's no space under the tanks."

"Oh yes there is. I can see a gap of about an inch or so, maybe two."

The searcher crawled closer to the tanks and shone his torch under. "There's something under there. Pass me that pole." The pole, a rod about three quarters of an inch in diameter and three feet long was passed up. After a bit of poking there came a shout of "Bingo!"

Ryecroft moved forward. "Give it to the man on the ladder." It was handed down. "Now, you give it to me." Ryecroft was handed three plastic bags, each containing about one kilo of a white powder. "Time fifteen-twenty. I am sealing these bags in a plastic bag."

Hughes had been allowed to watch the proceedings and was now ushered out to one of the cars. Two more uniformed officers appeared from the back of the bungalow.

"Anything from the sheds?" asked Ryecroft.

"Only this, sir. It's a piece of tubing and it has recently been used for some sort of fuel oil, not petrol."

Ryecroft produced another bag and the tube was deposited in it. He felt he now had enough evidence to charge Hughes with a drug offence, and with a good report from the forensic lab he might make an arson charge stick. Either way, Hughes was going to be in custody for a long time. Just how long that would be could depend on someone else — Jeff Cavanagh. If he would talk perhaps they could put Hughes away for a very long time. He decided to pay a visit to the prison.

Eleanor had been to the shops and when she arrived home she carried her shopping bags into the kitchen then went into the sitting room. "Mum, I've got everything —." She stopped. "Mum! Are you all right?"

Ruby was stretched out on the settee, one arm hanging limply down the side, her face very pale.

"Mum, what's the matter?"

Ruby stirred and looked at Eleanor. "I'm a bit — er — I don't know, I haven't got any energy left."

"Shall I call the doctor?" asked Eleanor.

"No, I expect I'll manage." She tried to sit up, then with a sigh fell back again. "Oh what's the use" she moaned, "I've had enough. I just don't care any more. It's all your father's fault, the stupid silly idiot!"

"He was thinking of you, Mum, really he was. He just didn't foresee the consequences and he's paying for it."

"Paying for it!" she almost shouted. "It's we who are paying for it. We could have managed all right. Now things are worse than ever."

"They're not!" chimed in Eleanor. "We shall not be badly off if we get the insurance, surely?"

"There's nothing to do, nothing to live for. A lifetime's work gone and now we're too old to start again." Ruby broke down and sobbed.

Eleanor comforted her and then went into the hall. She called Ruby's doctor. "Dr Gibson? It's Mum. She's terribly depressed. I think someone ought to see her."

Priscilla had not heard from Ruby or Bill for over two weeks. They had parted on the day they had all met at Ruby's. She, Priscilla, had carefully avoided eye contact with Bill while they were there, in fact they had not spoken directly to each other that afternoon. Also, she was anxious to know what had transpired about the suspected arsonist. She would ring Ruby.

Mrs Richings answered the phone. "No. This is Mrs Richings, you know — I come in every day."

"Oh yes Mrs Richings, I remember. Is Mrs Cavanagh there?"

"No, she's at the hospital."

"Oh dear. What happened?"

"Nothing's happened. She's had some extra treatment, but she is going to a therapy session twice a week. Eleanor takes her there."

"How long will she be?"

"About two hours I think. Just a minute, here's Eleanor."

She passed the phone. "Hello Priscilla" said Eleanor, "can I help?"

"I wanted to speak to your mother. I need an update on what's happening."

"Well" said Eleanor, "Mum's at the therapy department. I take her there and then fetch her two hours later."

"I could come over later" said Priscilla.

"Why don't you come over now" said Eleanor, "have a cup of tea, then we'll both go and fetch her, then you two can chat on the way back."

"Right. I'll come over, say fifteen minutes. Bye."

When Priscilla arrived at Ruby's Eleanor opened the door to her. "Come in, Mrs Richings is just going." They went into the sitting room.

"Has anything materialised since I last saw you?" Priscilla asked.

"Oh yes, lots. That man I identified that I'd seen with Dad. It seems he's still in the drug racket so if he doesn't get convicted on the arson charge it's almost certain he will on the drugs charge."

"When shall we know?"

"Apparently it will take weeks to put the case together, and it's more than likely that Dad will have to give evidence."

"What a mess this all is" said Priscilla. "I shall be glad when it's all over."

"You didn't know what you were letting yourself in for when you joined up with Mum, but then, neither did any of us."

"No, it seemed that we were blotting out the past when we refurbished the business, but now it has all come back, only twice as nasty."

61

"What will you do now, Priscilla?" asked Eleanor.

"I just don't know" she answered. "Nothing I suppose, until after the trial of this chap Hughes, and of course the insurance settlement."

They chatted on for a while then Eleanor said, "Come on, let's go and fetch Mum. My car."

When they reached the hospital they went into the reception area.

"If we wait here Mum will come from the lift."

Presently the lift doors opened and they could see Ruby in her wheelchair. They had no need to go to her for her wheelchair was being pushed by a very striking-looking man of about fifty.

They came towards Priscilla and Eleanor. Ruby's face brightened as she spotted them. "Hello Priscilla, this is a nice surprise." She partly turned to the man behind her. "This is Mr Mowbray. Arthur, this is Mrs Thurston."

Priscilla put out her hand. "Hello Mr Mowbray."

"Nice to meet you, Mrs Thurston" said Mowbray.

Priscilla was thinking — what's a healthy looking fellow like that doing here?

As if reading her thoughts Ruby said "Mr Mowbray — er — Arthur has been looking after me on my visits here. He's in the same group as I am."

Eleanor went to take the chair.

"No, it's all right" said Arthur, "I'll take her to the car."

They all went to the car park and Arthur helped stow the chair in the boot. "Cheerio Ruby. See you next time."

"Goodbye Arthur, thank you." Ruby was slightly flushed.

When they got to Ruby's home they all went in, and Priscilla, who was curious to know more about Arthur Mowbray soon got round to it. "What's Mr Mowbray doing at a therapy group — or you for that matter?"

"Well, first of all" said Ruby, "after the fire I felt all my old symptoms returning and the doctor advised me to try this therapy group, more to settle my mind than my body, so that's what I am doing."

"Yes, you look better already, but what about Mr Mowbray?"

"Arthur Mowbray is a widower. Apparently his wife's death almost unhinged him. He once had a thriving electronics business, but he was so depressed that he had to sell it. He has been going to the therapy for some months and he has improved so much that he is now able to give support to others, which is the whole point of the group really."

Priscilla had been quite impressed by Arthur Mowbray but he did not look as though he needed therapy. She said as much to Ruby.

"Well" said Ruby "he has probably got over it, almost. I am certainly finding it beneficial."

"In what way?" asked Priscilla.

"In the first place, I was so shattered by the fire following on the other catastrophe that I hadn't given a thought to the possibility that there could be others in the same boat. Yet when I sat there at first, listening to the others talking about their problems I realised almost immediately that I was not unique, in fact their troubles seemed to be much more severe than mine. That appeared to be the crux of the whole procedure. Each one of us went there with the feeling that ours was the worst thing that had ever happened, and each one of us has realised that a catastrophe is a catastrophe. It's not the size of the catastrophe that matters, it's how it affects the victim. I have managed to put the whole thing in perspective and I feel much better."

Eleanor had been watching her mother as she spoke. She noticed a new sort of radiance about her, like she used to be when Eleanor was a child.

Priscilla was speaking. "Have you heard from the insurance people yet?" she asked.

"Only that they are still investigating. They are pretty sure it was deliberate, but proving who did it is not going to be easy."

"We'll just have to wait then" said Priscilla.

She left soon afterwards and drove home.

Eleanor sat looking at her mother. "Mum" she ventured slowly, "this Mr Mowbray, how well off is he?"

"Oh, I should say he has a substantial bank balance. I know he has his own house over at Angmering, and he had a really good business, so it would have fetched a good price, probably a million. Why?" asked Ruby.

"It's only that — well — I thought that if he's showing a lot of interest in you he might — er — well, he might be looking for a bit of cash or something."

Ruby laughed. "That's absolute rubbish. He's a very kindly person, genuinely interested in all the people in our group. I admit he has shown me more attention than most but I like it — it makes me feel I am not on the outside."

"But what about Dad?" Eleanor asked.

"What about him? He's not here. He hasn't wanted me since the day I became ill with this wretched disease. Oh yes, he has not failed either of us in providing for our welfare, but he is only tolerant. He hasn't wanted me as a person for years, but he is loyal, I grant you that." She reached over and patted Eleanor's hand. "Don't you worry" she said, "I can look after myself. You are only eighteen and I wouldn't expect you to be able to appreciate how older people feel."

"I'm sorry Mum, I'm sure you know best."

The weeks passed slowly. Priscilla had taken up some of her former voluntary jobs that she had dropped when she went into the taxi business. Now that she had time on her hands she was desperate for anything that would keep her occupied. With the coming of spring she had started to tidy up the garden and was considering getting a greenhouse.

She was pottering about on the terrace when the phone rang. She hurried in to the kitchen extension phone. "Yes?"

"Hello, is that Priscilla?"

"Yes, who's calling?"

"It's Michael Eldon."

"Oh, Mike! Of course, I'd almost forgotten you."

"Oh dear, that's a bad start, I was going to ask you if you would like a day out."

"When?" asked Priscilla.

"Today, now, if it's convenient." Mike sounded eager.

"Where are you speaking from?"

"Worthing. I've been in Worthing on business and stayed overnight, so as I've a free day I thought I'd call you."

"It's a nice thought. What had you in mind?"

I haven't been to the Isle of Wight for several years, so I thought I'd like to re-visit. We could take the ferry from Southsea and drive round the island, have some lunch say at Ventnor or where ever you like."

"It sounds a lovely idea. What time would you be going?"

"I can come straight along to you now, say half an hour, that means we could get a ferry about eleven o'clock. Can you be ready?"

"Yes, I've had breakfast and will be ready as soon as you arrive."

"Right. See you later then." He rang off.

'Solid old Mike, fancy him coming down again.' He was good company and she began to look forward to the day ahead.

Mike arrived on schedule and they set off at once.

"It's good to see you again" said Mike when they were settled in the car. "How have you been?"

"Well, you know, it has all been a bit traumatic, but the worst is over."

"It must have been a shock after all your efforts, and for Mrs Cavanagh."

"Yes, Ruby was quite seriously affected by it, but she's making a remarkable comeback."

"I'm glad. What about you? Have you any plans for a second go, or what about Mrs Cavanagh, is she going to try again?"

"No, I shall not try this one again. There are criminal undertones to the whole thing and I don't want to be mixed up in it any more."

"OK then, let's forget it all for today and enjoy the trip."

They were able to get the eleven o'clock ferry, so by twelve they were driving round the west road.

As they reached Bembridge Mike pointed out a side road. "That's where we used to take the children when we had a holiday here. They loved it." He sounded wistful. Near Sandown Mike reminisced again. "We often went to the little airport and watched planes landing. The weather was always fine."

Priscilla could not remember ever having been to the Isle of Wight before, so she began to feel irritated by Mike's continual references to his family from whom he had been separated for several years.

Through Shanklin to Ventnor. They found a restaurant that was open all year. As it was the week before Easter the other smaller establishments were not open yet. They went in. There were several tables occupied. The fine weather had brought out lots of trippers.

Over lunch their conversation was trivial, and each avoided any reference to the fire or business of any kind.

"How's your home and garden?" asked Mike. "There must be a lot to do keeping the lawns and shrubbery tidy."

"I shall get the lawns cut by a contractor who goes to several houses in the district. I should be able to manage the rest. Actually I was thinking of asking my mother if she would like to live with me. She's quite active and would probably like to potter about in the garden."

"Wouldn't you find that restrictive? I mean, you would be responsible for her at all times, and what if you wanted to entertain or have people stay?"

"I don't entertain much and I —" she was thinking of Bill and the day he and she had been in the bedroom. If there had been someone else living in the house that episode would never have happened. That would have been a shame, she thought. Perhaps Mike had ideas too, ideas that required Priscilla being on her own. "Oh, I don't know" she went on, "I'll probably carry on as I am now."

Suddenly Mike said "Have you ever thought about marrying again?"

'What's he up to now>' thought Priscilla. 'Has he got ideas?' "No. Well yes, I have thought, but not seriously." 'His own marriage has foundered,' she thought, 'so I hope he's not going to tell me I ought to remarry.'

"I think you should remarry. You are much too attractive to become a recluse or a parent minder."

'So he is thinking along those lines.' She didn't answer.

They left the restaurant and set off again along the coast road. When they were getting near the Needles Mike started reminiscing again. "It was somewhere along here we stopped and went to the sea. Little Trevor had a big ball and he bounced it and it went down and into the sea. He ran after it down the slope and fell over into the water. I ran down to get him and ended up knee deep in the sea, grabbing Trevor and squelching back up the beach. The ball went out to sea and I had soaking shoes and trousers. We laughed afterwards but it could have been serious." He sighed. "Ah well, water under the bridge."

They drove along for a while in silence. Priscilla suddenly sat up very straight. "Pull in somewhere please Mike."

"What's the trouble, don't you feel well?"

"No, I'm all right, I want to say something."

They came to a lay-by, Mike drove in and stopped. "What's the problem?" he asked.

"It's you Mike" said Priscilla. She was amazed at how cool she felt. "It's obvious to me that you have lots of regrets about what happened to your marriage. You really miss your children although they are much older now. But —."

Mike started to interrupt.

"No, let me finish" she went on. "You didn't spend enough time with them, only on holiday. Your wife didn't see much of you because you were too busy working. It may be presumptuous of me to say this, but I have the feeling that you are seeing me as possibly the next Mrs Eldon. I think you should ask the present Mrs Eldon to give you another chance. From what you told me previously she must have been a sort of recluse in her own home. Any wife and mother deserves more. You failed her, them. I don't want to be picked up and dropped. So please put any thoughts about you and me out of your head. Can we go straight home now, please."

Mike said nothing. He re-started the car and they drove off towards the ferry terminal. For about ten minutes Mike was inwardly fuming. He knew he had been rumbled, he also knew he had been a fool to presume that he was eligible to compete for Priscilla. His track record was poor and he would need to make drastic changes in his approach if he wished to become an attractive prospect to any woman.

As he drove along he gradually calmed down and tried to visualise himself as Priscilla was seeing him. "You are absolutely right Priscilla. I'm sorry. I had no right to bring up the subject of marriage, even hypothetically."

"It's all right, it's over now" said Priscilla quietly.

They arrived at the terminal, drove on to the ferry and finally arrived at Southsea.

As they drove off the boat Priscilla said "Can you drop me off in the town, I'll get a bus to Chichester, please."

"As you wish, but it's no trouble to drive you home."

"No, I'd like to stay and look in some shops."

He found a street where he could stop safely. "How will this do?"

he asked.

"That's fine." She got out, looked back through the door of the car and said, "Thank you for the trip, it was quite nice. Take care." She closed the door and walked away up the street. For the first time she felt very lonely.

She wandered through some shops, then found the bus station where she got on to one for Chichester. Ironically, in Chichester she had to get a taxi to take her home. The driver was courteous and pleasant, she tipped him generously.

"What's your firm like to work for?" she asked.

"A1. Couldn't be better. Lots more work since that fire a few weeks ago."

"Yes, I suppose so. It's an ill wind." She went in.

Easter came and went. The summer began brightly enough but by July it had become dull and mostly wet, Priscilla could hardly get her garden into shape. All the ground was soaking and flowers were drooping, being full of rainwater. She was sitting indoors watching more rain pelting down when the phone rang.

It was Eleanor. "Can I come and see you, I must talk to someone."

"Of course, I'm doing nothing. Come over now, I'll get some tea ready."

After twenty minutes a car drew up outside. Eleanor got out and ran up to the front door. Priscilla was waiting by the door. "Come in quickly. What weather!"

Eleanor shed her coat and followed Priscilla into the sitting room. "How nice it is in here" she said.

"Yes. You haven't been here before have you? I'll show you round later. First let's have a cup of tea." Priscilla poured the tea, passed a cup to Eleanor and said, "Now, what's on your mind?"

"It's Mum. No, she's not ill, far from it."

"That's good anyway."

"Well, up to a point. You know that Arthur Mowbray Mum got friendly with. You saw him that day at the hospital."

"Yes, I remember."

"Mum is besotted with him. She has already spent two days at his house in Angmering."

"There's nothing wrong in that, is there, not these days anyway."

"No, that's not the worst of it. She's going to divorce Dad!"

"Oh dear, that is something else indeed. I don't know what to say."

"Poor Dad. He'll be shattered, but I know he will not put up any opposition. He'll say that if that is what she wants she shall have it."

"I know. But look where it got him. He was doing that stupid thing for your mother. But there is something you are overlooking. Ever since your mother's illness started they have not been man and wife, do you understand?"

"You mean they haven't slept together?"

"Yes. Apart from the sclerosis symptoms your mother is a normal woman with a woman's needs."

"You can't mean that she wants to — well — make love?" said Eleanor.

"Of course she does. But your father is in no position to fulfil her needs even if he wanted to" said Priscilla.

"I don't suppose he would anyway, not at their age" said Eleanor.

"Their age!" Priscilla almost shouted. "You've a lot to learn Eleanor. The sexual urge is strong at all ages. You often read of couples in retirement places getting married. Your mum is only a little older than me, so there's nothing unusual in her wanting a bit of comfort, a bit of loving or whatever."

"It seems a bit sordid to me" said Eleanor.

"Present-day teenagers jumping into bed as soon as they meet seems sordid to me, but they don't affect me so it's none of my business."

"Well anyway, I don't know what I should do" said Eleanor.

"You don't have to do anything as far as I can see. When do you go to university?"

"September, three months time. I've got a place at Hull."

"And so you'll be away from home leaving your mum to her own devices" put in Priscilla.

"Yes, I suppose so, but I have to complete my education."

"Exactly" said Priscilla triumphantly. "Everyone has a goal, an ambition, call it what you like, but it's an incentive to fulfil oneself, and your mum's no different."

"But what about Dad then?" Eleanor asked.

"Your dad made an error of judgement and he's paying for it. When he finishes his sentence I don't doubt he will have very different aims and ideals."

"And no one to look after him" said Eleanor.

"He'll survive. Don't forget it will be years before he is free. A lot will have changed by then, not least yourself. My advice to you is — get on with your life, leave your mum to sort hers out herself. If she decides she wants to live with Mr Mowbray it would solve your problems."

"I suppose it would, in a way." She got up from the settee. "I think I'll be off now. I think I am beginning to see Mum's side of it now. So, thanks for the chat."

"I think I went on a bit, but if it has been of any help then that's all right." Priscilla went with Eleanor to the door. "Keep me in touch with developments. I don't want to pry but it's nice to know about things."

"Sure I will. Goodbye."

Towards the end of July Ruby had a phone call from Detective Inspector Ryecroft. "Ah, Mrs Cavanagh. I'd like to see you down here at the station, tomorrow if possible."

"Yes, I'm free tomorrow, in fact any time" said Ruby.

"Good" said Ryecroft. "Now I'd like Mrs Thurston here as well, so if I ring her and arrange for two o'clock tomorrow that suits you then?"

"Yes. If it doesn't suit Mrs Thurston I can fit in at any time to suit her."

"Right. I'll confirm with you later."

Ryecroft rang Priscilla and put the same request to her. She was free and agreed to meet there at two o'clock.

When Priscilla arrived at the station Ruby was already there in the waiting room accompanied by Arthur Mowbray. Priscilla greeted them both warmly, taking particular note now of how their relationship appeared to have blossomed.

At two precisely Ryecroft called them into his room. "Sit down please. Now ladies, first of all the trial of Edwin Hughes will take place in October. He has been charged with drug possession and a second charge of arson. You will both be summoned to appear as witnesses for the prosecution on the arson charge, mainly to do with the business you ran. You will have interviews with the prosecuting counsel later on. Then on the drugs charge you Mrs Cavanagh will be called because this relates to the previous case that involved your husband. Incidentally, your husband will be appearing as a witness for the prosecution in the drugs case, a fact that may eventually do him some good."

"How do you mean?" asked Ruby.

"Well, it is possible that evidence might be proferred that could support an appeal against your husband's sentence. No, not a pardon. He was guilty as charged, that stands. Now your daughter Eleanor will also be called to say she had seen Hughes, but she knows about that."

"She'll be at Hull University in October" said Ruby.

"That's all right. She will be given time off and expenses." He looked from one to the other. "Are there any questions? No? Well I won't keep you. Thank you for coming in."

They went down to the waiting room. Arthur Mowbray rose from his seat and took Ruby's arm. "All right dear?" he said.

"Yes thanks."

Priscilla had watched this little scenario with interest. This was a new Ruby. She was a woman who was being appreciated and she was enjoying it. Her disability was almost forgotten, she was very much alive.

69

Priscilla made as if to leave but Ruby put out a hand. "Come back to my place and have a chat, please."

"Yes, all right, I was only going back home."

At Ruby's there was no sign of Eleanor. In response to Priscilla's question Ruby answered "Eleanor? Oh she's having a few days in Hull, sizing the place up after her interview."

They all sat down and when they were settled Ruby looked at Priscilla and said. "Arthur and I have come to an arrangement. If I get a divorce from Jeff we shall be married and I shall live at Angmering. This house will be sold and the money put in trust for Eleanor when she is twenty-one."

"You are looking a long way ahead aren't you" said Priscilla. "What if you don't get a divorce?"

"Everything will go ahead just as if there was a divorce."

"And you?" asked Priscilla tentatively.

"We" said Ruby, looking at Arthur, "shall live together no matter what."

Priscilla did not know what to say. She looked from one to the other. "How does this affect me then?" she asked.

"I would like you to be a sort of trustee to look out for Eleanor during her next three years. I know it's a lot to ask but believe me it's the only solution I can think of."

"Solution to what exactly?" asked Priscilla.

"Well, as yet Eleanor doesn't exactly approve of Arthur, or rather of my going with him. She's not ready to trust us yet, not as a couple. If she had someone she could call on for advice or guidance she would soon come to accept my relationship with Arthur."

"There's another very important aspect that needs resolving" said Priscilla, "and I'm not sure I should get involved."

"What's that then?" asked Ruby.

"Your husband Jeff. Does Eleanor visit him in prison? Do you still visit him? Are you expecting me to visit him? Where exactly does he fit in to your new scheme?"

"Oh dear" said Ruby, "I must admit to being a bit selfish in that when I decided on my new life I have behaved as though he didn't exist anymore. What you have got to understand is that I have had this sclerosis bug for several years, and that from the outset Jeff and I were as good as divorced. We lived in the same house, that's all. I have now made the separation. I shall not voluntarily see him again."

"I don't know what you are asking me to do" said Priscilla. "Am I to be a surrogate mother, because I am not qualified to do that. In any case Eleanor is eighteen and officially an adult citizen, so in actual fact no one has any power to control her life anyway."

"Perhaps I can put in a word" broke in Arthur. "When Ruby and I are living at Angmering there will be a room for Eleanor. She will be free to use it or not, and if she does she will have complete freedom to come and go as she pleases without restriction. I hope she will take advantage of it and come to regard me not as a second father, more of a guardian and companion to her mother." He looked at Ruby. "We two have a second chance for continued happiness. We have love and security, and both are available to Eleanor if she wishes."

Priscilla began to feel like an intruder as Arthur exposed his feelings for Ruby. She needed to end this discussion. "Well, I'll need time to think about it, Ruby. When are you thinking of making the change?"

"Not until the arson and insurance are settled, so that you can get your capital back and we can dispose of the yard. Could be months and months." Ruby sighed.

"Should I speak to Eleanor about all this?" asked Priscilla.

"I wish you would, it might save her the embarrassment of us seeming to plan her life for her."

"Very well then." Priscilla rose and turned for the door. "I'll be in touch, but in any case we'll meet at the assizes in October."

"Goodbye Priscilla" said Ruby, "you really are a brick."

'Yes,' thought Priscilla, 'I must be solid from the neck up.'

On the way home she continued to think over what had been said, then reached a decision. 'I shall leave things as they are and let nature take its course.'

It was early in September, Priscilla was watching the evening sun go down behind the trees. The phone rang. "Hello?"

"Hello, Priscilla?" It was Bill Hopkins.

"Oh Bill, how nice to hear from you. It seems months."

"That's what I was thinking. I was ringing just to see if you were all geared up for the assizes next month."

"I had almost forgotten about it, but anyway it will not be as much of an ordeal for me as for you" said Priscilla.

"I've never been in a court before" said Bill, "so I hope they treat me kindly."

"I'm sure they will. You are an important witness you know."

"Yes, I suppose I am" said Bill. "Anyway, how are you keeping?"

"Oh, I lead a quiet life. It gets a bit boring, but I can't see there being any change until after all that unfinished business is resolved."

"Why don't you have a night out somewhere" said Bill.

"How do you mean?" queried Priscilla a little cautiously.

"I don't mean a dinner dance like our last outing, our only outing actually. What about a nightclub in say Brighton."

"Do they admit over forties?" joked Priscilla.

"Any age, not minors though. The lights are low so nobody cares how well you dance or whatever, what do you say?"

"When?" asked Priscilla tentatively.

"Tomorrow night" said Bill.

Priscilla thought for a moment, 'Well, what the hell!' "OK you're on. What time?"

"Say nine o'clock at your place, we'll be there from ten onwards. Miniskirt and lots of lipstick" he laughed.

"I won't let you down" said Priscilla.

At nine precisely Bill rolled up at Priscilla's door. She called "Come in."

Bill stepped into the hall and saw Priscilla standing in front of the long hall mirror. He gave a long low whistle. "That's some outfit. Where did you get that?"

"Actually I've had it for some time but have not had a chance to wear it."

"What exactly is it, a Dior or something?"

"No, but it's a creation with a good name. They described it as a kind of sheath in a pseudo gold lamé, cunningly drawn to one side from shoulder to waist, giving a twenties' look but not disguising the female form. Definitely not mini but the length short enough to be interesting. An intermittently secured back opening down to the waist allows for dissipation of warmth generated by dancing."

"A winner all the way" said Bill admiringly.

"And what about you then, how would you describe your outfit?" asked Priscilla looking him up and down.

"Well, these are taup chino slacks, a silky material shirt — don't ask me what — in stripes of black and gold, plus a lightweight single-breasted jacket in biscuit, to be discarded to dissipate heat when dancing" he mimicked.

In happy mood they set off for Brighton.

On the way Priscilla had a sudden thought. "Won't you feel restricted about having a drink when you've got to drive home after?"

"I shall only have two alcoholic drinks. You can have as much as you want, but I don't expect you will have that many will you?"

"I never over indulge. I like a couple, maybe three if the 'do' goes on for any length of time."

"We'll see how it goes" said Bill.

They were able to park not too far away from the club, and a little while later were seated at a table being served by a young waiter. Priscilla looked around and saw that this was a larger place than she had imagined. It was almost square with one end semi-circular. The top end had a small raised dais on which the five-man combo played. There were two bars, one each side of the semi-circle and all the space between was polished maplewood floor.

Down the right hand side was a larger stage for the cabaret artistes, and at floor level on the right of this stage was a synthesiser used for accompanying the cabaret spot.

A third bar was situated near the entrance door and was for the use of waiters only who were serving the tables. Half the tables were occupied and there was a growing bunch of people at each of the bars. A young lady was playing the synthesiser and her accomplished playing greeted the customers as the tables gradually filled up. She finished her spot with a sustained chord and stood to appreciative applause.

That was the signal for an MC to appear at the far end. "Thank you Marguerita. Ladies and gentlemen, the first cabaret performance will be at eleven-fifteen. Until then you may enjoy listening or dancing to the Sonic Five, thank you."

The group went straight into a foot tapping rhythm and soon many of those around the two bars were on the polished floor gyrating to the beat.

Bill and Priscilla were content at this stage to stay at their table and sip their drinks. The nightclub atmosphere intensified as the crowd dancing around the bars became more excited by the rhythm.

Eventually Priscilla found that she was becoming affected by the beat and could no longer just sit still. She downed her drink and said, "Come on Bill, let's go and shake!"

"Right!" He leapt to his feet, took Priscilla's hand and threaded his way between the tables and on to the floor. There was still plenty of room, and as they faced each other and started jumping to the music they could see that the other people were mainly thirtyish.

Priscilla felt better at that and any inhibitions she had just fell away. Bill had good rhythm and was putting in lots of jive steps. Priscilla could match these, plus a few innovations of her own, but basic to all their movements was the pounding beat that ennervated all the dancers.

As Bill became more energetic he caught Priscilla's hand and twisted her first this way and then that. Priscilla responded with a lightness that surprised him, but they never stopped moving. As the bass thumped on they became more and more abandoned, and the dancers near them stood tapping their feet and watching them.

Priscilla felt the years dropping away — forty? — not on your life. Thirty? — no, at this moment she was Bill's age, they were as one, and their enjoyment was that of two equals.

The music stopped with a thump. They held each other for a moment then went back to their table. A waiter came by so they ordered another drink.

"You did better at my sort of dancing than I did at yours, remember?" Bill looked at her admiringly.

"Yes I do" said Priscilla. "That seems like another life away."

The spotlight came on and illuminated the side stage where the MC had appeared again. He was also the stand-up comic. "Good evening ladies and gentlemen. I'm the dogsbody for this evening. I'm supposed to stand up here and make you laugh. Talking of which, did I tell you about my new girlfriend with one leg shorter than the other? No? She was an absolute pushover!"

A party of chaps at a table near the stage fell about laughing at this, and the rest of the customers soon joined in, the guffaws from the chaps at the table helping to start others laughing. From then on the MC had them all laughing at anything he said, the mood was set and this first show of the evening was assured of a receptive audience.

Bill and Priscilla were no less receptive and enjoyed the unicycle act and the plate jugglers. The first show ended with a very attractive girl vocalist reminiscent of Dionne Warwick, then the MC came on and announced more dancing. On cue the group started playing and soon the floor was full of jumping couples. By this time Bill and Priscilla had had their second drinks as well as a snack.

"How about another bash at physical exercise?" said Bill.

"Lead me to it" said Priscilla, squeezing out of her chair.

They took up where they had left off, and for a good five minutes flung themselves about as in a frenzy.

Then, abruptly the music stopped, the lights were turned low and the group went into a slow romantic love song with a sensuous beat. Priscilla slid into Bill's arms and he pulled her closer to him with both arms round her waist. They shuffled round to the music, other couples pressing closer as the floor filled up. The song seemed to go on for ever, and when the music eventually stopped they were reluctant to release each other. When they did come down to earth they walked in silence back to their table.

Priscilla looked at Bill. "I think I'd like to go home now Bill."

"Sure, anything you say." They picked up their things and went to the exit.

On the short walk to the car park Priscilla said "I really enjoyed this evening, Bill."

"So did I" said Bill, "but it was just enough."

"That's what I thought" said Priscilla, "had we stayed longer it might have palled a bit, but that was just OK."

They got to the car and then drove straight home.

A little over an hour later Bill pulled up at Priscilla's house. He got out and went with her to the front door. "Perhaps we can do this again sometime." He was preparing to say good night.

"Tonight's not over yet" said Priscilla. "Would you like to come in for a coffee or another drink?"

"Well perhaps a coffee. Are you sure it's not too late?"

Priscilla had already opened the door. They went inside to the hall. Priscilla went on into the sitting room and put a light on.

Bill followed her, they stood facing each other. "I don't think I want a coffee" said Bill.

Priscilla moved towards him, looked up at him and said "Neither do I."

Bill slowly took her into his arms and as soon as their bodies touched Priscilla clung to him, offering her lips to his. Bill crushed her to him, and the passion in their kisses rose to a crescendo.

Priscilla broke away. She took Bill's hand saying "Come, you know the way."

They went up the stairs together and into Priscilla's bedroom.

She indicated the bed. "I'll be a couple of minutes she said.

She went into the next room, Bill slipped quickly out of his clothes and slid between the sheets. When Priscilla returned she was wearing a see-through negligee.

Bill gasped "Wow!"

Priscilla sat on the bed, switched off the light, discarded the negligee and crept in beside him. Their bodies touched and the passion was rekindled. Bill showered kisses on her lips and neck and down to her breasts. His hand stroked her body from her breasts to her thighs. Priscilla squirmed with pleasure and then pulled him on to her. She gave herself up to his intense passion.

She felt his penetration and put her hands on his buttocks pulling him tighter. "Don't leave me, don't leave me, I've taken precautions" she gasped."Oh Bill oh!"

Together they reached a glorious climax and as they subsided their bodies were glistening with perspiration. They separated slowly and lay on their backs.

Priscilla pulled the bedclothes back up over them. Bill threaded an arm round her shoulders. She snuggled her head on to his chest.

As she regained her equilibrium she thought about the whole evening. She had really enjoyed it, and coming here as a finale had been superb. But — she knew it was not what she would want to do regularly. She had gone all through that in her courtship and marriage. She had got over the flaming passion that consumed young couples and now was more mature, needing quality rather than quantity.

She nudged Bill's chest. "You can have a shower before you go" she said quietly.

That morning Priscilla slept late. She finally got up to a sunny morning and went down to the front door to get the milk. As she stood on the step she thought back to a few hours ago when she had stood on this same step with Bill about to leave.

"Bill" she had said, "this has been a wonderful evening and I have thoroughly enjoyed myself." She had paused to think out what she would say next. "It really isn't right for you Bill. You are young and have lots to look forward to. I think you should seriously think of finding a girl of your own age."

Bill had protested.

"No, Bill" she had gone on, "give it some thought, and please — leave me out of your plans for the future."

Bill had mumbled something about thinking it over and had left.

She picked up the milk and went inside. She started wondering how she should spend her time now that the taxi project was finished. Ruby was planning a new life, Eleanor was off to college, she had given Michael Eldon the fond farewell and now she had virtually dismissed Bill from her life. She would not find the answer for some time yet.

Chapter 4

The Truth — at Last

Eleanor had taken up her place at Hull University and had made arrangements for time off to go down for the trial of Hughes on a drugs charge.

She had made friends with several of her year's intake but one young man was paying her quite a lot of attention. When Eleanor had first seen Don Metcalfe he had not impressed her that much. She was making sure she missed nothing during these first weeks and so was not looking for male attention. Her good looks and pleasant appearance made her a target for amorous students but Eleanor was not ready for any sort of relationship yet.

Every day Don pressed her to join him on little outings and in fact she did accompany him for coffee or tea some days, but mostly in company with several of her girl friends.

On the Sunday before Eleanor was due to go down to Chichester she was in her room when there was a knock at the door. She opened it and was surprised to see Don standing there. "Hello Don, what brings you here?"

"It's a nice day. I'm going on the bus to Beverley to see the Minster and I wondered if you'd like to come along. We would have tea there and be back here by seven o'clock."

Eleanor motioned to him to come in. She was considering his request. "I have my car here, if I came could we go in that?"

"I'd rather not. I've planned to go by bus and as I'm asking you to come I would like to stick to my plan."

"All right Don, what time are we going?"

"The bus leaves at two. I'll call for you at one-thirty and we can stroll down to the bus station."

"I'll be ready" said Eleanor.

Later that afternoon they left the Minster and made their way into the town and found a little cafe where they ordered tea.

As they sipped their tea Don was looking at Eleanor and was almost overwhelmed by the pleasure he got from gazing at her. "How are you enjoying it so far?" he asked.

Eleanor suppressed her desire to make a flippant remark about the tea and cakes, instead she answered steadily, "It's been very pleasant. Not only looking round Beverley Minster but being out in the countryside."

Don looked pleased. "There you are. I'm not so bad to be out with, am I?"

"Of course not, silly. I don't want to let social activities spoil my keenness to study and get a degree."

"Oh dear" said Don, "you've just knocked my feet from under me."

"Why, what did I say?"

"There's a good play on at the theatre this week and I'd like to take you to see it."

"I'm sorry Don" said Eleanor. "It isn't that I don't want to go, it's — er — well, I have to go home on Wednesday and Thursday."

"Home? Already? How come?" Don was incredulous.

"I have to go down to Chichester on Wednesday, that's all there is to it. I've got permission from my tutor and the dean."

"Can't you tell me why, or is it personal?" Don asked.

"It is personal I suppose, but I'd rather not say."

"Well then" said Don, "can I help in any way? How are you going to travel, train or coach or what?"

"No, I'm driving down in my own car. I shall leave directly after the last lecture on Tuesday, then it will be a three-hour journey."

"You can't do that by yourself, it's madness. What if some lout accosts you? You need an escort and if you can't get one I'll go with you."

"You are being alarmist. I shall be all right." But her voice wavered, Don had sown the seeds of doubt in her mind.

Don tried a different approach. "I don't want to pry into your family affairs" he said quietly. "I could drive you down there, disappear for a day or so and then escort you back to Hull, how's that suit you?"

Eleanor sipped her tea and thought about it. Finally she said, "If you can get permission then I'll accept your offer" she said.

"Now you are being sensible. Have another cake."

That evening Eleanor telephoned her mother to tell her that she was being escorted down on the Tuesday night.

"Who is he? What's he to do with us and our problems?" Ruby was apprehensive and protective.

"Oh Mum, he's a student friend. He thought I shouldn't drive down

78

alone. He's not even asking to stay with us."

"Oh well, I'm sorry. I'm just as concerned for you as anyone else. I thought you would be coming down by train."

"That would have meant going down to King's Cross and then getting another connection for Chichester. It's quicker this way."

Ruby was mollified. "Look, why not let him come here. He can have the little bedroom, it only needs some aired linen. I'll do that on Tuesday, or Mrs Richings will for me."

"That'll be lovely. He'll have to get his midday meal out somewhere, but he'll manage, I'm sure" said Eleanor.

"What have you told him?" asked Ruby. "I mean, does he know about the trial and you being a witness?"

"Oh no, I've not told him anything about that" answered Eleanor.

"I think you should give him some idea of what you are coming for. There's nothing to stop him from going in as a member of the public. Give him the choice."

"If I do tell him he might want to opt out of coming down altogether. What then?" Eleanor was in a dilemma.

"It would be better than having him find out for himself. He's bound to find out about your father sometime, especially as your father is being brought here as a witness. Oh dear, it's all such a mess. I wish it was all over."

"Look Mum, I'll go and tell him about it. If he backs out, no harm done. I was coming down on my own anyway."

"All right then. Let me know what he says."

"Right. Bye Mum." Eleanor rang off and sat deep in thought for a while. Then she got up, left the foyer and went to find Don's room.

As she went up the stairs to the next floor Eleanor had misgivings. It was not going to be easy to confess to anyone that your father was in gaol through being mixed up in drugs, and now there were more drugs and arson as well.

She stopped and started to turn prior to going back down again, but just then a door opened above her and out came Don and his roommate Jack.

They stopped next to her. "Eleanor." Don was surprised to see her there. "Were you coming to see me?"

"Yes I was. Well, I rather wanted to talk to you alone."

Jack waved his hand. "I'll be over in the cafe. See you." He was gone in a flash.

"Do you want to come up" said Don.

"No, let's go outside."

They went down the stairs and out into the half-paved area in front of the building. They strolled along the front. Eleanor plucked up courage and started to tell Don why she was a witness. To make any sense of it she had to tell the whole story starting with her mother's illness, then her father's involvement with this evil-looking man, her father's trial and sentence. Then the business venture with Mrs Priscilla Thurston and then the devastating fire.

Don was fidgetting. "But where do you come into all this?" he asked.

"If you'll be patient I'll get to it" Eleanor answered. She then went on to tell how she recognised the photo of the man accused of the arson attack as being the same man she had seen with her father years before, and that now he too had been found with drugs. "So it's on his other charge about drugs that I shall be called as a witness to his involvement with my dad." Eleanor felt relieved that she had got the whole story off her chest. She turned to Don.

"I expect you won't want to be involved with me now. I should be grateful if you would not mention it to anyone though."

"Just a minute" said Don, "I haven't said I would or I wouldn't. I haven't come across anything like this in my life before and quite frankly I'm not sure how to deal with it."

"I knew I shouldn't have told you, but my mum thought otherwise. Actually she was right. I was right in the first place when I didn't want you to come with me. Now you will have to make the choice. Let me know by Tuesday afternoon please."

Eleanor got up and with a brief wave of her hand she went back to the student block.

After Eleanor had rung off, Ruby was beset with worry over her advice to her daughter. She was sure that it was best that this Don knew all about Eleanor's immediate family, but what effect would it have on her life at college when others found out? She, Ruby did not think Don would go through with his offer, but if he did the least she could do would be to offer him accommodation. He was most likely dependent on his grant as much as any other students. It probably would not be a good idea for him to stay in the same house as Eleanor, so what to do?

Suddenly she had an idea. Mrs Richings, her daily woman. She would ask her in the morning.

When Mrs Richings came to the house next morning Ruby broached the subject. She explained that Don was escorting Eleanor down and back, and would be wanting a bed for two nights, could she put him up if he came down as promised?

"Of course I can. There's only me and Charlie so it'll be no trouble." Mrs Richings was quite enthusiastic.

"If you can give him breakfast" said Ruby "he'll get any other meals out, or with us here, and I'll see that you are paid for your trouble."

"It's no trouble. It will be a change for us, anyway."

So that was settled. But, Ruby wondered, would he be coming or wouldn't he? She would have to wait for Eleanor to ring.

Up at the university Eleanor was keeping a lookout for Don. She had not seen him when lunch-time came, but she spotted him in the large dining hall, and when she had finished eating she waited until she saw Don leaving then ran after him, catching him up as he went out. "Don, Don!"

Don looked round. "Ah, Eleanor, I was going to come and see you later on."

"Don, I have to phone my mother after tea and she will want to know whether she has to get a bed ready for you."

Don looked down at his feet and then looked past Eleanor to anywhere except her face. "I can't do it Eleanor. I just can't get involved with anyone who has anything to do with drugs. Oh I didn't mean you personally, but — well — your family, or at least your father has been running drugs and it's contrary to everything I believe in."

Eleanor looked crestfallen. "So, I'm back to square one. I can't go with you to see a play this week Don" she mimicked the conversation of Sunday. "I am driving down to Chichester on family business."

Don was embarrassed. "I'm sorry Eleanor, I really am sorry. I was too impetuous."

"When you offered to drive down with me I thought it was because you were concerned for my safety. Does this mean that you are no longer concerned or what?" Eleanor was beginning to get angry.

"No" said Don. "I could still drive you down, but I wouldn't want to stay down there. If there was some way I could get back I would still drive you down. I just don't see how I can do it." He sounded genuine.

"There is a possible solution" said Eleanor more calmly now. "Suppose you come down with me, stay overnight in a bed and breakfast place, and then you can take my car and drive back on Wednesday morning. That way you would only lose half a day at college. I could come back by train and you would pick me up in the car at the station."

Don spent a long time thinking about this.

Eleanor spoke again. "You wouldn't have to pay for anything, Mum would cover any expenses you might incur."

"That might be possible" said Don. His face brightened and he looked Eleanor in the eyes as he said "I'll see my tutor this afternoon and try to arrange a morning off. If he agrees, I'll drive down with you on Tuesday — tomorrow — evening, and return here in time for the afternoon lectures. That's what you meant, wasn't it?"

"Yes, that's about the size of it. Are you happy with that arrangement then?"

"Yep. I'll get cracking and let you know about four o'clock, that's if my tutor doesn't decide to go off somewhere."

"All right then Don, I'll wait to hear from you."

They parted and went to their billets.

Thomas Tait Esq. MA was going over his notes for the next period. To a knock on his door he called "Come in."

The door opened and Don entered. "Excuse me sir, could I have a word?"

"Certainly, come and sit down." When Don was seated Mr Tait said "Well, what's on your mind?"

Don explained as much as he felt he ought, not mentioning Eleanor's father. "So you see, it would only mean that I would miss a morning really" he finished.

"And you would be whacked with the driving and not fit to do anything for the rest of the day." He was silent for a while then he spoke again. "Wouldn't it be more useful for your friend if you could escort her back as well, or is that not possible?"

"Yes sir, it would be possible" said Don, "but that would mean me staying for two nights, or even three, and I don't particularly want to do that."

"Well if it's a case of you being away from your studies you know you can take work with you, seeing that you are not involved in the actual proceedings. I mean, you are not attending the court presumably, so your time would be your own."

"Yes, that's true, I don't want to attend there, it may be a bit unsavoury." Had he said too much? He was anxious not to have to mention Eleanor's father.

Mr Tait was speaking again. "You can't isolate yourself completely from everything 'unsavoury' as you term it, in fact I think you could benefit from the experience of seeing what goes on in other communities. After all, experience of whatever kind is always of some value, not least in helping one to make up one's own mind. Or perhaps it would cost too much for accommodation, yes?"

"Oh no" said Don, "that won't cost me anything I believe."

"Then I can see no reason for you not staying to see this young lady through this episode. I can prepare enough for you to take for one, two or three days. More than enough to ease your conscience I should think."

"I'll talk to the young lady again. May I come and see you tomorrow morning and let you know what I'm doing?"

"Certainly. If I were you I'd opt for staying over."

"Yes, right, thank you sir."

Don left his tutor's room and went to find Eleanor.

He caught her between lectures. "Eleanor, I've seen my tutor. He says it's all right for me to go, and also he's quite willing to provide me with some work to do if I should decide to stay over."

"That's lovely Don, except —."

Don chimed in with "Except what? You're not having second thoughts are you?"

"No, silly. I was going to say except that you haven't said what exactly you are intending to do."

"No. Well, it depends really on the accommodation. I cannot afford to spend thirty pounds a night for bed and breakfast."

"Don, I told you Mum would arrange it. She wouldn't expect you to be out of pocket, neither would I. Look, I'm phoning Mum at five o'clock. You come with me and we'll get first-hand information from her. You can decide then."

"I'll meet you in the hall foyer at five then" said Don.

"Oh Don" said Eleanor.

"Yes?"

"Please don't dither. I'm rather pent up anyway and any further uncertainties will have me worried sick."

"Don't worry. I think I know what to do" said Don.

Promptly at five they met in the foyer where there were three telephones. Eleanor went to one of them and dialled the number. "Hello Mum, it's me, Eleanor."

"Oh hello dear, how are you, all set for Wednesday?"

"No I'm not. I've got permanent butterflies. How about you, are you coping all right?"

"Oh yes, no real worries except about your journey. Now, what's this young friend of yours going to do? Is he coming or not?"

"Yes, he's definitely coming. The real sticking point seems to be what he's to do about staying and —."

Ruby broke in, "That's all arranged, I've asked Mrs Richings to make up a bed for him at her house. He can have his breakfast there as well, and it's available for as long as he can stay."

"What about the cost?" asked Eleanor.

"It will cost him nothing. He will be our guest."

"Just a minute Mum, I'll tell him. He's here beside me." She turned to Don. "Mum says she's arranged for you to stay each night at Mrs Richings' house, she comes in to help Mum most days. It will cost you nothing. What do you say?"

"Tell your Mum thank you very much, I'll be delighted to stay a couple of days."

Eleanor turned back to the phone. "Mum, it's all right. Don says he will accept your kind offer, thank you very much."

"Well that's a load off my mind, what time will you be here?"

"If we get away say four-thirty, it will be nine at the latest."

"Right. We'll expect you about nine. Drive carefully."

"We will. Bye Mum." She turned to Don and said, "You know, I feel better already."

Ruby put the phone down and sighed. She went back to the settee where Arthur Mowbray was sitting. "All right dear?" he asked.

"Yes, that's all settled. Eleanor and this fellow Don will be here tomorrow night about nine."

Arthur placed her cushion. "Remember what I said, Ruby. I'll take you to the court each day they want you, and I'll bring you back. Then I'll go back to my own place and leave you and Eleanor on your own."

"You are very kind, Arthur. I don't know what I'd have done without you. You won't feel you are being pushed out, will you?"

"No, not at all" said Arthur. "One day we shall be together for always, so I think I should not give Eleanor the impression that I'm coming between you and her."

"I'm sure she will soon get used to you, but it must be very difficult for her. She loves her dad, and as far as she's concerned nothing has changed yet."

"No, but it will, and when it does Eleanor will have no obligations to anyone. I shall be taking care of you and she will be making her own way in her own life, knowing that she can see you any time she wants and that you are in good hands. What more could a girl want?"

"What more indeed" said Ruby. "I'm longing for this trial business to be over and done with so that we can get back to normal, whatever that is."

Eleanor had arranged to meet Don in the college dining hall next day. Don was already in the queue, and when Eleanor finally got her meal she took it over to Don's table. "Phew, what a rush" she said. "Are you all ready for the trip?"

"More or less. I've just got to collect some books from the library then I can go, so if you can get away any earlier we could go."

"I'll try. Where will you be?" she asked.

Don thought for a moment. "I'll be in the library. You come over or get a message to me and we'll take it from there. How does that suit you?"

"Excellent."

By half past two Eleanor had managed to arrange things so that she could leave. She phoned the college library and Don was brought to the phone.

"Don, I'm all straight and can be ready to leave when you are."

"Right then" said Don. "I'll meet you in the car park in ten minutes, OK?"

"Fine, see you then."

Some twenty minutes later they were on their way, Eleanor driving the first part down the M18 and the M1, and Don taking over for the second part. The weather was fine and with luck they would be in Chichester long before nine o'clock.

Ruby was pouring tea for Arthur. He was going to wait until Eleanor arrived and then he would go back to his own house.

"What do I say when I introduce you to Don" asked Ruby.

"How do you mean? Why not just Mr Mowbray?"

"You know what I mean Arthur. Youngsters like to have people in their proper pigeon holes, and the pigeon holes in a set pattern. Where will you fit?"

"I don't know. How about this is my fellow sufferer?"

"Don't be silly. I'm serious. I don't want you to be thought of as an interloper, an alien."

"You're too sensitive. As long as you give a plausible reason for my being here he'll be happy."

On the M1 Eleanor was looking for a service station before she had to leave the motorway for the A road to Oxford. One appeared about two junctions from their turn off. Eleanor swung on to the slip road and into the car park. "Come on, let's get a cup of tea and a snack before you take over" she said.

They made their way to the buffet and selected tea and sandwiches.

At the table Eleanor voiced something that had been worrying her. "Don, there is one thing I haven't mentioned. It may not be important but it could be embarrassing to you if you didn't know."

"Now she tells me" said Don half jokingly.

"Listen Don. My mother and father are separating, getting a divorce."

"That's nothing new, lots of people are doing it" Don replied.

"It's not just that. You see, when Mum was having therapy recently she met a man who was very kind to her and helped her over a difficult few weeks. She has become very fond of him. When you and I get home he will probably be there. He spends a lot of time at our house during the day and goes home to his own place in the evening. He's a widower."

"I see. I think you are saying that they will one day be married."

"Yes, I think so. Anyway, if he's there when we arrive you at least will know how he fits into the scene."

"A kind of friend of the family eh? Well, I expect I shall not say anything out of place, so just relax. Now, where do we turn off for Oxford? I'm driving now."

They made good time for the journey and were in Chichester soon after eight. Eleanor directed Don through the city and out to the house. There was a car — Arthur's — in the short driveway but Don found room to park next to it.

They went in. "Mum, we're here!"

Eleanor went through to the sitting room. Ruby was on the settee and Arthur was in one of the easy chairs. He got up. "Hello Eleanor."

"Oh hello. Hello Mum." She bent down and kissed Ruby's cheek. "How are you?"

"Oh I'm fine" said Ruby.

Eleanor called out to Don. "Come on in Don. Mum, this is Don Metcalfe."

Ruby held out her hand. "Hello Don. Did you have a nice trip?"

"Hello Mrs Cavanagh. Yes thanks, we had a good run down."

Eleanor moved towards Arthur. "Don, this is Mr Mowbray, a friend of the family" she said.

"Hello Mr Mowbray, nice to meet you."

"Hello Don. How does college life suit you?"

"Oh fine. I didn't realise there would be so much to do or take part in. One could fill every hour of every day."

"Then this little break won't help, will it?" said Arthur.

"Well, my tutor has given me work to do while I am here, so it will not be so bad really."

As Don was talking Arthur was looking at him quizzically. "You sound as it you might come from Somerset way" he said. "Where do you come from exactly?"

"Taunton" said Don, " and all my family before me."

"Ah, I thought so" said Arthur. "I've got a good ear for regional accents."

Ruby broke into their conversation. "Now, Don and Eleanor, this is the arrangement. You can have a meal now, we have something prepared in the kitchen. We have had ours so you can have yours whenever you like. After that, Don will go down to Mrs Richings who has everything ready."

"How far is it?" asked Don.

"Only a few minutes" said Ruby.

"It's all right, I'll take him there" said Arthur, "it's on my way."

"Thanks very much" said Don.

"That's settled then" said Ruby. "Now, how about your meal."

When it was time for Don to go Ruby felt in her handbag and produced a key. "This is the front door key and this is a card with our address and telephone number. We shall be gone by ten o'clock so you can come here and get on with your work. Make sure you lock up if you decide to go out. I don't know if court cases interest you but if they do then ours starts at eleven. They say the actual proceedings don't start till the afternoon because of all the preliminaries. If you want a midday meal Mrs Richings will be here from eleven till twelve, so ask her to get you something. Or you can go down the town and get a meal. We shall probably get a pub lunch."

"Thanks very much Mrs Cavanagh" said Don, "and good luck for tomorrow. I hope all goes well."

Don and Arthur went out. Don collected his bag from Eleanor's car and got into Arthur's car.

Eleanor came out and spoke to Don. "Thanks a lot Don. I appreciate your coming down with me."

"That's all right Eleanor, I've enjoyed it so far."

Arthur started the engine and drove off. "Tell me" said Arthur when they had turned out of the drive, "what does your father do?"

"My dad? He's got a small engineering business, why?"

"Well, some years ago I did a business studies course near Henley-on-Thames and I met a nice bloke called John Metcalfe from Taunton. We —."

"That is my father. He did that course when I was a lad."

"Well I never" said Arthur. "We got on well together. I wish I'd kept up with him. How is he, by the way?"

"He's just fine. Business is doing well and he is in good health, my mother is too."

"I'm glad to hear that. If I'd had my full health I would still be in business, but that's the way it goes."

They arrived at Mrs Richings.

As Don got out Arthur came round and spoke to Don. "When you next go home will you remember me to John, your dad?"

"Certainly I will Mr Mowbray."

"Good, thank you. Now, I'll introduce you to Mrs Richings then I'll be off."

The day of the trial dawned bright and clear. Priscilla looked out from her window at the view. 'Today,' she thought, 'a man is probably going to be shut off from views like this for years.' Then she thought of Jeff Cavanagh, 'He has already been shut away for — goodness, it must be almost two years.' She had lost track of time, what with the dramatic events that led to her becoming a widow, then a business woman and now an ex-business woman, co-victim of an arson attack.

Yes, she of course had not seen Jeff since their little jaunt out to Arundel. 'I wonder what he looks like now?' she thought. 'And I wonder how Ruby will react.'

At ten o'clock she set off for the courthouse.

Bill Hopkins got his men off to an early start. They were good chaps, he could leave them to carry on knowing they would play the game. He went back indoors to shave. He started wondering about Priscilla. They had had a good time at the club, and afterwards too, he mused. She did dismiss him a bit abruptly he thought. 'She doesn't want a close relationship, I wonder why? Let's face it Bill, old sport, she is a bit old for you. Yes, she looks young, but that's not enough, you know.' He couldn't find any substantial pros for their present relationship. 'In fact,' he thought, 'I don't believe she will want to see me again, non-professionally that is.' He jumped in his car and went to the courthouse.

Arthur Mowbray called for Ruby and Eleanor at a quarter to ten. He put the wheelchair in the boot and helped Ruby into the car. Eleanor locked the front door and then got into the rear seat of the car.

"OK Eleanor?" said Arthur.

"Yes, all set," answered Eleanor.

When they were on their way Arthur said "That Don is a nice young fellow, Eleanor."

"Yes, I know, he's a brick really."

"I know his father" he went on.

Eleanor was very surprised. "How on earth is that?"

Arthur explained how he had made friends with John Metcalfe.

There was only one thing anyone could say to that and Eleanor said it. "It's a small world, isn't it."

Arthur shot a quick glance at Ruby and said, "So you see, I'm in the right pigeon hole, aren't I?" He laughed.

They drove on to the courthouse.

Bill was in the witnesses' room when Priscilla was shown in. He got up and went to her. "Hello Priscilla, everything OK?"

"Yes, fine. Not fancying the prospect of a long wait though."

"It may be longer than you think, they are doing the drugs charge first."

"Oh no! Oh well, it can't be helped. I'd rather be a witness than a juror though."

They looked up as the door opened. Eleanor entered followed by Arthur pushing the wheelchair with Ruby in it.

It had been arranged that one of the attendants would take Ruby where and when she was required, so Arthur did not stay. "I shall be in the public area" he said. "Good luck."

Inside the courtroom the preliminaries were gone through, taking almost all of the rest of the morning. The court was then adjourned until two'clock. Arthur left the courtroom and went round to the witnesses' room.

A police officer had gone into the witnesses' room a short time before and had read from a sheet of paper on a clipboard. "Mrs Cavanagh will not be called today. Mrs Thurston will not be called today. Mr Hopkins will not be called today. Miss Eleanor Cavanagh, please return here by one-forty-five today. Thank you."

Bill Hopkins got up and went to the door."I'll see you all tomorrow morning then, cheerio," and off he went.

Ruby turned to Priscilla. "We are going for a quick pub lunch just up the road. How about you, will you come with us?"

Priscilla had not thought about eating but she decided she would go with them. "All right" she said, "I'd love to."

Arthur came in, went over and collected the wheelchair and moved it towards Ruby. "Are you ready then Ruby?"

"Yes thanks." She lowered herself on to the seat and pulled her legs on to the step. "We're going to the Acorn, is that all right with you Priscilla?" said Ruby.

"Yes, of course, they do a good meal there."

They all left the building to walk the hundred yards to the Acorn.

While they were eating no one had mentioned the trial, but when they were just finishing their meal Ruby turned to Priscilla. "What are you going to do this afternoon? Will you stay and see what happens to this man?"

"I'm not sure. I'd like to see what sort of chap would want to burn our business down and why. So I think perhaps I'll stay and watch."

"Arthur and I will be there of course to give Eleanor our moral support."

They finished eating, paid the bill and set off back to the court.

Don had slept well and did not wake until well after eight o'clock. He went to the bathroom and when he came out Mrs Richings was coming up the stairs. "Morning Mrs Richings."

"Good morning Don. Did you sleep all right?"

"Yes, I certainly did. A comfortable bed and no noise, lovely."

"Well, you can have breakfast any time now. Cereal, bacon and eggs, toast marmalade, how does that sound?"

"Marvellous. I'm ready for anything you put before me."

"Right. Come down when you are dressed." She went back down to the kitchen.

Don had an excellent breakfast alone at the table. Mr Richings was out starting on the autumn jobs in the garden and Mrs Richings was busy with other chores.

When he had finished he told Mrs Richings his plans. "I shall go down to Mrs Cavanagh's now and do some reading. What time are you coming down?"

"About eleven" answered Mrs Richings. "I shall do a bit of dusting and that, then if you are feeling hungry I'll get you something to eat."

"I don't think I shall want much for a few hours. Anyway, I'll be off now, see you later."

He walked down to the Cavanagh's house, let himself in and went into the dining room, where he spread his books out and settled down to read. He soon got immersed in his work for it seemed only minutes before Mrs Richings was there.

She came through to where he was sitting. "Now" she said "I'll just close this door and I'll get on with my work and you won't be disturbed for another hour."

"Right Mrs Richings."

Soon after twelve o'clock Mrs Richings tapped at the door and poked her head in. "I've finished my jobs. Now what do you fancy to eat?"

"Anything you like Mrs Richings" said Don.

"How about a bowl of soup with some crackers, then there's a bowl of fruit you can choose from."

"That'll do fine, thank you."

Ten minutes later Mrs Richings called him again. "It's all set out on the kitchen table."

Don went into the kitchen and sat down.

Mrs Richings hovered for a moment then said, "Are you staying in all the afternoon too?"

"Well yes, I think so" answered Don.

"Won't you be going down to the court then?"

"I wasn't planning to" said Don.

"Poor Eleanor" went on Mrs Richings, "she hasn't seen her dad since, well, you know. They say he's being called as a witness today, whatever will poor Eleanor think. It'll be a terrible ordeal for her, I shouldn't wonder."

"I'm afraid I don't know much about it really" said Don.

"Oh don't you? Oh well, her dad, Mr Cavanagh, he's a lovely man really. I can't believe he was a drug sort of person. He never took any himself, nor did anyone else round here as far as I know. They were pretty hard on him you know, what with Mrs Cavanagh and her sclerosis and all. I feel very sorry for all of them."

"I only met Eleanor this term, and this is the first time I've seen Mrs Cavanagh so I don't know much about any of them."

"What Eleanor will do when she sees her dad, I don't know. I reckon it will be a shock for her. Well, I'd better be off. If you do go out don't forget to lock up. They've all got keys to get in. Goodbye."

She left, and Don heard the front door slam.

He finished his soup then munched a banana. He thought about Eleanor. He was beginning to see why she was upset when he, Don, dithered about coming with her. She'd virtually lost her father, her mother was on the way to leaving her, then to top it all he had almost let her down. She deserved better than that, if not from them then from him. What was it his tutor had said? 'Experience of any kind is of some value.' Well, all this was a new experience but should he add to it? Reluctant though he was to get further involved, he was now imagining Eleanor seeing her father in court, probably handcuffed if he was being brought from prison. He could get to the court easily for the afternoon session, it was only just after twelve-thirty now. He would go. Perhaps they wouldn't let him in. He decided he would try anyway. He packed up his books and left them on the table, grabbed his jacket and went out.

He didn't know where the court was but he would ask when he got to the main street. As he swung along he felt slightly uplifted. He had made the decision and was feeling better for it.

When Priscilla and the others arrived at the courthouse Eleanor went straight to the witnesses' room. She had not waited for her mother to say anything, she just hurried away, her stomach churning, not because she was nervous of going into the witness box, more the thought that she would be seeing her dad. She knew she was going to be embarrassed for him. In her mind he didn't deserve to be in this humiliating position. Their lawyer had told her what questions were likely to be asked of her, but she had no idea of what her father was going to say.

Priscilla hung back from Arthur and Ruby as they approached the doors. "You go in" she said to Ruby, "I'll come in later, if at all."

Arthur and Ruby passed through into the room.

Don had asked someone to direct him to the courthouse so he arrived in good time. There did not seem to be a queue so he wandered back up the street to waste a bit of time. He strolled up past the cinema and back down to the courthouse. As he approached the doors he saw a smart lady go through ahead of him.

Don went up to the policeman at the door. "Can I go in?" he asked.

"In what capacity sir?" asked the policeman.

"Nothing really. I'm a student."

"Oh that's all right then, there's still some seats left for the public."

Don went in. The lady he had seen entering before him was in the back row to the left. Don found a seat to the right. He looked around. Well over to the right he saw Mrs Cavanagh still in her wheelchair

91

and Mr Mowbray on a seat near her.

At the appointed time the judge and entourage filed in and the trial began. Hughes pleaded not guilty to being in possession of drugs. The trial proceeded and eventually the barrister called for Jeffrey Cavanagh.

Don was watching intently. Where was Eleanor? He couldn't see her anywhere. He was not to know that she could not enter the court until called as a witness.

A door at the side opened, in came two officers and between them a man in a blue shirt and trousers, Jeff Cavanagh. They led him to the witness box.

Priscilla gasped as she saw him for the first time in two years. He was leaner, not so suntanned and looking all of his forty-five years.

Ruby looked at her husband then looked down again. Arthur took her hand. Ruby felt guilty. She knew that in a sense she had betrayed him but she consoled herself in the knowledge that he had brought all this on himself.

Don saw the rather dejected looking man brought forward. So this was Eleanor's father. He began to feel nervous. 'How could he have got himself mixed up with all this?' he thought. Police, criminals, barristers and reporters. He felt very uncomfortable.

The barrister had got to the point of asking Jeff questions about Hughes. "Do you know the accused?"

"Yes."

"How did you first become acquainted?"

"He approached me one day at the marina about seven years ago."

"Had you been sailing?"

"Yes, I owned a thirty-footer."

"Did anyone crew with you?"

"Yes my daughter, then aged twelve. My wife used to crew with us, but she developed a form of sclerosis."

"I see. Tell us about the meeting with the accused."

"We had been sailing and had just berthed when this — the accused — came up to me and asked me how would I like to earn some money."

"He did say 'earn' some money, not 'make'?" asked the barrister.

"Yes, earn some money. I said 'How and how much.' So he said 'Fifty grand.' So I said 'What do I have to do for that sort of money?' He said 'You just have to take something from A to B and I shall be at B to collect.'"

"What prompted you to accept this offer?"

"My wife was getting disabled with the sclerosis, and I thought that if she got worse in the future she might need specialist treatment or operations that would be expensive."

The barrister interrupted again. "But weren't you comparatively well off?"

"We had a good standard of living, yes, but my taxi business absorbed most of the capital, so even though we were doing well there wasn't much spare cash for anything out of the ordinary."

"So you felt you needed the money. What happened?"

"I asked him how to go about it, what was involved. He said he would accompany me on the first trip and would give me the co-ordinates for the rendezvous in the Channel."

"Mr Cavanagh," said the barrister, "where was your daughter while this conversation was being carried on?"

"She was in and out of the cabin getting out things together for going home."

"I see. Please continue."

Don was getting interested in the story now. He was thinking — 'How could this man be so naive, so gullible?'

Jeff was speaking again. "He said we should be prepared for a full day's sailing there and back, and if the weather was bad he would cancel it on the day. We arranged it for the following Saturday, so I told my daughter she would not be able to come the following week."

"And what happened on the day?" asked the barrister.

"The accused showed up as arranged. He was carrying an empty water container, about a four gallon size, and a length of line. He came aboard, gave me the co-ordinates and we set sail. We got to the place after about four hours. We saw a vessel waiting, a sort of high speed launch. We drew alongside and Hughes — the accused — said 'Watch this.' A man on the other boat appeared with an identical water container with a line attached. With one well-aimed swing he slung the container on to our boat. Hughes grabbed it, unhitched it, hitched the empty one on the line, and the other man hauled it rapidly on to the launch. It was all over in seconds. The launch then sped away and I was told to turn for home. We got back some five hours later. When we had berthed he reached into his pocket and gave me a waterproof packet. He said 'As promised, fifty grand in cash.' Then he said 'I'll be in touch,' picked up the container and left."

"Was that the end of him?" asked the barrister.

"No sir. About a fortnight or three weeks later he phoned me at my office. He said he had another fifty grand. I said 'No thanks once was enough.' He said 'But not for me.' He then said I was to be ready the following Saturday, but I said 'No.' He then said 'Your little daughter, is she well?' I said 'Yes, of course, why?' And he said 'If you want her to stay that way you'd better be there on Saturday — do I make myself clear?' I could not ignore this threat so I agreed to the plan. This time he was waiting in the car park. He gave me the container and told me I was on my own, he would meet me on my return. We did this nine times in all, the money was always paid to me, although it got down to thirty thousand on the last two occasions. Then, as you know, the customs people caught me."

"And now you are serving your sentence. Why haven't you told this story before?"

"My daughter was being threatened. No father could fail to protect his child, no matter what the cost."

"At your trial you never implicated anyone else. Why?"

"For the same reason. The threat was always there, but now I feel free to speak."

"Thank you. That is all Mr Cavanagh."

Arthur Mowbray turned to look at Ruby. She was in tears as the story of Jeff's self-sacrifice came to light. He patted her hand.

Priscilla had sat nervously as Jeff's story unfolded. The antipathy that she had felt originally was slowly diminishing, and in fact that antipathy was being replaced by a feeling of protectiveness. She wanted to mother him and tell him how sorry she was that she had misjudged him

She looked up again as the judge was speaking. "I would like to mention to the counsel for the prosecution that this last evidence could possibly be of some advantage at a later date."

"Thank you m'lud."

"What does that mean?" Ruby whispered to Arthur.

"Grounds for appeal against his sentence" Arthur whispered back.

Jeff had been taken to the side of the court. Everyone waited for the next move.

Counsel for the prosecution rose again. "I would like to call Miss Eleanor Cavanagh."

A little buzz went round the courtroom. Don clenched his fists and looked towards the witness box. Eleanor appeared through the door. She looked around, saw her father, gave him a little smile and went to the box.

She was sworn in and the barrister rose once more. "Now Miss Cavanagh, you are, are you not the daughter of Mr Jeffrey Cavanagh?"

"Yes I am."

"Do you see him in court?"

Eleanor turned slightly to look at her father. "Yes. He is over there." She pointed.

"Now Miss Cavanagh, in your statement you told of your last sailing trip with your father. Would you please tell the court of that day."

"Yes. I can't remember the exact date, but it was a Saturday, and we'd spent several hours at sea."

"Just you and your father?" asked the barrister.

"Yes. My mother used to come with us but she became ill and so

94

was unable to continue with it."

"Go on, Miss Cavanagh."

"On this Saturday we had just berthed when this man came up and started talking to Dad."

"Miss Cavanagh, do you see this man in court?"

"Yes, it's him." She pointed.

"The accused?" said the barrister.

"Yes, the accused."

"Did you hear what they were saying?"

"No, I was busy packing up and they were on the quayside talking. I didn't like the look of him, he frightened me. I was only twelve at the time."

"Why were you frightened Miss Cavanagh?"

"I don't know. A child's instinct I suppose."

"Did he speak to you?"

"No. When they had finished talking he went off. Then my father said I wouldn't be going with him on the boat next week as that man would be with him."

"And have you seen him since?"

"No, not until today."

"Thank you Miss Cavanagh, that is all."

Eleanor stepped down, she looked round the courtroom, saw her mother's wheelchair and went over to her. She sat down on the seat Arthur had vacated. He moved to a seat behind.

Don had not missed a word. As the story unfolded he saw that weak Jeff Cavanagh had become a victim of circumstance and poor Eleanor was just a pawn, ignorant of the fact that she was unwittingly the cause of her father's long sentence. He felt protective towards her.

The counsel was summing up. Eleanor listened astounded as he recalled her father's evidence and his fears for her safety that led to his conviction when he was forced to continue carrying the drugs. It was enough to sway the jury and they returned a verdict of guilty.

The judge said sentence would be pronounced after the verdict on the other charge. Court was adjourned until the following day at ten-thirty.

Don slipped out of the door and stood to one side. When he saw Arthur and Ruby appear he moved towards them. Behind them came Eleanor. Now her head was up and she had an almost defiant look.

She saw Don who had gone past Ruby to greet her. "Don!" said the surprised Eleanor, "I thought you were studying."

"I was. I felt out of things somehow. I had to see what it was all about. I'm glad I did. You have been through an awful lot."

"Not as much as my poor dad. It's been hell for him all this time."

Don took her arm. "Let's walk home" he said.

Eleanor called to Ruby. "Mum, we're walking home. See you later."

At that moment their lawyer pushed his way towards them. "Mrs Cavanagh!"

They stopped.

"Mrs Cavanagh, Miss Cavanagh, I've got permission for you to see Mr Cavanagh in a security room here before he goes back. Can you come?"

Arthur looked at Eleanor. "Here, you take your mother. We'll wait here for you."

He and Don moved away to the waiting room. The lawyer walked with Eleanor as they pushed the wheelchair with Ruby along the corridor. A policeman stood by the door.

"You go in Mum. I'll wait here."

Ruby had not said a word since leaving the court. She was churned up inside, a mixture of guilt about the forthcoming divorce, pride at Jeff's fortitude having to bear his situation alone, anger at Jeff's stupidity in the first place and sorrow that all this could have been avoided. With these mixed feelings she eased herself out of the wheelchair and shuffled slowly into the room.

Jeff was standing on the other side of the room with a police officer next to him. "Hello Ruby. It was good of you to come."

"Hello Jeff. You must be relieved after what you've had to bottle up all this time."

"Yes I am. But what about you? How are you in yourself?"

"Oh I'm not too bad, some days are better than others."

"I must say you look as well as I've ever seen you recently."

"So do you. Are you keeping busy?"

"Oh yes, I have lots to do, mentally and physically."

They were awkward with each other.

Ruby said, "I thought you did well in there."

"It was the truth. It's easy to tell the truth and people believe you."

"Yes, I suppose so."

The police officer broke in. "That will have to do I'm afraid."

Ruby turned. "Goodbye Jeff and good luck."

"Goodbye Ruby. Thanks for coming along."

Ruby went out. The lawyer motioned to Eleanor. They entered the room together. When Eleanor saw her father she made as if to go and hug him.

"I'm sorry Miss, no contact today. Regulations."

"Dad, I didn't know anything about that," meaning the threats on her life.

"Eleanor, never mind about that, it's over. I'm so glad to see you. Tell me what you have been doing."

"I'm at Hull University. It's very nice. I met Don, a student there, he drove down with me in my car."

"Your car? My goodness how you have changed. I lost my little girl, at one time I thought for good, but now I've got a very sophisticated daughter and I'm proud of you."

"Dad, are you staying for the next thing, tomorrow?"

"No, I'm not required for that. I shall be going back shortly."

"You do understand about me not coming to visit you?"

"Yes, your mother is right. I don't want you to see me in there."

"Right Miss" said the officer, "you'll have to go now."

"Goodbye Dad, keep your chin up."

"Goodbye Eleanor, make sure you get that degree. Goodbye."

The lawyer ushered her out. She brushed a tear away with the back of her hand. They got behind Ruby's wheelchair and pushed her towards the waiting room.

Arthur and Don reappeared and as Arthur took over the wheelchair Eleanor went towards Don. "Let's do what you said, walk home. See you later Mum," she called as they moved out of the courthouse. When they got outside Eleanor took a deep breath and said, "Oh that's better, good clean autumn fresh air."

They walked together through the streets, neither spoke. When they were about halfway they stopped, and looking between the houses they could see the sea.

Don was anxious to say something, anything. "How do you feel now that it's all over?" he asked.

"I don't know" answered Eleanor. "Relieved I suppose. I wish I could have seen my dad giving his story, I only got the summing up."

"Well" said Don, "it was like something out of a film or book. Your father told his story very naturally, you couldn't help but believe him, in fact I couldn't believe that he was actually serving a sentence for a crime."

"He was doing it for Mum."

"No, you are wrong there. The first time he did a trip it was for your mother's future. After that it was out of his hands. It was for you, your safety. He hardly deserved to go to gaol at all, really."

"Oh Don, how nice you are. I am so glad you came down with me."

They left the view and continued walking. "What happens now?" asked Don.

"Well, tomorrow there's the arson trial. Mum and Priscilla and Bill Hopkins will all be called" said Eleanor.

"Who is Bill Hopkins then?" asked Don.

"Oh, of course you don't know any of them do you. Well, Bill Hopkins is a builder and he was the one who caught this fellow running away from the fire. He also has done work on what was our taxi place."

"And Priscilla, who's she?"

"She came in with Mum into the revitalised taxi set-up. She put money in, helped run the business with Mum, but it only lasted a few weeks before this bloke Hughes set fire to it."

"He seems a really nasty chap. Revenge I suppose."

"Yes, I suppose so" said Eleanor. Then suddenly "What a bloody mess!"

"Steady on Eleanor" soothed Don, "you know, the worst is over."

"It may be. But our family will never be the same. If their divorce goes through we shall all split up."

"If?" said Don. "Is there any doubt about it then?"

"Only in my mind" answered Eleanor, "but in the end Arthur and Mum will be together, Dad will be on his own and I shall be on my own."

"You won't, you know. You are in a better position than they are. You are already going out on your own, as I am, so in a little while you won't need the family. But you will always be able to see them. It isn't as if they were dead, is it?"

"No. Now what about you? I've done what I came down for. I'm free to go back to Hull, except that I'd like to see the outcome of this thing."

"So would I" said Don."We can stay quite legitimately, so there's no point in rushing back just yet."

When the court was adjourned Priscilla hurried out of the courtroom. She did not stop to speak to Ruby or Eleanor but dashed away to get to her car. When she got there she just sank back in her seat. She, like Ruby and Eleanor, had been through an emotional experience. She had sensed in the courtroom that Jeff had aroused the sympathy of many of the spectators and probably the legal people as well. She herself was in a special dilemma. She realised now that what she felt for Jeff was not sympathy but love. She also felt that Jeff was not equipped for hard-headed business. Yes, he had had a successful taxi business, but she had seen him when he had just returned from sailing alone and free in the Channel. He was naive and easy going, people would take advantage of him. She could help him a lot, she could protect him from predatory people, men or women. But, she thought, 'I can't go sailing; I love the sea but I get so seasick. That can wait.'

The point was — what should she do now? After tomorrow she would keep clear of Ruby until they knew if the divorce was going through. Then she would get in touch with Jeff and see how he reacted to seeing her again.

The next morning Ruby and Eleanor had just finished their breakfast when there was a ring of the front door bell.

Eleanor went to the door. "Don! What are you doing here?"

Don had decided he would accompany them to the courthouse again, although of course Eleanor was not involved in today's proceedings.

He went inside and greeted Ruby. "Here's your key Mrs Cavanagh" he said, "I'm coming with you this time, so I'll not be needing it again."

A little later Arthur Mowbray arrived to take them in his car and off they went.

At the courthouse Priscilla had arrived early and was shown in to the witnesses' room. A WPC was on duty at the door with a list of the witnesses on her clipboard. She ticked off Priscilla's name.

Bill Hopkins was the next arrival. As he got to the door he saw the WPC and asked "Anyone else in there yet?"

"Only Mrs Thurston" she answered.

"Oh, Priscilla, good" said Bill.

"Priscilla is it? Isn't she a bit old for you?"

"She might be, but you're not" he joked back.

"Watch it, cheeky, or I'll put you behind bars" she said.

"I wouldn't mind that if you were in there too" Bill laughed.

"Come on now. What's your name?"

"Bill Hopkins."

"Right, you can go in." She ticked off his name. Bill waited. "Well, what is it now?" the WPC asked.

"You know my name, so what's yours?" he asked.

"WPC Scott" she answered shortly.

"WPC Scott" Bill repeated. "I'm sure your mother doesn't call you that. What's your first name?"

"It's Angela" she replied. "Now, you'd better get inside, there are others arriving."

Bill went in and sat next to Priscilla. She avoided his eyes as he greeted her.

"Hello Bill" she said "here we are again."

"Yes. How did it go yesterday, did you stay all day?"

"Oh yes. Hughes is in trouble I think, or he will be today."

Some other witnesses came in, then after a few minutes in came Ruby pushed by Arthur. Ruby greeted the other two and Arthur left to go to the public part of the courtroom.

Don and Eleanor were already in there so Arthur joined them.

There was a new jury to be sworn in and then the proceedings proper commenced. Hughes was charged with arson to which he pleaded 'Not guilty'.

Ruby and Priscilla were called to explain whether or not their business was failing. Their auditors confirmed that the business was solvent thanks to Priscilla's injection of funds. The insurance company was called to clarify the cover on the property. It was established that there was no link with Hughes prior to the blaze.

Bill Hopkins was called to tell how he had caught Hughes running away.

Detective Inspector Ryecroft had been painstaking in his search for evidence and it soon became evident that Hughes hadn't a leg to stand on. It was a clear case of malicious arson, and the jury came back quickly to give a 'Guilty' verdict.

Hughes was given seven years on the drugs charge and a further three years for the arson.

As he was led away Eleanor shuddered. "I hope that's the last I'll see of him" she said.

Outside in the foyer they all met up again, Arthur, Ruby, Priscilla and Bill. Ruby thanked Bill for the major part he had played in the capturing of Hughes and for his clear evidence. Bill seemed anxious to get away and was looking over his shoulder. He left them, and soon afterwards Priscilla saw him in earnest conversation with the WPC who had been on the door of the witnesses' room.

Priscilla said goodbye to Ruby and they agreed to get together again when the insurance company paid their claim.

There was still a part of the afternoon left when they arrived at Ruby's house. Ruby suggested that Don and Eleanor would like to relax by going to the theatre or a cinema.

"I feel I've had enough drama" Don said to Eleanor, "but I'll tell you what I would like to do, and that is — I'd like to see the marina or jetty or whatever you call it, where you used to have the boat moored. It would make all this seem more real somehow."

"All right" said Eleanor, "we'll go in my car. Mum!" she called, "we're going to the marina. See you for dinner."

Mrs Richings was coming in as usual to help with the evening meal so Eleanor was free.

They went off together and were soon on their way to the marina. Eleanor drove into the car park, they got out and walked towards the berths. As they approached the spot where her father used to moor his boat Eleanor felt a sudden pang that just as suddenly went. They saw a wonderful collection of boats of all sizes and designs, all bobbing in the late afternoon sunshine.

"This is the life, eh?" said Don. "When I've made some money I wouldn't mind having a boat here."

"You didn't say you could sail" said Eleanor.

"I can't, but I can dream, can't I?"

The following morning Don and Eleanor set off on their journey back to Hull. They reached the university buildings in the afternoon.

As soon as they arrived Don grabbed his bags and said, "I might just catch my tutor to thank him. I'll see you tonight if you like, OK? Goodbye."

He ran over to the Ed. Block and found the tutor's room. In response to his knock he was relieved to hear his tutor's voice say "Come in."

"Ah, Don Metcalfe, welcome back" said Mr Tait.

"Hello sir. We've just got back so I came over to say thanks for the time off, and I haven't done much work except on the first morning."

"But was the trip worth it in other ways?" asked the tutor.

"I think so, yes. I've learned a little about good and evil, quite a lot about compassion, a little about the legal system and about tolerance."

"That doesn't sound too bad for a start. What about the — what did you call it — unsavoury aspects?"

"They were there, but not where I expected; there was a degree of suffering though in place of it."

"Well, if any of that filters through to your studies I think your trip may have been rewarding."

"Thanks again sir. See you on Monday."

Don left in a jubilant frame of mind. He felt as he had years before when he had obtained his 'A' levels.

It was the week before Christmas and Ruby was alone in the sitting room. Mrs Richings had been in and had gone home.

Ruby picked up the phone and tapped Priscilla's number. "Hello, is that you Priscilla? Ruby here."

"Oh, Ruby, seems ages since we spoke."

"Yes, it must be almost two months. I was wondering if you would like to have lunch, say tomorrow, or whenever it suits you."

"Tomorrow would be fine" said Priscilla. "Where were you thinking of?"

"Oh, Galotti's restaurant is quite nice, how about there?"

"Yes, all right. Who will bring you, or shall I pick you up?"

"No, I'll get a taxi down. Eleanor's away so I'm on my own except for Mrs Richings coming in now and then."

"If you're sure. Then I'll meet you inside, say twelve-thirty?"

"Yes. I'll book a table just in case they are busy."

"Right" said Priscilla. "Look forward to it. Bye."

Ruby was already at the table when Priscilla walked in. "Hello Ruby," she said, "how are things with you?"

"Well, I seem to have a lot on my mind, some of which concerns you."

"What's it all about then?"

"Let's order first then I can settle my mind to talking."

A waiter came over and they ordered from the à la carte menu. That done, Ruby heaved a sigh and said "First the good news."

"Don't tell me there's bad news as well" said Priscilla half jokingly.

"Well, not for you perhaps. Anyway, first things first. You will be glad to hear that the insurance claim has been met. My solicitor is working it all out with the accountants, but you will receive all of your investment back, plus ten per cent, so that you are not out of pocket at all."

"But where is that extra money coming from?" asked Priscilla.

"I've had an offer for the site as it is and I shall accept it. The rest of the money I shall put on deposit for Jeff when he is released."

Priscilla was reduced to silence. The waiter brought their first course and Priscilla busied herself getting ready to eat.

Finally she said "That is good news. I really was not expecting to make a profit after that catastrophe, but as long as you are not robbing yourself I suppose it will be all right."

"We've worked it out and my solicitor says that's how it will be settled subject to agreement by all parties."

"Agreed then." They both continued eating for a while then Priscilla looked up and said, "Come on then, what else is on your mind?"

"Well, it concerns only me really, or rather me and Arthur."

"Oh" said Priscilla, "I don't really —."

"That's all right. I have to speak to someone and there's no one else. Eleanor's off on a skiing trip with a party from the university, but I couldn't speak to her anyway. No, this is my problem, but I need some assurance. You see, this Christmas is going to be a test for Arthur and me. I am going to spend five days at his house. We shall live as man and wife. It will be a sort of trial period, and it worries me that I might fail. I have grown to love Arthur and if I disappoint him I don't know what I shall do."

"But didn't you spend a weekend with him before?"

"Yes, but separately, if you see what I mean."

"Oh, I thought it was — you know."

"No, it was too soon. We just wanted to get to know each other a bit more. Now this will be different and I'm getting cold feet. It isn't as if I'm fully fit and —."

"But he knows that" broke in Priscilla. "Wasn't that how you met?"

"Yes, mutual attraction. We still have it, but will it be enough?"

"Look, Ruby, Arthur has made all the running, hasn't he; he's the one who has asked you to his house. Perhaps at this moment he is wondering whether he will fail you."

"Oh I shouldn't think so, he's so —."

"He's a semi-invalid like you, only it doesn't affect him as it does

102

you, so I don't think you should worry. In any case, you are not divorced yet, and you are not married to Arthur either, so there's nothing irrevocable. If it doesn't work out you are not fully committed, but it will work out I'm sure, and being entirely on your own will be ever so much better for both of you. Now, how about a sweet?"

"Yes, I will have something. I think you may be right, I was perhaps worrying too much, but you've helped a lot. Now, what about you, isn't it time you found yourself someone?"

It was as though the ceiling had fallen in. Priscilla made a pretence of going through the menu to hide the embarrassment she felt. What could one say in reply to the woman whose husband one was in love with? She decided that whenever she answered questions she would think of Bill Hopkins. "I have my moments" she said gaily.

"Someone serious?" asked Ruby "or am I being nosey?"

"No. It's all right, you are not nosey. I'm not serious about anyone, but anyway there's plenty of time."

"It would be a pity for an attractive woman like you not to have a good man by her side. I do hope you find someone."

"No doubt I shall, one day."

A week after Christmas Eleanor returned from her skiing holiday tired but very fit. It was the first time she had skied and she had got on well, with the skiing and the instructors.

When she saw her mother she was greatly surprised. "Mum, what have you been doing? You look as though you've been on holiday yourself."

"I have not been on holiday, you know that. I was away with Arthur for a few days."

"You're looking much healthier anyway, so that's good."

"How much longer is your vacation?" asked Ruby.

"Five more days. By the way, the day after tomorrow I shall be going to see some friends at Southsea, so if you can arrange to have someone come over I should feel better."

"I expect I'll manage. You go ahead."

The phone rang and Eleanor answered it, "Hello."

"Hello Ruby?"

"No, I'm Eleanor, who is that?"

"Priscilla. Is your mother in?"

"Yes she is. Mum! Take the other phone, it's Priscilla."

"Priscilla, this is Ruby. How are you?"

"Fine thanks. I was just ringing to say that I am going to have a winter break in Barbados, so anything to do with the business will have to wait until I get back."

"How long will that be?"

"Fifteen days. About the twentieth. Now, how are you? How did it go?"

"Well, the first day we were almost like strangers but after that it was marvellous."

"So it was successful then?" asked Priscilla.

"Oh yes, very. We are extremely happy."

"That's good, and I'm happy for you too."

"Now Priscilla, let's hope you meet a nice tall handsome man in Barbados, it would make your holiday."

"Well you never know, I might. Anyway I'm glad you are happy. See you when I get back. Goodbye."

It was with a light heart that Priscilla went about her packing. Ruby's liaison was working out, by February Ruby and Jeff would be divorced and she would be free to pursue her own path to happiness without fear of hurting anyone. She began to sing as she sorted her clothes.

Two days later Eleanor said goodbye to her mother and went out to her car. She drove off to the west and along the coast road to Havant and Portsmouth. At Southsea she drove on to the Isle of Wight ferry for Fishbourne. She then drove to Newport and had a snack lunch. She looked at her watch. Another half hour then she could finish her journey. When she was ready she drove off and eventually arrived at Parkhurst Prison. With pounding heart she left her car and joined the rest of the visitors. She showed her card to a warder at the door.

"First time here Miss?" he said.

"Yes. I'm to see Mr Cavanagh."

"Go on to the next door Miss."

She went along to the next door and then through to a large hall with lots of tables. Seated on one side of the tables were blue-clad men of all sorts and ages. She scanned the faces hurriedly until she saw her father anxiously watching the visitors.

She rushed over to his table and sat down in front of him. "Hello Dad" she whispered.

There was a tear in Jeff's eye as he looked at his daughter. "Eleanor, I didn't ever want to see you in here, but I have wonderful news. They've allowed my appeal to be heard."

"Oh Dad! When will it be?"

"April, and if the warders are to be believed I could get at least two years knocked off, so you keep your fingers crossed."

"Oh I will Dad. That's marvellous news." Then Eleanor went on to tell him all the other news, about the insurance money and that Mrs Thurston had gone on holiday to Barbados.

"And your Mum, is she all right?"

"She's fine, yes, she's fine."

There was nothing more she could say about her mother without distressing her father so she refrained from mentioning Arthur or the Christmas holiday her mother had had.

After half an hour she got up. "Dad, I have to get the ferry. I shall be back at college next week until Easter, so I shall not see you again before your appeal. Good luck. Write to me at home when you get the result."

"I will, I will. Goodbye Eleanor, I'm so glad you came."

She left without turning round. She couldn't bear to see him among those other — criminals? She put that thought out of her mind and concentrated on the good news about the appeal.

When she arrived home she found her mother in her chair in the sitting room.

"Did you have a good day dear?" she asked Eleanor.

"Yes, very nice." She sat down next to her mother. "Mum, I've been to see Dad."

"Oh Eleanor, we'd all agreed that you shouldn't."

"I know, but when I saw him at the courthouse I just couldn't let him go day after day without seeing anyone, it didn't seem fair, and now we know the truth about what made him do it, well, he deserves a lot of sympathy."

"Believe me Eleanor, I have a lot of sympathy for him, and I was just as moved as you were when I heard of the threats that forced him to carry on against his will. However, I have chosen my life now and nothing will alter my decision."

"Well it's not all bad news. They've allowed Dad's appeal against his sentence of seven years and it will be heard in April."

"I'm glad. Any remission will be well deserved. When you write to him tell him I wish him luck."

"I will" said Eleanor. She knew at that moment that their family life was finished for ever.

Priscilla had had a wonderful holiday. It had been such a change from everything that had been filling her life over the last year that she felt completely refreshed. The warmth had been of special benefit but the colours and the music were all part of what was to her a very therapeutic holiday.

Now she had to get back to everyday life doing — what? She had so much time on her hands, her charity commitments only took up a few hours a week, she felt she needed something to do. At first she could only think of ordinary things like bridge clubs, typing and home visits.

Then she thought she might try doing a course in something. Book-keeping? No. Needlework? Definitely out. Languages? A possibility.

Perhaps a course in Italian would be useful. Then she thought of computing. That was being more widely used than ever and it seemed that one would have to know something about computers and their uses in order to be in business or to work for other firms. Yes, that is what she would do. She decided to investigate where computer courses were available.

When she had been home a week she received a phone call. It was Bill Hopkins. "Hello Bill, nice to hear from you."

"I was wondering if I could come and see you."

"Of course. Any particular reason?" Remembering the last time they went out together Priscilla thought she had made it clear that she was not in favour of a continuing relationship.

"Yes. I want to tell you personally why I shall not be coming to see you again, socially that is."

"Oh." Priscilla was slightly affronted. This was so unsubtle. "Why can't you tell me now?" she asked.

"I can, of course, it's just that it seems sort of cold."

"Nonsense. Tell me now, you silly boy. But I think I can guess."

"All right then. Do you remember when we went to the courts?"

"Yes, quite clearly" said Priscilla.

"There was a WPC at the door checking the names."

"That's right, I remember."

"Well, her name is Angela Scott. We hit it off at once and now I am seeing her regularly."

"Is it serious?" asked Priscilla.

"I think so" said Bill. "We have a great deal in common and our ages are only a year apart."

"You know, I always said you should find someone nearer your own age and now you have, and believe me I'm very pleased for both of you, really I am."

"Thanks Priscilla, I knew you would be. Well, there's nothing more to say except that I shall value your friendship in the future."

"And I yours. I shall call you if there is any building work to be done, and don't you dare refuse."

"Of course I won't. Goodbye Priscilla."

"Goodbye Bill and good luck." She put the phone down. 'Good,' she thought, 'that's the way it should be.' She went back to her chair and flopped down.

She picked up the local paper and flicked through the pages. Suddenly she stopped. Her eye had caught the name Cavanagh. There it was. A small paragraph, *Mr Jeffrey Cavanagh, currently serving seven years for possession of drugs has been given leave to appeal against the sentence. The hearing will be in April.*

She tried to remember when Jeff had been convicted. It was about the same time that her husband Lionel had been murdered, almost two years already. She felt she would like to go and see Jeff, but she had resolved to do nothing until Jeff and Ruby were divorced, then there would be nothing to stop her going. Except one thing, she now knew what she felt for Jeff, but she did not have any idea how he would react if she revealed her feelings. She recalled how they had enjoyed each other's company that day at Arundel, and was fairly sure she could build on that.

She had been too late for the start of a computer course at the Education centre but they had agreed to let her take the second half of the term that lasted until April. She attended twice a week and began to absorb the rudiments of using a computer as well as the completely new vocabulary of the computer jargon.

Eleanor had come home for the brief half term break. She suspected something was up when she received a short letter from her mother asking her to come down.

Only her mother was there when she arrived, and after she had greeted her she sat down next to her. "Well Mum, what's it all about then?" asked Eleanor.

"You have probably guessed, but anyway your father and I are divorced" said Ruby.

"Oh Mum, now what happens? Do I get thrown out or what?"

"No dear, of course you don't. Arthur and I will be married at Easter and we shall live at his house in Angmering. You will have the use of this house until you are twenty-one, then you can choose whether to keep it or sell it and have the money from the sale to finance your career, whatever that career is."

"I can't run a house, I have no income" said Eleanor.

"I know, I know. I shall pay for the upkeep until you are twenty-one, so you need have no worries there."

Now Eleanor came to the question that was in both their minds. "What about Dad, where does he fit into all this?" Eleanor asked.

"I don't really know" said Ruby. "It will be three years before he is released, even with remission. If his appeal comes off he may get a bit off, nobody knows as yet, but whatever happens there will be the money from the sale of the yard, about a hundred thousand. That will be there for him only."

"I shall have to stay here" said Eleanor, "otherwise where will Dad go when he comes out. Wouldn't it be better to give him the house and me the other money?"

"No. When he comes out he will not want to stay around this area. He will want to make a fresh start where he is not known."

"I suppose you are right" sighed Eleanor.

Ruby now began to feel uncomfortable as she framed her next pronouncement. "There's one other thing Eleanor, and I don't want you to misjudge me because of it. When Arthur and I are married we are both going to have to make adjustments to our lives, and we shall need time to do that, without having any outside worries. You know what that means, we wouldn't be able to have anyone to stay, probably for six months or so until we are properly settled. Of course we want to see you during your holidays, but not to stay." Ruby was apologetic in her delivery and waited for Eleanor's reaction.

"If I hadn't this house to come home to I should have felt slighted, but as it is I do understand, Mum, even thought it will be a big upheaval for all of us."

"It most certainly will" said Ruby with a sigh. She suddenly remembered something else. "Do you remember me mentioning about keeping Priscilla in mind if you had any problems? I feel guilty about Priscilla. She's been a good friend. She saved the business only to lose it all because of that Hughes. I know she has got her money back, but she has nothing to do and as far as I know she has no one close to her. Try and see her now and then, and if you should need support yourself in any way, ask her, involve her in some way."

"Sure I will Mum, if the need arises, but what we have in common I don't know, except that she was your partner for a while. I should think she has had enough of us and our goings on."

"Perhaps" said Ruby, but she also has had her own share of 'goings on' as you call it, when her husband was murdered by that woman's husband. That was horrible."

"I didn't take much notice of that at the time" said Eleanor, "there was too much happening with Dad's trial and all that."

"Oh dear" said Ruby with another big sigh. "I shall be glad when Easter comes."

Chapter 5

New Beginnings

Easter was early that year. Arthur and Ruby were married at the register office on the Wednesday before Easter in order to avoid the busy time at that weekend. Only a few people had been invited, including Priscilla. A small reception was held at the Evenbridge Hotel and afterwards the bride and groom went straight back to Angmering. They wanted to spend their first weeks together in the privacy of their own home. There would be plenty of opportunities for a honeymoon or holiday when they were used to each other's company. Ruby knew that if they had gone anywhere strange as a 'honeymoon couple' they could easily become figures of ridicule, especially as she had to have the wheelchair handy for moving any distance more than about thirty yards.

When Arthur and Ruby had departed the guests remained for a little while. Priscilla saw Eleanor and went over to her. "Hello Eleanor, so they've actually done it then?"

"Yes" said Eleanor in a resigned tone. "Here beginneth the second lesson."

"For you perhaps" said Priscilla, "but for some of us there have been several new beginnings, not least your mother."

"I know. I suppose it is too much to ask that things should go on serenely for ever. People are always saying that there has to be change, but right now I wish that the past two years could be wiped out and that we would be one happy family again."

"For you maybe, but not for me" said Priscilla. "Two years ago my life was steadily becoming worse. My husband's murder was a kind of catalyst; it solved my immediate problems and brought me a few more, but nothing that would make me prefer the old days before then. I can think of lots of cliches that would fit the bill, like 'it's an ill wind' or 'count your blessings'. So when I'm feeling low I do just that, and it helps. Yes, I have regrets but — another cliche — 'time will tell'."

"I miss having Dad around. I suppose you heard that he's had his appeal allowed?"

"Yes, I heard. When is it?"

"It's just before I go back to college" said Eleanor. "Why don't you come along with me, I shall be on my own." Then suddenly she said "Did you know Dad? Have you met him?"

Priscilla was momentarily disadvantaged. "I met him, yes, but only briefly. I can't say I know him. I saw him at the Hughes' trial of course. He stands a good chance of winning his appeal, I should say."

"Well, what do you say? Could you come with me?"

"I suppose I could. Yes, why not, my time's my own."

"Oh thanks" said Eleanor. "I shall not feel entirely alone now. I'll phone you when the actual date is."

"Righto. What are you going to do for the next two weeks?"

"I have my car. I shall visit some friends and have a day here and there."

"When you know the date of the appeal come round and have a chat."

"All right, I'll ring you when I'm coming round."

"Good. Well I'll be off now. Bye."

A week later Eleanor phoned Priscilla. "I've got the details of the appeal court. Can I come round and have that chat?" said Eleanor.

"Come about two, I'll have finished my jobs by then."

Precisely at two Eleanor arrived at Priscilla's house. She admired the outside then rang the door bell.

Priscilla opened the door. "Come in Eleanor." They went into the sitting room. "Now, sit down and give me the news."

"It's a week on Thursday, ten-thirty, court number three."

"Thursday, yes I can manage that all right, that is if you still want me to come along."

"Oh yes, I do" said Eleanor. She paused and looked puzzled. "You know" she went on, "Dad's lawyer, when he phoned me to tell me the date and time, he said 'take your father a complete change of clothing', and when I asked what for he said it was 'just in case'."

"That was odd, Do they have to wear civilian clothes in court, or their uniform?"

"I don't know. When I said 'just in case what' he said 'just in case he needs it, that's all'."

"That's very interesting" said Priscilla. She was silent then. She was contemplating the possibilities and the only reason she could think of for Jeff needing his own clothes were if he was released. She thought back to the Hughes' trial and remembered Jeff's story of how he was blackmailed. He could possibly be released if they reduced his sentence low enough. She did not voice her thoughts to Eleanor. "I expect all will be revealed next week" she said. "Come and look round the house and garden."

Eleanor stayed for another hour, as she left she said "Will you go straight to the court?"

"Yes, I'll see you there at ten-fifteen."

On the Thursday morning Eleanor walked into the courthouse carrying a small suitcase. At the entrance was Jeff's lawyer.

He went towards Eleanor. "Miss Cavanagh. This is a good day. I'll take the case and if it's not needed I'll return it afterwards."

"Thanks. I still don't see why you want it though."

"No, yes, ah well, it's one of those rules, really" he said.

Eleanor looked round as the doors opened again, it was Priscilla. "Hello Priscilla, I'm glad you are here, I feel nervous again."

"I'm not exactly settled either, and I'm not involved." But she was. She thought, 'What happens to Jeff today will be of great concern to me as well as Eleanor.' "Shall we go in?" she said, forcing a smile. They found seats and waited.

An hour later when the preliminaries were over, Jeff was brought in and the appeal began. They went over all the old evidence and then Jeff was called to the stand. The questioning was similar to that in the Hughes' trial, and once again Eleanor and Priscilla listened while Jeff related the story of his involvement in the drugs affair.

The proceedings came to an end. The judge adjourned for lunch. Eleanor and Priscilla popped out for a snack meal.

"What do you think?" asked Eleanor as they were eating.

"I think they will reduce his sentence" said Priscilla confidently.

"Do you? Do you really?" said Eleanor. "Oh I do hope so, poor Dad."

They returned for two o'clock.

The officials filed in, then the judge. He asked Jeff to stand up. The judge recalled various pieces of the evidence in his original trial and then the Hughes' trial. He said "My brief today is not to decide whether the defendant was guilty or not guilty. That was decided by the jury at the original trial. He was guilty as charged. What concerns me now is whether or not his sentence properly reflects the seriousness of the crime. In my opinion it does not. In the original incident the defendant had not known that what he was receiving and passing on to others was anything but say jewellery, diamonds or some other form of contraband. It was only subsequently after threats that he was forced to agree to continue with the moving of narcotics. I am satisfied that the defendant's story is correct and that he was indeed intimidated by threats on the wellbeing of his daughter. I find that the sentence of seven years therefore is excessive. Accordingly I now reduce that sentence to two years. I understand that with remission he has already served that term, and so Jeffrey Cavanagh you are herewith discharged and free to go."

Eleanor and Priscilla looked at each other and instinctively clasped hands.

Priscilla was ecstatic. "Oh Eleanor, how marvellous. I never thought it would be as good as this."

Eleanor was more subdued. "Good old Dad" she said. "What a pity there will be no one to welcome him home."

They went out into the foyer.

There they saw the lawyer again. "Mr Cavanagh is waiting to see you in the interview room" he said. "Come, I'll show you."

They followed him to the room.

At the door Priscilla suddenly said "Eleanor, I would be intruding. Ring me when you are settled." Before Eleanor could answer Priscilla turned quickly and left.

Eleanor went into the room. The two officers with him left, one of them saying "See you later."

Eleanor hugged her father and then said "What did he mean, see you later?"

"Oh, I'll explain that in a minute, now let's look at you again." He hugged her again and then sat down. "I am overwhelmed. The lawyer said I might expect a good outcome but I never expected this." He went silent and hung his head. Eleanor heard him sniff as he bit his lip to hold back the tears, but the emotion of the moment was too much for him, the tears streamed down his cheeks. After a moment he found a handkerchief and dried his eyes. "I'm sorry Eleanor, you've no idea the relief I feel after two years in there. I shall not believe it until I'm home again."

"Tell me what you have to do next" said Eleanor calmly.

"I'm being taken back, once I've put my own clothes on. I have some formalities to complete. They will put me up in a separate non-prisoner room for tonight, then tomorrow I shall leave of my own accord. I shall get the ferry and if you will pick me up at the terminal we'll go home together."

"I can manage that all right Dad" said Eleanor.

Jeff was now calmer. He spoke again. "When I get home it's going to feel a bit empty, so I'd like you to phone up a few people and ask them to a small kind of reception party."

"What people Dad? I'm not sure what you mean."

"Well, there's Mrs Richings and her husband, there's Tim Freshman who was the taxi foreman, and his wife of course, and two of the original engineers from our shed, only for an hour or two, just to make a bit of noise."

"What about Priscilla? You know, Mrs Thurston, formerly Mrs Bulmer, she was with me today to keep me company."

"If you like, though she's not likely to be kindly disposed to someone who has caused all this trouble" Jeff said sadly.

"I think she will. She has been very sympathetic towards you."

"All right then, I'll leave it to you."

After a few more minutes one of the officers returned. "The transport is ready Mr Cavanagh, so when you are ready."

"Right. Now Eleanor, try and make my homecoming lively. Don't get to the terminal before five o'clock, then we can get home about six. Arrange it for six precisely, there's a good girl."

"All right Dad, see you tomorrow then."

Jeff went off down the corridor carrying his case. Eleanor waited until he disappeared then went to her car.

When she got to the car she was surprised to see Priscilla. "I waited" she said. "I wasn't sure what you would be doing."

"I'm glad you did" said Eleanor. She quickly explained the arrangements that her father had asked for and then said "You will come, won't you, I shall need some support."

"Yes, of course I'll come. About ten to six? Fine."

They went to their cars. Eleanor sighed with relief then went home to do her phoning.

Mrs Richings was overjoyed at the outcome of the appeal and offered to come in and make some snacks to go with the drinks. Eleanor gratefully accepted the offer and promised to go shopping for the ingredients.

While she was pottering around that evening she suddenly realised that the bed would have to be aired, but which one? Her mother had had the small study to sleep in since she became almost unable to manage the stairs, so there were still three bedrooms available. She decided to prepare the larger spare room instead of the one where her parents used to sleep. Then she decided to tell her mother the news.

With some trepidation she dialled the number. Ruby answered, "Hello."

"Hello Mum, it's Eleanor. I've some news for you."

"Yes." Ruby waited expectantly.

"I went to the appeal court today Mum."

"Yes, I know. What happened?"

"Dad got his sentence reduced to two years, so he's free to come home tomorrow."

"Oh, I really am glad, really. For all his faults he never deserved a long sentence anyway. Justice has been done, as they say."

Eleanor told her about the people coming to welcome him home.

"I hope your father settles down quickly. I expect it will all seem strange for a while. He must find something to occupy him."

"I expect he will do that eventually, but anyway he's in good health but a bit thinner."

"That's good. You may give him my good wishes and tell him the solicitor has all the information on the money for him."

"Thanks Mum. I'll come over the day after tomorrow, before I go back to college."

The afternoon of the homecoming saw Mrs Richings busy as a bee. She was a good cook, and a small party posed no problems for her.

Eleanor had managed to get the lawyer and his wife to come to the reception, all the others had accepted, about six couples and Priscilla.

At half past four all was ready and Eleanor left for the terminal leaving Mrs Richings to receive the guests.

Her father was waiting for her with his few belongings in the case, he got into the car and they drove off.

All the guests had arrived by six as requested. Mrs Richings had given them all a drink and they awaited Jeff's arrival.

Jeff and Eleanor arrived just after six o'clock. Eleanor went up to the front door and opened it. "Welcome home Dad" she said. "Come on, let's see who's here." Eleanor led the way in. "He's here everybody" said Eleanor.

Jeff entered, looked all round the faces before him, then looked down at his feet. "Would you mind if I had a little drink first before I welcome you?"

Eleanor rushed to get him a sherry.

He drank half of it and said, "That's better. I thank you all for coming here today. It helps restore one's faith in the human race. For two years now I have had to mix with people from what I always regarded as another race, human maybe, but of the criminal league. I was almost one of them, but in my heart I knew I was not a criminal as the law interprets it. It has been partially put right but it can never be erased. It has altered my life and that of some others too. To save you all the bother of asking me what I am going to do, the short answer is I don't know exactly, but I do not intend to stay in Chichester. It would place too much of a strain on some who knew me but now wish they hadn't, and it will be much easier for friends who might be embarrassed. So when I talk to you individually please tell me what you have been doing, you know about me." He finished his speech and drank the rest of his sherry.

The lawyer then stood up. "Ladies and gentlemen, I shall take it upon myself to welcome Mr Cavanagh, Jeff, back home. He has, as they say, paid his debt to society and is as free as you and I. So I say welcome back to the fold, and may your future be as bright as I'm sure we all wish it to be. To Jeff."

They all raised their glasses and drank To Jeff.

Eleanor went to the CD player and put on some soft background music. Immediately a buzz of conversation started and Jeff moved from friend to friend chatting about their lives during the last two years.

He was particularly interested in his former employees, especially Tim Freshman who had been on the microphone for so many years. He had got a similar post with one of the larger hire companies who had benefited from having Ruby's Taxis annihilated by the fire. Apparently all the drivers had managed to get jobs so Jeff felt relieved.

Jeff thanked Mrs Richings personally for being such a help. He hoped she would continue to come in on a few days per week to help prepare a meal as he was no cook.

Eventually he came in front of Priscilla. He shook her hand formally. "Hello Priscilla, that is — er — Mrs Thurston now isn't it?"

"It is" said Priscilla, "but please call me Priscilla."

"Not shortened I believe" said Jeff, remembering their second and last meeting.

"That's right" said Priscilla. Now that they had met once more she found herself tongue-tied. He once had seemed so masterful and self-possessed, she knew now that he was weak, vulnerable and surprisingly naive.

Eleanor came up to them. "I see you've met Priscilla again Dad. Priscilla's been a great help to me and of course to Mum when they ran the business together."

"Yes, I know" said Jeff. "I was amazed at the way you two managed to turn around the business. You can imagine how shocked I was to hear about the fire, and of course" he said guiltily, "it was through my folly that that happened."

"It's all over now" said Priscilla quietly. "The financial side of it has been settled and I have lost nothing except an occupation. So you are not to go on blaming yourself. Forget it, look ahead to something better, I am."

"You're right, but it will take time."

After an hour or so the guests started to leave, and soon only Mr and Mrs Richings, Priscilla, Eleanor and Jeff were left.

Eleanor went over to Mrs Richings. "You've been a brick, coming in like this. We're very grateful but you are not to do any more. Stay and have another drink, I shall do the washing-up and clearing away." She laughed. "I'm not helpless you know."

"I know dear, but I'm more at home in a kitchen than anywhere else. Still, I will have another sherry, then me and hubby will be off."

Priscilla felt it was time to go. She got up from her seat and approached Jeff who seemed a bit deflated as the room emptied. "Thanks for asking me here. I'm so glad everything is beginning to work out for you." She offered her hand.

Jeff took it. "I never expected to see you here in such circumstances, but I'm glad you came."

"Goodbye Jeff,"

"Goodbye Priscilla."

Priscilla called to Eleanor "Goodbye Eleanor, have a good trip back."

"Thanks. Goodbye Priscilla."

Priscilla went to her car and drove home. When she arrived home she sank into an armchair and started to recall the whole evening. She had been expecting — what exactly?

Whatever she had been expecting it was not what actually occurred. The intense sympathy she had felt when Jeff was giving his evidence at Hughes' trial had been replaced by — she did not know what, but she knew that she would like to be with him again, he was more her type than Mike Eldon. She discounted Bill Hopkins because he had never been her type. She decided to give Jeff time to settle down.

Back at the house father and daughter were alone.

"My God it's quiet" said Jeff. "I'm not used to this sort of atmosphere. There was always some noise going on in there."

"You'll soon get used to it again Dad" said Eleanor. "You can start by watching TV or having the radio on, that will make the place seem not quite so empty. Come and see the room I've got ready for you. They went upstairs, Eleanor went into the large spare room. "There, what do you think of that?" she said.

"I'm glad you didn't put me in our old room. This will be just right for me for a while."

"You're not going just yet are you Dad?"

"Oh no, like I said before, I shall have to look around before making any decisions."

"Well I shall not be here after tomorrow so you'll need some means of getting about, won't you?"

"I had thought about that. I expect the money I've got allocated to me by your mother will run to a small car. Anyway, time enough for that next week or the next" said Jeff. When they were downstairs again Jeff said to Eleanor, "How is your mother, is she happy?"

"She's fine. I think she's happy. They have a nice little place at Angmering." Eleanor did not think she should be any more enthusiastic about them.

Her father seemed satisfied. "That's all right then" he said. He

116

switched on the television.

The solicitor had rung Jeff to ask him to come down to his office to sign a paper to do with his money from the sale of the former taxi site. He had also asked Priscilla to come down as former partner to sign in confirmation.

They met in the solicitor's office and were greeted formally.

"Sit down please" said the solicitor. "This is just a formal acceptance of the sum of one hundred thousand pounds, and the waiving of any claims you may have against the former car hire firm. Yours, Mrs Thurston is a similar acceptance and it absolves your former partner from any other claims."

They signed the appropriate documents and prepared to leave.

"Just a moment Mr Cavanagh, I have something else to discuss with you. It's about the house."

Priscilla made as if to go but Jeff said "You may stay if you wish, after all, you were nearly part of the family."

"Very well then" said the solicitor. He turned to Jeff. "The house is in Mrs Cavanagh's or rather Mrs Mowbray's name. She was going to put it in trust for your daughter Eleanor, but she has now decided to gift it to her immediately. This means that probably next month the property will belong to Miss Eleanor Cavanagh and she may keep or dispose of it as she wishes. I must of course point out that you Mr Cavanagh have no legal right to any part of this property."

"In other words" said Jeff, "if Eleanor doesn't want me there I have to go."

"I'm sure she won't, but legally — yes — that is about it."

"Thanks" said Jeff. "Now we all know where we stand."

He and Priscilla left together.

Outside, Jeff made as if to move off but Priscilla laid a hand on his arm. "Just a minute" she said, "most men would at least offer one a coffee."

"I'm sorry" said Jeff. "It never occurred to me. You see, one forgets how to deal with the fairer sex. Where would you suggest we go?"

"That's better" said Priscilla. "I know just the place. Come on, I'll take you in my car." Priscilla had suddenly perceived how she was going to deal with Jeff. He needed educating, she thought.

When they got to the edge of the town Jeff said "Where is this place then?"

"You'll see" said Priscilla.

Two minutes later she swung the car into her own driveway and pulled up at the front door.

"My place" she said. "Come in."

They got out of the car. Jeff looked around and said "This looks

117

like a nice little house."

"And we make good coffee. Come on in" said Priscilla.

When they were sipping their coffee Jeff looked at Priscilla and said "Do you remember the last time we had tea together, it seems a lifetime ago."

"It was, and I didn't bring you here to reminisce. Lots of things have happened since then. We all had different lives, you had your boat and everything was plain sailing. Now there's no plain sailing; we've had storms and tempests, probably there will be more. We're not going to weather them by dwelling on the past but by learning from it." She paused. "Now, drink your coffee then I'll show you the garden."

"Jeff was taken aback, so much so he was unable to think of any reply except "Yes, I'd like to see it."

They wandered out to the rear of the house where a large but rather unkempt garden, lawn and shrubbery had been originally arranged tastefully. Now, in the middle of May it was already beginning to get overgrown.

"You need someone on this for a week" said Jeff, "otherwise you'll never overcome it."

"I can get the grass cut easily enough but finding a jobbing gardener is difficult. I may have to get a landscape firm in eventually, I suppose."

"I don't want to appear pushy" said Jeff, "but I have nothing to do at present. I'm not entirely useless at gardening so if you are agreeable I'd like to offer my services, reasonable rates to my friends." He laughed.

Priscilla laughed too. "If you were serious I'd take you up on that" she said, "but I —."

"I believe I am serious, though I wasn't when I said it, but I am now, why not?"

"Think of the neighbours, they'd be shocked."

"Why, what's wrong with having a friend to help in the garden?"

"I think you mean it" said Priscilla.

"I do" said Jeff. "What do you say?"

"I would have to pay you" said Priscilla.

"All right, I'll give you my terms." Jeff was really warming to the idea now. "I shall come here in the mornings, three days a week, Mondays, Wednesdays and Fridays, and in return I shall expect coffee free at ten-thirty, lunch free at twelve-thirty and a cup of free tea at three. How does that sound?" They had got to the end of the garden now. Jeff looked at the rough vegetable plot. "I hope you have got some tools, mechanical if possible" he said.

"There's a mower and a small rotovator and lots of hand tools" said Priscilla.

"That'll do. When can I start?"

"Tomorrow is Wednesday, how will that do?" she answered.

"Right. Now suddenly I feel useful."

"There's one more thing though" Priscilla said. "I know you have not got transport yet, so how will you get here?"

"Mm. How about if I got a bus from town out to here, then perhaps you would run me back in the afternoon."

"Yes, I could do that. If it clashes with my charity jobs you could get a taxi" said Priscilla, still not quite sure whether he was joking about the whole thing.

Jeff looked her straight in the eyes. "I am serious about this. I'd like to do it, so what about it?"

"All right Jeff. Wear your oldest clothes and toughest boots and we'll give it a try."

The weather was kind during those two weeks in May. Jeff worked like a demon, sleeves rolled up, no hat, the sun shining down; he soon looked a browner fitter man than the one who had come home only a short while ago. Sometimes Priscilla helped him or worked on the front borders, but mostly she left him alone, only calling him for the breaks. Jeff found the work therapeutic. He was able to think and plan and square his mind up about all the things that had bothered him, not least his return to society and how that would be resolved.

As they lunched on the Friday of the second week Jeff was noticeably quiet.

"Something worrying you?" asked Priscilla.

They were in the kitchen and could see the garden clearly.

"Take a look out there" said Jeff.

Priscilla looked out. "It's lovely already. You've done well" she said.

"That's it. There's really no need for me to come any more. It's manageable now and you could easily keep it tidy, and get the travelling lawn keepers in now and then."

"Look Jeff" said Priscilla, "you don't have to stop coming here. I've enjoyed your company and would appreciate it if you would do another week, could you?"

"If you really don't mind. I would like to do a bit more. It's helping me more than you know."

When Jeff looked at her she felt that wave of sympathy that she had experienced in the courtroom. She wanted him to stay working in the garden for weeks and weeks, but she knew that if she appeared too eager Jeff might not react favourably. She had to wait for him to become less institutionalised and to rediscover his emotions. "As far as I'm concerned you can come and go as you please. For now let's say one more week and see how you feel next Friday." Priscilla saw his face brighten.

"Right then, one more week" Jeff said happily.

The following Wednesday it was a much livelier Jeff who sat down to lunch. "I've got some news" he said suddenly.

Priscilla was interested. "Oh, what's that then?" she asked.

"I'm going to look at a possible restart for me."

"I'm dying to hear what it is. Tell me."

"Well, I've been studying the Auto magazines since I've been home and I found an advert for a small car-hire firm for sale with a small house. I've telephoned them and have an appointment for next week, Tuesday to be exact."

"That's marvellous" said Priscilla with obvious delight, "but where?"

"Norfolk. Quite near Norwich but not in the city."

"It sounds ideal for you. Is that a place you know?"

"No. I've been to Norwich but I can't say I know the area."

"Well, I wish you luck then" said Priscilla. "How will you travel?"

"I had been hoping to get a car but I'm reluctant to dig into my capital yet in case I need it all."

"Why not borrow my car?" said Priscilla impulsively. "As long as I give the charity people a few days' notice I don't have to go in, and I've no other commitments that require driving anywhere."

"That's very generous of you Priscilla, I don't know why you bother with an old lag like me" said Jeff self-pityingly.

Priscilla was incensed. "What do you mean Jeff Cavanagh, an old lag like you? Unless you stop thinking of yourself in those terms you'll never rise above the ex-con level. You've been virtually exonerated by the legal people, so take advantage of your good fortune and stop moaning. I've made you the offer of my car, are you going to take it or not?"

Jeff was shaken by Priscilla's vehemence and it took him a little while to compose himself. "Thank you Priscilla" he said quietly, "I suppose I deserved that. I would like to accept your offer and your advice. I apologise if I have seemed to be ungrateful. Shall we discuss the details?"

"Yes, all right. You will be coming here this Friday, why not come again on Monday, you can drive my car to your home and it will be ready for you to go off early on Tuesday."

"It's about a four or five hour trip I should think, best part of two hundred miles. You know what I think? I should go on Monday, stay in a B & B overnight then go along fresh on Tuesday morning, look around a bit and come back Tuesday afternoon and evening."

"Or even stay another night for a second look round" put in Priscilla.

"Yes, I could do that as well, but that would depend on what I thought of the place. I'll leave that option open, I think."

When Priscilla returned after taking Jeff home she sat thinking about him. Why on earth was she bothering with him. She thought, 'He not only doesn't know how to deal with the fairer sex, he doesn't seem to recognise them.' She had done everything except throw herself at him, but he didn't see her as anything other than a person being kind to him. Perhaps she should withdraw and let him get on with his own life.

It would not make any difference because fate was on hand to provide the boost. Jeff had taken the bus up to Priscilla's on Monday morning, collected the car and driven back to the house to get his bag and maps. As he put the bag in the boot he noticed that his next-door neighbour was going to have some work done on the house. Outside on the road were two vehicles, a van and a small lorry.

A man came down the drive and went towards the van, turned, saw Jeff and came over. "It's Mr Cavanagh isn't it?"

"Yes, that's right."

"I'm Bill Hopkins, I was at the trial of Hughes."

"Oh yes, I remember. You caught him by the taxi yard. You did well."

"I never had chance to congratulate you on your appeal. You must be relieved" said Bill.

"I am indeed."

"That car looks like the one Mrs Thurston owns. Is it?"

"As a matter of fact it is. She has lent it to me for two days."

"She's a good sort" said Bill. "We've done quite a bit of work for her. A pleasure to deal with her."

"Yes, she is very nice."

"Very nice, that's an understatement. She's a fine-looking woman. I can't understand why some handsome millionaire hasn't snapped her up before this."

"I expect she has plenty of admirers" said Jeff.

"I know different" said Bill. "I've seen her a lot when we've been working there and I think she's saving herself for someone."

"I'm sure I don't know. I haven't noticed anyone at her home while I've been doing a bit of gardening."

"There you are then. I tell you, if I was her age no one would stand a chance. I'm spoken for anyway."

"Yes, well, Bill I have to get going, up to Norwich you know."

"Right. Nice talking to you. Have a good trip."

Jeff got the rest of his things, locked the front door and was soon on his way.

It was early afternoon when Jeff arrived in Norwich. He found a car park and then walked round the city. He found the agent and explained who he was. They had given him the appointment when Jeff had phoned them, and now they gave him a more detailed description of the place.

"There was no figure mentioned in the advert" said Jeff. "Have you any idea of the asking price?"

"He's hoping to get over a hundred and fifty thousand, lock, stock and barrel, but we advised him to set his sights a little lower. Try an offer then you will know where you stand."

After he had returned to the car he drove off to find the yard and cottage, intending to look it over from the road, he would then be able to assess it better on the morrow when he came for the appointment.

He found the place easily, just off the main road but in a good built-up area. 'Plenty of customers' thought Jeff. He parked in a side road and walked back to the yard.

It was a spacious yard with what looked like an office and a large workshop building, brick built. At one end of the yard was a small brick cottage. The whole site was sandwiched between a busy garage that had a very large car park. On inspection he found that the proprietor had been enterprising. He had a park and ride system without the ride. People could pay to park there and then take a bus into the city or go next door for a taxi. It appeared to be very busy. Jeff liked what he saw and was already looking forward to his appointment. He went to find a bed and breakfast place.

The next morning he was up bright and early and after a good breakfast he paid the bill and drove up to the taxi yard. He drove right in and parked near the cottage.

As he got out of the car a man came from the office. He looked to be about sixty years old. "Are you Mr Cavanagh?" he called.

"That's right" said Jeff.

"I'm Jim Stephenson." They shook hands. "Come into the office, I'm on my own."

In the office Jim Stephenson went straight to the swivel chair and resumed listening. Jeff noted the radio set-up and was pleasantly surprised.

"This is the control room" said Jim. "We've four cars, they're all out, two on regular runs and two on city runs. When one of them comes in we'll go over to the house and look around, the driver will take over here."

The phone rang, Jim took a message and booked a car for eleven o'clock. He wrote it in the big ledger then got up and chalked it in a big blackboard with 'Today' at the top in white letters. There were two other times on the board.

A few minutes later a clean black taxi swept into the yard. Jim got up and called to the driver "Take over here please, I'm going to the house."

They left the office and went first to the workshop. It was well equipped, it even had a hydraulic lift. On one side of the shop there was one car with a wheel off.

"We don't have a mechanic full-time. When any driver has an hour to spare he can do a bit in here. Usually I do the more complicated jobs."

"And what about major repairs or servicing?" asked Jeff.

"We have an arrangement with a repair garage about two hundred yards down the road."

They moved off towards the house. Inside they were met by Jim's wife. She offered to make a cup of tea but Jeff declined with thanks. She showed Jeff round the house and was obviously very proud of it. They had lived all of their married life there, she said, and were very fond of the place. It was in a good state of repair.

The two men went round the yard and back to the office. Jim led the way through the office to a cosy rest room. A door off it led to a clean cloak room and toilet. They sat down in the rest room.

Jeff went straight to the point. "What are you expecting to get for it?" he asked.

"One hundred and fifty thousand. The cars will be at their used-car list price at the time of completion of the sale."

Jeff thought hard. That means two hundred grand all told. He couldn't do it. Where was he to get another hundred thousand, he had no security for a mortgage. "What do you intend to do if you sell it. Where will you go?"

"I don't know. I'll have to buy a little place somewhere. I shall miss our little cottage though."

"Why exactly are you selling?" asked Jeff.

"Well, I've had a bit of hernia trouble and I can't put into the job as much as I'd like, so I thought I'd retire early."

An idea was forming in Jeff's mind. This set-up was similar to how he and Ruby had started over twenty years ago. They hadn't lived on the premises ever. "Here's something for you to mull over. First of all, if you didn't include the cottage what would you be asking?" said Jeff.

"Oh — er — I don't know, about half what I said I suppose, plus the cost of the cars."

"Here's something else. Suppose you stayed as you are and I put some money into the firm to give me say 60% control, what sort of figure would you be thinking of?"

"I couldn't say off-hand, I suppose I'd have to get advice."

"All right then. I'll say sixty thousand for the 60% one. If you like either of those two options get in touch with me again. But, one thing, I cannot afford to buy you out completely. I know this business and I would work hard to make a go of it. I shall go home this afternoon. Remember, on either of those options you get to stay in the house. I shall rent a flat somewhere near if you accept."

As he went back to the car Jeff went hot and cold. He sat in his seat thinking it over. Had he been hard on the old man, was his offer really fair? He had felt a return of his old business flair while he had been assessing the potential of the little firm. If Jim Stephenson had any sense, he thought, he would see that he would be having the best of both worlds, whichever option he chose. He was just about to start the engine when there was a tap at the window. It was Jim.

Jeff wound the window down. "Excuse me Mr Cavanagh, you did say that on those two options we can stay in the house?"

"Yes, I did. The house would be your capital in the firm, so if ever I wanted the whole firm I would have to pay you an agreed sum."

Jeff was not committing himself. "Well, I think I shall be taking one of those options, but you understand I shall have to wait to see if there are any other people interested in it."

"Yes, of course, I understand. I'm in no real hurry anyway. Talk it over with your agent and solicitor. Give me a ring when you've made your decision."

"I'll do that. Thanks for coming up. So long."

Jeff wound up the window and then drove slowly out of the yard. On the way he found himself singing little snatches of songs — like 'Whistle while you work', he was decidedly happy.

Jeff arrived home in the evening. He rang Priscilla immediately and offered to bring the car back to her, but she would not hear of it. "You come over tomorrow morning then you can tell me how you got on. No, not now, tomorrow."

He was still cheerful when he woke next morning. He was looking forward to seeing Priscilla again although it was only two days. He put his old clothes on.

Priscilla noted that he was dressed for gardening but she refrained from making any comment. It was still only ten o'clock but Priscilla said, "Come on, let's have some coffee and you can tell me about your trip."

Jeff's enthusiasm for the whole project was obvious as he launched into a detailed description of all that had happened the day before. "So" he said finally, "we left it that he would see if there were any better offers. If not, well, it looks as though I might be in business again."

"Oh Jeff, I'm so happy for you. Mr and Mrs Stephenson sound a lovely couple, are they?"

"They are. That little cottage is the whole of their married life. It would be a shame if they had to move out, however much money they were paid. I think my suggestions suit them so I'm keeping my fingers crossed."

"What about you though? You'll have to find accommodation. Have you any ideas about that?" Priscilla was determined to sow seeds in his mind, perhaps they would bear fruit later.

"I should have to rent a flat or something, and it would have to be not too far away."

"But what about meals, laundry, cleaning and all that?" said Priscilla. "You'll be on the go twenty-four hours a day."

"I'll cross that bridge when I get to it" said Jeff, "and anyway it would not be for long, I should probably look around for something more permanent after a while."

"We shall see. Now, you've obviously come dressed for gardening, so let's go and see what there is to do."

Priscilla intended to use his visits to try to open his eyes to what she had to offer, so she encouraged him to continue with the gardening even though it was now just a maintenance job. She also suggested that he get an answering machine in case Mr Stephenson phoned while he was with her.

One morning about two weeks later a letter arrived for Jeff from Norwich. It was from the solicitor who acted for Jim Stephenson. *Dear Mr Cavanagh, Mr Stephenson has instructed us to inform you that he is mindful of accepting one of your proposed options in respect of the property and business known as "Stephenson's Taxis". Would you therefore kindly telephone this office and arrange to meet with us and Mr Stephenson so that we can discuss this fully. Yours etc.*

Jeff almost shouted with joy. He would have to borrow Priscilla's car again, or hire one.

He went to the phone and called her. He gave her the gist of the letter.

"Look Jeff, I'd like to talk about this with you. No, not now. I'll come over to your place this afternoon."

Priscilla had decided that enough was enough. She would have to force him to notice her as a woman and not as a therapist.

That afternoon she drove over to Jeff's place.

He answered the door. "Come in" he said.

"No, Jeff. I'm not coming in, you are coming out" she said.

"Why, what's the matter?"

"Nothing's the matter. Get your jacket and come with me."

"All right, if you insist."

Priscilla went back to the car.

Jeff came out, locked the door and got into the car beside her. "Where are we going?" he asked.

"You'll see" she answered. She drove skilfully out to the main road and took the road to Arundel. It was a sunny afternoon, the beginning of June, there was blossom everywhere.

As they approached Arundel Jeff once more said "Where are you taking me?"

"I thought we'd have tea in Arundel" she said.

"That'll be nice" said Jeff. He was beginning to recall their previous visit.

When they arrived in Arundel Priscilla went to the same car park.

She locked the car. "Come on" she said, "let's skip the tea." She took his arm and steered him towards the road that led upwards past the castle and up to a high point where they could see over the hills. She found a patch of grass and sat down.

Jeff came and sat beside her. He was aware of her presence more strongly than before. "What's it all about?" he asked quietly.

"When we came here before, over two years ago, we spent an hour together. We enjoyed each other's company. Then suddenly both our lives were completely shattered. Everything we had known had gone and we separately became different people. You lost your freedom in the physical sense then gained your freedom twice, from Ruby and from prison. I lost my husband and have been coping with life in a different way. What I want to say to you Jeff, is that you are about to embark on a new adventure. In the fine weather one copes capably, but when the weather turns rough its comforting to have someone to help with the handling of the boat or gear or —" she faltered. "I want to help. I want to be aboard in the bad weather and the good. We are alone, you and I; we owe nothing to anyone, we are as free as the gulls over the sea, the future could be so —" she sighed deeply, "so lovely."

Jeff was silent. Then he slowly put his arm round Priscilla's waist. "What a fool I've been" he said.

* * * * * * * *

126

Broken China

Andrew and Olivia were having a leisurely lunch. Their dining room window overlooked their wide terrace and beyond that a large plantation of pines and larches. On the broad white-painted windowsill stood a bowl of flowers freshly cut from their garden and just behind the flowers a tall blue and white vase.

Andrew gazed intently at the vase. "You know" he said "that really is a lovely shaped vase, I wonder if by any chance it could be valuable."

"If it had been valuable it would hardly have been in a Kirkcaldy shop for £15 would it?" replied Olivia.

"No" said Andrew.

He thought back to that day last summer when he and Olivia had joined a coach trip on a day's outing from their village to Kirkcaldy.

They had lived in Ayrshire for several years and often went by car to visit some of the towns within fifty or sixty miles, returning the same day, places like Irvine, Troon, Largs, Kilmarnock and Strathaven. This time though they took the coach and so were able to enjoy the journey without having the strain of driving. They marvelled at the Forth road bridge and the view to the east over the Forth, and as they passed Aberdour they noted its character and vowed to visit it on their own one day.

Soon they were in Kirkcaldy and after finding out the arrangements for reboarding the coach they went off together. They had a most enjoyable day and were pleased to discover what a fine old town Kirkcaldy is. All too soon it was time to meet the coach, so they made their way to a spot in one of the shopping streets. They had a bit of time in hand so they sauntered along the street looking in the shop windows. They had not gone far when Andrew spotted a shop full of earthenware, china and porcelain, and as he had a liking for anything of that kind they stopped for a better look.

There was a good selection on display, but right in the middle of the window on a pedestal was a blue and white vase of exquisite shape and aesthetic design.

"Look at that!" exclaimed Andrew. "I'll bet that's expensive."

"Why not go and ask" said Olivia, so in they went.

"It's £15" said the assistant in reply to Andrew's question, "and there are some more over there" pointing to a shelf at the back.

There were several similar vases but this one was in a class of its own.

"We'll take this one" said Andrew, and within minutes it was wrapped and they were outside in the street waiting for the coach.

When they arrived home Andrew took the parcel into the dining room, unwrapped the vase and placed it on the wide windowsill.

"There" he said, "it looks absolutely right."

So, as Andrew gazed at the vase he made a decision, he would get an expert to look at it, then there would be no doubt as to whether it was anything more than just a good reproduction.

One of his colleagues at his firm's office on being asked where Andrew might take the vase suggested that perhaps one of the museums in Glasgow or Edinburgh could give him some indication as to its date of origin and whether or not it would be worthwhile having it valued.

On his next weekday off Andrew, with Olivia drove up to Glasgow and took the vase into a museum. They found the right department, then having located the porcelain expert, Andrew unwrapped the vase and placed it carefully on the table in front of him.

The man inspected it thoroughly inside and out, then went to a shelf and selected a large volume that seemed to be full of information on early ceramics. After studying this for quite a while he marked a page and then turned to Andrew and Olivia. "Well" he said, "it isn't Ming." He laughed as he saw their faces drop. "But I do believe that it is rather rare." Their faces brightened again. He continued "The first blue and white pottery was made in the early 14th century, the Yuan dynasty, but this is not that! Later on, other bright colouring was introduced and used extensively during the next three centuries. In the early 17th century there were some small rural potteries producing blue and white wares that were not for the export market, but were bought and sold locally. A few of these have survived to the present day and I truly believe that this is one such as those." Then he added for good measure "One of the auction houses should be able to assess its value, but I think it will be worth at least £30,000."

Olivia was quite excited. "What'll you do with the money Andrew?"

Andrew looked surprised. "I'm not thinking of selling it" he said. "I bought it because I liked it." But he was not thinking of letting the matter rest there.

Lee Fing Lua gave a little grunt of annoyance at the sound of someone calling from the sleeping part of the small worker's dwelling that was one in a row of similar bungalows on the outskirts of Canton in southern China.

All his life he had lived there. His father and mother first had the bungalow, then when his father died Lee took over the tenancy. His aged semi-invalid mother was a permanent part of the household, seldom moving from her small partitioned area next to the bedroom of Lee and his wife who were now in their late forties. They had had two children, but ten years earlier a virulent flu epidemic had claimed both the children's lives within a week.

Lee's family had had quite a lot of bad luck. He thought back to when it first began, when his father was well, just before his grandfather had died. Lee's father had come back from the funeral carefully carrying a paper parcel. He placed it on the table and unwrapped it. It was a blue and white vase, about fifteen inches high with a beautiful traditional design covering the whole of its graceful shape. This vase was a kind of heirloom and it was now the property of Lee's father. As he recalled that day he remembered also that it had been only a few weeks later that his father had developed the lung trouble that was to kill him only five years later. The vase then passed to Lee.

His mother called again. "All right, honourable mother, I'm coming." He shuffled into her closet and looked down at the bundle on the couch.

"I'm cold, son" she whined.

He pulled the bedspread over her frail body. 'We could do with more blankets,' he thought, 'in fact more of everything.'

His meagre wage from the packing department of the ceramic firm where he worked was just enough to keep them in food, warmth and clothes, there was nothing left over for extras.

He was very superstitious. If things were bad there must be someone or something responsible for it. Why should his children have died and so soon after inheriting the vase?

He went back to his chair and looked towards the window. On a small wooden stand stood the vase, the only thing of value in the house. It was only since it had come to him that their troubles had increased. If he sold it, everyone would soon know that he had, and his mother would never forgive him. The more he thought about it the more he blamed the vase for their misfortunes.

He decided that he would get rid of it somehow and hopefully he could prevent his mother from knowing. A plan was already forming in his mind. His job was as a packer of ceramics for export, and through his department passed a variety of vases and bowls. If he could get his vase in amongst those, then he could truthfully say that he did not know where it was because it would have been packed and despatched by other people. He could not put it with his own batch because they came to him in baskets of twenty and they were all accountable. No, the only way of getting rid of it was to put it in the reject basket outside the inspection room. The reject basket was wheeled away when it was half-full, and went to a final checker and rectifier whose job was to sort through the rejects, repair any with slight defects and pass them on for sale as seconds in the local market, the rest to be smashed into small pieces.

Lee set off for work the next morning. In his bag he had secreted the vase, unwrapped. It had not been easy avoiding his wife, but she had not noticed anything when he left. At the depot he went to his bench as usual and took up his boxes and tape. Breaktime came, Lee picked up his bag and walked quickly, not to the canteen but up to the door of the inspection room, outside which stood the reject basket. A quick look round, a swift movement from the bag and the vase was deposited among the dozen or so objects already there. He turned about and went to the canteen. He had done it, he had removed the jinx from his life. He felt better already.

But fate had other ideas. When the basket arrived at the bench of the rectifier he could not find any flaws in the vase. He had not come across this situation before so he reasoned that it should be returned to the inspectors. He took it himself and was told by the inspector to leave it there and he would reinspect it.

Of course they could see nothing wrong with it except that it looked slightly less bright than those they were used to inspecting. So it went into the onward basket and was transferred for packing for export.

The next few days Lee waited nervously to see if there were any developments, and by Friday he was convinced that the whole matter was over. Then the supervisor sent for him.

"You have been here two years now."

"Yes sir, I have." He bowed.

"And you have worked satisfactorily, I believe."

"Yes sir, I think so."

"Well starting Monday you will be moved to the export loading bays, and because it is important work you will receive a rise in wages."

The relief Lee felt was apparent in his face, and as he left, mumbling "Thank you sir, thank you sir," he knew that he had beaten the jinx, his luck had changed. He would now be able to tell his wife what he had done and that their troubles were at an end at last.

The winter passed, spring came and the summer drifted in. Everything was serene, the vase forgotten, his mother was more tolerant and his job secure.

Then one day when he was at home his wife called him, "Lee, your brother Cho is here. He is very angry."

Cho came storming in. He confronted Lee. "What have you done with the heirloom?"

Lee looked disconcerted. "It was mine by right to do what I liked with."

"No. You had no right to let it leave the family."

"There is a very good reason" Lee said quietly, and he went on to explain how their troubles had started with coming of the vase, and had now lessened.

Cho was not satisfied. "That vase should have come to me and my family next, now we shall have nothing."

"The vase was not valuable" Lee argued, "it was an heirloom but it had an evil spirit. Where it is now I do not know. I am well rid of it, and you should be thankful that you will not be affected by it ever."

"It would have been mine, and I intend to get some payment for it." Cho was still angry, and as he turned to leave the bungalow he paused, then asked "What exactly did you do with it?"

Lee thought for a moment then answered him, "It can't do any harm you knowing now. I put it in the reject basket and after that I never set eyes on it again, and that was six months ago."

Andrew sat deep in thought. If the vase was worth £30,000 how had it come to be in a Kirkcaldy shop for £15? He decided to try and find out, so his first port of call was to be the shop where he had bought it.

The following Saturday Andrew and Olivia set off in their car for Kirkcaldy and were there by lunchtime. They soon found the shop and asked for the manageress. She was very helpful and showed them the boxes that the ceramics came in. All the boxes had the same letters and numbers stamped on them as well as *'Canton, A product of China'*. She had no other identification but she said that all her wares came through the same wholesaler whose head office was in Liverpool. Andrew made a note of the numbers and letters and the address of the wholesaler, thanked her and left.

Back home they decided that the next step could be taken by telephoning the wholesaler, but that would have to wait until Monday.

Monday came, and after lunch Andrew used the phone in his office to call the Liverpool number. He managed finally to locate the secretary to the person in charge of imports from the Far East who was helpful but suggested that they write to her formally for the information quoting all the data they had acquired so far.

They sent a letter off that night and settled down to await the reply.

Four days later the letter came and they learned that the Chinese exporters were based in Shanghai and the manufacturer was the Orange Porcelain Company of Canton. So they were perhaps a step nearer towards solving the mystery of how that vase came to be exported from China, but why should a valuable antique be so disposed of? And also who would do that? There were so many questions to be answered that Andrew felt inclined to forget it and just be grateful for having such a piece of luck come his way.

Then out of the blue fate again stepped in to replan their lives. Andrew's boss, manager of a computer software company, said that they would be sending two representatives to a trade fair in Canton in November and would he be interested. The sales rep had been selected and Andrew would be the technical rep.

Andrew accepted immediately and enquired about the itinerary. They would travel by charter flight with reps from other British firms, then one day for setting up the stand, three days for the fair's duration, two days to pack up and do a little sightseeing, returning on the eighth or ninth day.

When Olivia heard about the arrangements an idea came into her mind. "How about if I come too?" she asked.

"Well, you couldn't come with the party as you are not employed by our company, but I suppose that if we paid for your trip and hotel costs ourselves it might be possible."

"That's great" said Olivia, "and I could perhaps get to visit that Orange place where your vase came from."

Andrew put the plan to his manager and apart from a few small difficulties to do with visas and accommodation it appeared that it was feasible. In fact, during the next two months of hectic activity all the snags were successfully ironed out and Olivia's inclusion was ensured.

Andrew and Olivia checked in at their hotel in Canton. There was an English-speaking receptionist on duty so their arrival formalities were processed fairly quickly. Their room had a window that looked out over the river, its English name being Pearl River.

When they had rested awhile they went down to the desk and Andrew produced the details of the Orange Company. He asked if she could write down instructions for getting there which they could show to the taxi driver. This she did, also giving them the address of the British consul, saying that he might have names of interpreters who could be engaged for a fee.

The following day they travelled to the exhibition centre by taxi and after a quick look round Olivia left Andrew to his work at the stand and went out to the front of the building. She found a taxi and showed the driver the address of the consulate, and on arrival there she paid off the driver and went in to find an official. They were very helpful and were able to find her an interpreter, although she had to wait another half-hour before he arrived.

It was nearly lunch time so he suggested they get a meal before starting off. This they did, and by two o'clock were outside hailing a taxi.

They arrived at the Orange Company's buildings and found their way to the supervisor's office. Here Olivia explained how they had come by the vase. She showed him the data that had been on the packaging and then produced the photographs.

The supervisor studied them for a long time, then to the interpreter he said, "This is not one of ours. It is very similar but this pattern is a very old traditional one. If it came from here it must have been 'planted' by someone. I don't know how we can find out but the people who handle all the products are the packers. Maybe one of them can remember."

Olivia agreed, then on an impulse she said "Can you mention that this vase is valuable, and if we can find out where it came from there will be a reward paid."

They went into the packing department and the supervisor went along the two rows of packers, questioning most of them. Some were new, so they were passed by, but the others had all been there when that particular batch was packed.

They had almost got to the end of the second row when a young woman indicated that she just might have handled it. It was, she said, a bit shorter than those she had been packing and it needed a bit more of the filling material than the others.

Olivia pounced on this piece of information and asked how the vases got to the packers.

"In baskets from the inspection room over there" answered the supervisor, so off they went to see the inspectors.

The head inspector looked at the photos, then he said, "There was a strange incident last winter. We had a visit from the rectifier who had found a vase that had nothing wrong with it, so he brought it back to us. He was correct, so it was passed through for packing."

"Was it this one?" asked Olivia, tapping the photographs.

"It could have been, but after several months I can't really be sure. I do remember that it was slightly different from most of our wares, not so new looking."

They all went back to the supervisor's office and discussed the possibilities. The one thing that was definite was that it had been packed right there, but by whom?

"What about the packers who have left?" asked Olivia.

"It would be difficult to trace those now" said the supervisor, "although we did promote two of them, one two months ago and one eight months ago."

"Can we interview them then?" asked Olivia, already feeling excited that they might be getting near.

The supervisor sent for the two and some ten minutes elapsed before the door opened and in came two men. One was quite young, and after being shown the photos he said he definitely knew nothing about it, he hadn't seen it before.

Lee Fing Lua shuffled towards the desk when the supervisor gestured. The photographs were laid out on the desk. "Now, Lee" said the supervisor, "have you any knowledge of this vase?"

Olivia was watching Lee's face as the supervisor spoke and for a moment she thought she glimpsed fear and then perhaps despair.

Lee picked up one of the photographs, his hand trembled.

"We only want to know how it came to be in our department. There are no criminal inferences, in fact there could be a reward if we get good information."

Lee continued to gaze at the photograph, then at the other photographs on the desk. Finally he heaved a huge sigh then quietly said "All right, I know about this vase."

The other worker was sent out, Olivia got out her notebook and prepared to jot down some of the translation. Lee proceeded to tell them how troubled his life had been and how it had led to him blaming the heirloom. He explained it all, and when he had finished he looked very relieved. "I didn't steal anything, I just wanted to be rid of it" he said quietly.

Olivia finished writing then told the supervisor "My husband wishes to reward the previous owner. As the vase is worth a lot of money in Britain he feels that he should give some of its value back. If this man can come to our hotel my husband will give him the reward."

As the exhibition was on for three days Olivia suggested that the man Lee Fing Lua should be at the hotel in the evening of the day after that. She asked the interpreter if he could manage to come as well, and he said he could.

When Olivia had given all her particulars she bade the supervisor goodbye, and with a last look at Lee to make sure she would recognise him again, she was about to leave when she said, "Give Mr Lee Fing Lua the photographs so that when he comes to the hotel he will be allowed in."

The supervisor phoned for a taxi and soon she and the interpreter were on their way back. As the interpreter was getting out of the taxi he said, "This is such an interesting story, would you mind if I told it to our local news-sheet editor?"

"Not at all" said Olivia, "but don't overdo its value or we shall be overrun with reward grabbers!"

Andrew was amazed and delighted that Olivia had solved the mystery so quickly. The fact that the vase had been an heirloom, albeit to a poor family, explained its apparent age.

All they had to do now was to attend the exhibition through the three days, then meet with Lee, have one more day free and then fly home.

The exhibition, and the party afterwards, tired them out, so they were glad of a day's rest the following day. They pottered about doing nothing, then got ready to receive their guest, Lee Fing Lua.

In the poorer district of Canton, Lee's brother Cho was sitting in a small cafe reading the local news-sheet. Suddenly he spotted the article telling the story of Lee's vase, and how some people from Scotland had found it and were going to give Lee a present of some money because it was more valuable than they had supposed. It also mentioned that the people were from the exhibition that was finishing that day.

He wondered if Lee had got the money yet. 'It's really mine,' he thought, 'because Lee forfeited that right when he disposed of the vase.'

He resolved to find out more. He knew others who worked at the packing place, and he soon found one of them who seemed to know all about Lee. Lee was apparently going to see these people from Scotland the following evening at the hotel near the river. Cho decided he would be there too and would wait for Lee to come out.

Lee Fing Lua put on his best clothes and set out for the city. He felt curiously light-headed now, for he had come to a decision about the money. He had no idea how much it would be — £50? £100? Well, whatever it was it wouldn't matter because he would give the whole lot to Cho. Of course Cho was right, Lee *had* given up his right to the vase when he got rid of it, and Cho was next in line for the heirloom, so he *should* have it, every penny.

He arrived at the hotel, showed the receptionist the photographs and piece of paper with Andrew's name and room number and he was directed to the lift.

Olivia opened the door to him. Behind her stood Andrew and the interpreter.

"Good evening Mr Lua" said Andrew. The interpreter translated, then again as Lee replied.

Soon the transaction was concluded. On advice from the consul they had decided on the equivalent of £500. Anything more might invite trouble for Lee and his wife. They also gave him the photographs; they had served their purpose.

A few minutes more then the interpreter and Lee left Andrew and Olivia's room and went to the lift.

The interpreter called for a taxi and was soon on his way home.

In the foyer Lee was still holding the envelope containing the money, and in his coat pocket were the photographs. He went out on to the pavement, turned right and started to walk towards the bus stop.

A small dark figure emerged from behind a pillar of the hotel and crept quickly up behind him. It was Cho. "Lee!" he called in a hoarse whisper.

Lee turned. "Cho! I —."

Cho had slipped a thin dagger out of his pocket. "Where's the money?" he asked urgently. He saw the envelope in Lee's hand. He grabbed it with his left hand and with his right he thrust the dagger in and upward to the hilt. Lee never spoke another word. He fell to the ground, and as he did so the photographs fell out of his pocket. Cho turned quickly away and made to cross the street.

Upstairs in the hotel Andrew and Olivia had moved over to the window to look at the lights of the city. They saw the traffic going in both directions outside the hotel. As they looked down they saw a man start to run across the road. He looked neither to left nor right. Olivia screamed as the bus hit him. He was bounced several yards then lay still.

Andrew and Olivia raced to the lift and went down to the main hall. Andrew yelled to the receptionist "Call an ambulance!" then raced into the street. The traffic had all but stopped. On the edge of the road lay the figure of a man, all around him were notes in Chinese currency.

It was only then that he realised that a small crowd was clustered around something on the pavement. He and Olivia moved forward to see. They pushed through and there they saw the pathetic figure of Lee lying in a pool of blood, and there by his pocket was one of the photographs of the vase.

Olivia ran into the hotel and sank into a chair. Andrew waited. He unexpectedly found himself in the role of being able to identify the body.

Andrew and Olivia sat in the dining room looking out on to their terrace. They had arrived back the day before after flying up from Heathrow to Prestwick. In Canton they had not been delayed by the police who had taken statements from them about their connection with Lee. The murder was not their affair, but as Andrew reflected on it he knew that their actions over the vase had indirectly caused Lee's death. Fate, or something stronger had intervened and dealt with Cho, but that too was connected with Lee.

Andrew looked at the vase still standing on the broad windowsill. "Come on" he said, "we're going out."

"Where to?" asked Olivia.

"You'll see."

They put on coats and went to the car. Andrew put a parcel in the boot and they drove off.

Half an hour later they were approaching Stranraer. "Andrew! Where are we going?" Olivia sounded exasperated.

"Port Patrick" said Andrew sharply.

"Why?" she sighed.

"You'll see."

When they reached Port Patrick Andrew parked near the cliff. He got out and took the parcel from the boot, unwrapped it and put the wrapping back in the boot. It was the vase.

Andrew took Olivia's arm and they walked up a gentle slope to the cliff edge. Looking down they could see the jagged rocks being buffeted by the Irish Sea.

Andrew released Olivia's arm, got a little nearer the edge, then he swung his right arm back and hurled the vase as far as he could out from the cliff. The vase described a graceful arc then hurtled down on to the rocks. It smashed into tiny pieces and sank below the turbulent sea.

"There" said Andrew, "may Lee's spirit rest in peace."

They turned and went back to the car.

The Apple Barrel

Pastor Michael Hennessey got up from the bench against the clapboard front of the saloon and strolled to the edge of the boardwalk. The stagecoach was just coming in and the pastor was awaiting the arrival of his replacement.

Twenty years in one place was a recommendation that he had been well-liked and respected by the folk who lived in and around the midwest town of Veriton (pop. 1,750). He was still only sixty but he had decided to retire early and to go into retreat for a few months.

The stage rolled in putting up a cloud of dust. The passengers were helped down, and last of all came the new young priest. When his luggage had been handed down the pastor called to one of the men idling by the saloon. "Can one of you carry the bags for the new father?"

One of the men came forward and took up the bags. Father Hennessey then formally introduced himself to the young man and together they walked up the street to the manse next to the church.

"The manse will be yours of course" said the pastor. "I shall be leaving when the stage comes by in two days' time."

That evening, after they had partaken of their supper prepared by the housekeeper, they sat out on the porch talking.

"I was wondering, Father Hennessey, you look fairly healthy, so why are you giving up?"

The pastor thought for a moment or two then slowly answered, "You work for years doing what in your own heart you believe is good work. You expound your beliefs to the community and impress on them that we are in the hands of the good Lord, and that we should lead exemplary lives if we expect to go to heaven when we pass on. All my life I've firmly believed what I preached, without question, without doubt, with complete faith in the Lord. But last year something happened that caused me to doubt my faith, something so close to me yet so unacceptable that I now feel the need to creep away into retreat for a while. In this way I hope either to renew my trust in God or to reject Him for ever."

"Tell me Father, what could possibly have occurred to have had this tremendous effect on your religious morale?"

"Tomorrow my boy, tomorrow, after you have met a good number of our God-fearing community."

The following evening the two men sat on the porch. Father Hennessey began talking. . . .

. . . . It all started out of town, in a very happy homestead. When James Baker woke on that May morning in the year 1855 he got out of bed quickly and went to the window. A slight mist hung about the landscape, promising a good fine day in this mid-western state of America. In the bed behind him his wife Millie sat up and stretched.

They had been married for fifteen years and had worked hard to clear the land and grow crops. Their first child was Estelle, a fine intelligent girl now aged thirteen and a great help in keeping the homestead neat and tidy and tending the horses.

Their second child, Tommy, arrived some three years later. Now aged ten, he was fast becoming his father's right hand man, accompanying him on his own pony on their long trips round the boundaries of their property. Such a trip was planned for that day, and both father and son were looking forward to it.

During the summer months Estelle and Tommy rode their ponies the four miles to school in Veriton, their nearest township. On Sundays the four of them travelled to church in their two-wheeled trap. In Veriton there was a sheriff and one deputy and a pastor, a doctor who doubled as dentist when required. There were two saloons, a barber, and livery stables. Also a blacksmith and three general stores.

One of the stores was run by Millie's father, a widower of about sixty. He sold grain, oats, vegetables and fruit according to the season. The children, who called him Grandpa, looked in on him after school before going the four miles home on their ponies. He usually gave them a nice rosy apple from the wooden apple barrel that stood out the front of the shop together with boxes of other commodities.

It was Saturday, and James and young Tommy would be taking a packed meal and a water bottle, and would be away all day checking the fences. Millie provided them with a good breakfast, and as soon as they were finished James and Tommy saddled up and set off for the day. Millie and Estelle waved to them until they went over a rise and out of sight.

About eight miles from James' and Millie's homestead was a long strip of rough scrubland. Half a mile off the trail two men were stretched out under some bushes. They were both the worse for drink.

One of them woke, sat up and grabbed a half-empty whisky bottle. He took a long swig, belched and called to the other man "Hey Lanky, what we got to eat?"

Lanky stirred. "What? Eat? I dunno. Same as usual I s'pose." He sat up and looked for his bottle. He found it and took a long drink, making a wry face as he swallowed. "Cor, that's better." He looked over at the other fellow, named Critchley but called Critch. "What we gonna do then?" Lanky asked.

"I dunno. Best find a homestead and scrounge something."

The pattern of their lives had been unchanged for years. They existed by petty thieving. Their simple method was to wait until the last customers at a saloon had been ejected by the landlord. They would creep in the back, hold the landlord at gunpoint, grab a handful of cash from the till, take two bottles of whisky each and get out quickly, mount their horses and keep going until they were well clear. They never hurt anyone, so it was unlikely that the sheriff would be called, or if he was called he would not send a posse for a couple of small-time crooks. So inevitably they got away with it, got drunk and moved on to another patch.

They roamed round and round the county during the spring and summer. Winter forced them into the towns where they slept in dosshouses. On this spring morning they were hungry and their horses needed a good feed of oats if they were to continue.

The two men saddled up and rode out on to the trail that eventually came to Veriton. They rode on at a walking pace for a couple of hours until they spotted the Baker homestead. To them it spelt food for them and their horses.

Millie Baker and Estelle were baking in order to have a good meal ready for James and Tommy when they returned. As they busied themselves around the large table they heard a whinnying from one of the horses. Millie went to the window and looked toward the stable and then to the track that led down from the trail.

Coming down the track were two rough-looking men on horseback. They rode right up to the house and called out "Anybody home?"

Millie opened a window and asked "Who're you folks looking for?"

"We ain't looking fer nobody. We jest thought we might get a bite to eat and a feed for the horses."

Millie had never had to do this kind of thing before. She had only ever catered for the family. "Well we ain't got much ready" she said, "but you're welcome to a bite."

The men dismounted and hitched up to the rail. Millie went to the door and let them in.

Estelle crept back to the far corner of the room, feeling very shy in the presence of these two strangers. She knew about horses though, and when the men were settled on to their chairs she ventured forward. "If you like, I'll see to the horses."

Critch eyed her up and down. "My, there's a purty little miss, if it ain't. Sure, you go ahead."

Estelle ran out of the house and over to the stable to get the oats.

Millie busied herself with the frying pan and four slices of home-cured ham, very thick. This together with some hunks of bread and home-made butter provided a really tasty meal.

The two men tucked in to it and were soon sitting there belching. They had not said much up till then. Lanky spoke. "Could do with a drink."

Critch said "Yeah. Hey missus, got any whisky?"

"Oh no, we don't partake of liquor except for medicinal purposes in the winter."

"What you got then?"

"Only brandy, for medicinal purposes" she repeated.

"Let's have it then."

She noticed that he had become menacing. It was then that she saw they were both carrying guns. Inadvertently she glanced up to the space above the mantelpiece where a shotgun was lodged on two brackets. James kept it there, loaded, just in case, he always said. The days of Indian marauders were long since gone, but James said "You never know when it might be needed."

Millie went to the cupboard and brought out a bottle of brandy. Only a little had been used and when she set it down on the table Critch grabbed it, pulled the cork and took a good draught. It was much stronger than what he was used to, so when he swallowed he spluttered and his eyes watered. Lanky then took a swig at the brandy and was more appreciative and took a second swig.

By the time they had drunk half the bottle they were no longer the docile hungry travellers who had arrived an hour before. Millie wished they would go.

Estelle appeared at the door. "I've fed and watered the horses. They're all ready." She came over and stood by her mother and put an arm round her waist, protectively.

The men stood up. "My, ain't you purty" said Critch, reaching out and touching her cheek.

Millie and Estelle edged away.

"Come on." Critch moved towards them. "It ain't often we gets to see a purty creature like you." He took Estelle's arm and pulled her away from her mother. "Come here purty one, I'll bet you're lovely and warm." He noticed the door to the sleeping part. He grabbed her more firmly and pulled her against him.

Millie started forward. "Leave her alone!"

Lanky drew his gun and waved it at Millie. "Jest leave him be and no one'll get hurt."

Millie hesitated. This sort of treatment was new to her. She and the family led very sheltered lives.

Critch marched Estelle to the bedroom, holding her firmly by the wrist. He pulled her in and slammed the door.

Millie was almost frantic. "Stop it! Stop it! She's only a child!"

Estelle was screaming "Mum! Mum! No! No!"

There were sounds of scuffling and the creak of the bed as though it was being pounded. Millie made as if to rush in there, but the man called Lanky barred the way with his gun.

The screaming stopped. Not a sound came from the room.

This time Millie didn't care. She reached over the mantelpiece and grabbed the shotgun. She fiddled to find the safety catch and swung round to face the man. Lanky fired. Millie fell to the floor, a huge red stain on her chest.

The bedroom door burst open, Critch ran out still buckling his belt. "What the hell happened?"

"She got the gun down. It was her or me." He looked past Critch to where he could see the girl on the bed, not moving. "What's up with her?"

"She jest passed out. Where's that bottle." He reached for the brandy and took a swig.

"What you gonna do about her?" asked Lanky, pointing to the bedroom.

Critch walked slowly to the bedroom door, took his gun from the holster and shot Estelle through the heart. "Let's get outa here" he said, taking a last drink from the brandy bottle, and Lanky finished it off.

They hurried over to their horses, mounted and galloped off.

It was almost five o'clock when James and Tommy came over the rise and caught sight of the house. They could not see anyone. "Give them a call, Tommy."

They stopped, and Tommy cupped his hands round his mouth and called "Coo-eee! Coo-eee!"

They waited, not a sign of anybody. "Try again Tommy."

"Coo-eee! Coo-eee!"

"Well, they should have heard that" said James. "Let's go down and see what they're up to."

When they got to the house they could see the front door open. James had a sudden feeling of trouble. Something was wrong.

"Here Tommy. Take the horses to the stable and give them something. I'll see what your mum's up to."

He walked slowly into the house, pushing the door open wider as he went into the room. He took it all in in one glance. His wife, apparently dead on the floor, the shotgun under her, two empty plates on the table and an empty brandy bottle. He saw the partly-opened bedroom door. Slowly he moved towards it and gently pushed it open. Estelle, his little daughter Estelle, sprawled on the bed, violated and shot dead. He emitted a deep groan and a sob then rushed outside where he was violently sick.

"Dad! What's up?" Tommy was coming over from the stable.

James straightened up. "Tommy, finish doing the horses, then I want you to saddle up the other horse for me, and the other pony for you. We are going to Grandpa's."

"Why? What's the matter?"

"I'll tell you later, get the saddling done please."

James forced himself to act normally as he walked back into the house. First of all he took a long look at Millie's body. Then he went into the bedroom and got a bedspread with which he gently covered her. Next he went back to where poor Estelle was lying. He took a sheet from a cupboard and covered her body carefully. He went out and called Tommy.

Tommy came over and James took his hand. "A terrible thing has happened. Somebody has been here and killed your mum and Estelle. You may have one look, and that is the last time you will see them, ever."

They walked into the house together. James went to Millie's body and slowly lifted the cover from her face. Tommy looked quickly and then clung to his dad. They went into the bedroom and James drew back the sheet from Estelle's face.

"Is she asleep Dad?"

"Yes, asleep for ever, son." He replaced the sheet. "Right lad, now we've got things to do. Let's get down to Grandpa's and the sheriff."

James locked the doors and he and the boy went to their horses, mounted and rode away.

Forty minutes' hard riding brought them to the town. Grandpa's store was at the nearest end of the street through town, so they came upon it first, dismounted and went in.

Grandpa was alone in the front part of the store. "James! Tommy!

143

What you doing here at this time?"

"Listen Grandpa, sit down, I've got some real bad news."

As he related what he knew about the tragedy the old man's face showed incredulity, then horror and finally grief.

"Now hold on, Grandpa" said James. "Keep Tommy here with you. I'm a going down to the sheriff and we'll get a search going for these murderers."

The sheriff listened attentively to all that James told him. "It's getting late James, and I don't think we'll do much good riding posse in the dark, so I think we'll set out tomorrow morning and see if we can get a lead on 'em. You be here around eight and we'll head north for a bit. Got a gun?"

"I wasn't planning on going on no manhunt. I got to see Millie and Estelle brought down and properly laid out. I'll see you when you get back."

James went to the undertaker's office and explained what was to be done, and so they agreed to ride out the next morning.

"The doctor must come too," said the undertaker. "I'll go and see him now."

Next, James went to the manse to see me. He related all the events of the day, and when he had finished he asked me if I would ride out with him and the undertaker so that a prayer could be said for the souls of his wife and daughter.

I was extremely distressed to hear such a harrowing story, and I said I would ride out with them to the homestead in the morning.

There was nothing else for James to do. He made his way up the street to the store where Grandpa and Tommy were sitting miserably in the parlour.

"Grandpa, show me what food you've got and we'll have supper. We're going to need all our strength."

It was a sad little procession that left the township early on that Sunday morning. The sheriff joined the little party of men, having sent his deputy and four volunteers to search the local area.

When they arrived at the homestead James gave the key to the sheriff. "I guess I seen enough yesterday" he said. "I'll just stay here."

I was the last to go in. I entered slowly and gasped when I saw Mrs Baker, but when I passed through the bedroom door and saw little Estelle I ran out of the front door and dropped to my knees. Aloud I condemned the God that had allowed this to happen, then I rose to my feet and went over to James who was leaning on the buckboard containing the coffins and I said "Mr Baker, James, I apologise for my lapse. I cannot see the reason for this tragedy but

I will continue to pray for your family in the hope that a reason may one day become apparent."

The doctor and the sheriff completed their examinations and the bodies were put into coffins and placed on the wagon. James collected some of his and Tommy's clothes and put them on the wagon too. He decided he would stay awhile to burn the covers and anything else that had been soiled by the recent events. Then he followed on down to the town.

The funeral took place the following day. Afterwards Grandpa, James and Tommy went back to the store.

In the sitting room at the rear James sat silently for a while, then said, "Listen carefully. I'm going after those two murderers. I don't know how long I shall be gone, but I want you Tommy to stay here with your Grandpa and keep out of trouble. If I find 'em I shall kill 'em, but if I don't I shall come back and you and me Tommy will carry on at the homestead. I shall take some food for me and the horse, and a water bottle and my rifle."

"You ain't a killing man James. Why don't you leave it to the sheriff. The law will catch up with them sooner or later."

"No. The law's too good for them. They should be put down, kicked into hell!" He was getting agitated.

There was a knock from the store. "Anyone in there?" It was the sheriff. "Thought I'd tell you how the boys got on. Well, they didn't see anyone looking like crooks, but they did hear of a couple who had been in a saloon. They were strangers, but the barman remembers one of them being tall, he was called Lanky by the other one. And that's all we know, but maybe we'll hear something bye and bye."

At this Grandpa jumped up from his chair. "Sheriff, this here son-in-law of mine is going after them himself, and with a rifle. Tell him not to go."

"I can't stop him" said the sheriff, "but I say to you James — think about it. We've had enough violence, I would not like to see young Tommy here an orphan."

"My mind's made up, sheriff" said James. "I shan't be able to rest till I've had a try at finding 'em."

"Well don't say I didn't warn you. You'd be better off working your land than chasing criminals. So long now."

It was not going to be easy leaving Tommy, but James put the thought out of his head and once more allowed the prospect of revenge dominate his actions.

The following morning he rolled up his provisions and blanket and tied them behind the saddle, then with a brief wave of the hand he was off.

His plan was simple. He would take in the six nearest townships that lay in a roughly circular distance of twenty miles. If his quarry kept moving he might never catch up with them, but if their paths crossed he had a chance.

He would need luck. He had got one name. They did not know him, so he had the advantage. He eased his horse gently along the trail, no sense in tiring him out, it might take a long time.

The two priests sitting together in the parlour of the manse sipped their bourbon. "That family was hit fairly hard" said the younger man, "losing the mother and the daughter. Is that the end of the story?"

"Oh no, not by any means" answered Father Hennessey. He paused. "My faith was about to be tested as never before.". . .

. . . . James had been exploring the county for three weeks before he got any lead as to who or where the two men were.

He rode into a small town not fifteen miles from Veriton. He went to a saloon attached to a hotel and enquired about a room for the night. As he sat at the bar with a lemonade in front of him, he asked the barman if he had had any strangers in recently, particularly one tall one called Lanky, but both carrying guns.

"I sure have. A right couple they are too. They was right here last night."

James stood up quickly. "Where are they now?"

"Hold your horses man! They'll be too drunk to go far, I should think."

"What do you mean?" asked James.

"Well, they sort of held me up. I had almost finished the clearing up. I'd locked the front door. We only got one guest and he went to bed. Then these two roughnecks came into the bar from the back, waving their guns about. They had sort of kerchiefs over their noses, but one of 'em was tall."

"You don't seem very bothered" said James.

"No, I ain't. They just said 'Give us two bottles of whisky each'. So I put four bottles on the bar. Then one of 'em goes to the till and opens it and he don't take all the cash. He grabs a handful of dollars, stuffs 'em in his pocket, then they grab the whisky and hightail it out the way they come. They must have had their horses near the back, the next thing I hears 'em galloping past the front down the road to Veriton. I told the sheriff but he said 'Aw they ain't worth bothering about'."

"Not worth bothering about, you think" said James. "If you'd pulled a gun on 'em you'd have been dead meat."

"Nah, what makes you think that? They're drunks!"

146

"Listen to me mister, those drunks went to my homestead three weeks ago and killed my wife and daughter. If I catch up with 'em they won't be drinking no more whisky."

"There's customers coming in, I gotta go."

"Just one more thing please. Did the other one have a name, and what did he look like?"

"The one called Lanky did say 'Come on Titch' or something like that, or Rich. No, it was Critch. Yes, that was it. He was medium height, stocky, and he had a reddish shirt and a calfskin jacket."

"Thanks, I'll not be needing that room."

He left quickly by the front entrance, unhitched his horse, mounted and rode off towards Veriton.

Lanky and Critch rode for a couple of hours after leaving the saloon. They looked for a likely place to lay up until next evening. In the gloom they could just make out a rocky outcrop up to the right of the trail. They dismounted and led their horses up the embankment until they reached the rocks. They took them to the rear of the rocks and left them some oats.

They then found a sheltered niche where they could rest, even have a small fire to keep out the night cold, and if they were still cold there were two bottles of whisky each. They got through half a bottle each before settling down to sleep. As they had no definite plans for the future, this place would suit them until they ran out of liquor.

It was their second night there that James came trotting along the trail, looking to left and right for signs of men and horses. As there was no moon it was difficult to see anything with any clarity, but a lucky break disclosed the whereabouts of the two men. A flicker of light from the small fire was reflected from the high flat-faced rock above them and caught James' eye as he peered and listened.

He stopped and dismounted. He reckoned they were about half a mile away so would not have heard him coming. He could not know for sure that they were the two men he was after, or even how many were up there. He would have to hole up and wait until it was light enough to take a closer look.

He found a tree and some bushes, tethered his horse and settled down to wait. Whilst lying there he thought deeply, trying to decide what to do. Should he kill them in cold blood or wait until they moved and then shoot them on the run? The sheriff had been right, he should have left it to him. He could still avoid a gunfight by riding straight to Veriton now and rousing the sheriff. They could ride out and catch the two of them easily, especially if they were befuddled with the whisky. He dozed off.

He woke as it was getting light. He had made up his mind what he was going to do. He crept up the escarpment and made his way carefully towards the men's encampment by the rocks, stopping every few yards to listen. He got near enough to see the horses standing dejectedly on a piece of level ground near the rocks, but of the men he could see nothing.

He picked up a small stone and threw it towards the horses' feet. One of them snorted softly but did not move.

As he watched James saw a figure appear by the horses, giving them a reassuring pat on the neck. He was very tall, he could only have been the man Lanky. James retreated slowly until he was able to see his horse, then resumed his place under the bushes.

An hour later he took his rifle and went up the embankment once more. About halfway up he loaded the rifle and aimed at the rocks over the men's niche. He fired once, the sound echoing over the valley.

There was an immediate reaction. Both men rushed out and started to saddle the horses. James could clearly see Lanky as he came back round to fetch some part of his equipment. Lanky bent down to pick something up, and when he straightened up James seemed to see his wife Millie lying dead on the floor of their homestead, and poor little Estelle spread-eagled on the bed with that dark stain on her chest. He took careful aim at the man's chest and fired. The man dropped to the ground. James waited. After a couple of minutes the other man climbed on to one of the horses and galloped off.

It had been James' intention to scare both of them in to running off towards Veriton. He could then pursue them, hoping the sheriff would be there to stop them. The plan still held, but now there was just the one.

Doubt crept into his thoughts again. There was no proof that these two men were the murderers. If they were caught and tried for murder there was no witness to the events of that day at the homestead, and the two men led such a nomadic existence that they were only seen occasionally and then mostly at night. All this raced through James' mind but always the picture of the scene at the homestead spurred him on to continue the chase.

So, as the quarry came down to the trail and galloped towards the township James kept half a mile behind.

The man in front increased his speed to keep ahead of his pursuer. Who the hell was he and why did he kill Lanky? He wished he'd had time to have another drink, but seeing Lanky fall had put a fear into him he had never felt before. He looked back momentarily. He saw the dust being thrown up by the pursuing horse and rider.

Half an hour's hard riding brought Critch to the first shacks in the town. He reined in as he saw a young man loitering on the corner. "Hey you! Which way's the sheriff's office?"

"Right down the bottom end!"

This information caused Critch to give a sharp pull on the reins and gallop the horse round the back of the store opposite. It was Grandpa's store.

When Critch got to the rear of the building and out of sight of the road, he jumped down, pulled out his six-shooter and ran in through the back door of the store. Grandpa was there moving some grain as the man burst in. "Keep out of my way and you won't get hurt."

As he was knocked aside Grandpa shouted "Get out Tommy! Hide!"

Critch hollered at him "Shut up you old fool. Get out back!"

Tommy had heard his grandpa's shout, caught a glimpse of the man with a gun and he ran out of the front door, jumped on a box and then into the almost empty apple barrel that was standing out front every day. He could not see out of the barrel and he hoped the man could not see in. He crouched lower.

The man Critch took up a position behind the open front door. He could see the road where the man who was chasing him would come; this would be his chance to stop this hombre, whoever he was.

James was about two minutes' riding time behind Critch, so as he got to the first shack Critch was already in position.

The young man who was still standing against a shack, ran out and waved him to a standstill. "That one you're chasing, he's in the back of the store. Hey, ain't you Mr Baker?"

"Yeah. Did you see him come out?"

"Nope, but I heard the horse stop so I guess he's around there somewhere."

"Right. You'd better run down to the sheriff and tell him I got one of them murderers on the end of my rifle."

The lad ran off along the rear of the buildings on the opposite side to the store. James found a sheltered position behind a porch almost across from Grandpa's.

Inside the store the man wished he could see better. He peered round the doorpost. 'Damn,' he thought, 'I can't get my right hand round the post.' He edged out a little, no one in sight. He looked for a better vantage point and saw some boxes out front next to an apple barrel. If he could get behind them he would have a good chance of getting a shot at the man who was chasing him. He took a deep breath and bending low he ran quickly out of the door and down behind the boxes. Right in front of the box he was hiding behind was the apple barrel.

Tommy heard, and was frightened.

Over the other side James spotted the man as he went down behind the boxes. He got down on one knee, brought the rifle up to his shoulder and called out to Critch, "I know where you are. I'll give you a count of three. Come out or I shoot."

Inside the barrel Tommy heard the man breathing heavily. Tommy shifted his position a bit. The man hiding had no intention of coming out, but as he eased himself to get a clearer shot, he pushed the box against the apple barrel, jogging it slightly.

James had seen the movement. The man was directly behind the apple barrel. He took careful aim at the middle of the barrel. "One! Two! Three!" No movement at all. He fired two shots into the barrel of apples.

Critch heard the thud of the bullets. He was no hero. He scrambled to his feet, and in doing so he knocked the box against the barrel. The barrel toppled over facing where James was now striding forward, his rifle at the ready.

James watched with mounting horror as the barrel fell and a small blood-covered body rolled out. He dropped his rifle and ran the last few yards to his son's body. "Tommy!" It was a cry full of anguish.

Critch faced James. "I don't know who you are mister" he said, "but I do know you ain't fit to live." He pointed his gun at James' chest and fired twice. James fell beside the body of his son Tommy.

Old Grandpa had witnessed the drama being played out at the front of his store. In a daze he knew what he had to do. He had never fired a shot in anger, but when James fell he knew he had to do something. He went behind the counter and fetched his six-shooter, his bit of protection just in case. He released the safety catch and walked to the door. The man was still standing there thinking of going for his horse. He looked up and saw Grandpa, but before Critch could lift his gun Grandpa fired all six shots into him, then threw the gun down.

From the road the sound of horses galloping heralded the approach of the sheriff. As he came to a halt and dismounted he looked in disbelief at the carnage laid out in front of that friendly little store. Grandpa was sitting on the step, his head in his hands.

Father Hennessey had told the story to the priest exactly as it had been put together afterwards. He continued telling of his own involvement.

"I arrived at the store just after the sheriff. I saw the three bodies lying there. I'll never forget it. As I looked at that poor little Tommy. A victim not of a black-hearted murderer but a victim of his own father's revenge, I could not, indeed I would not believe that a loving God would allow such evil to exist in a world where there are so many loving people and families. When their lives are touched by evil they themselves become contaminated. You can argue that two wrongs don't make a right, but who is to say that those who grieve are wrong to want revenge? When we were killing Indians who were defending their property, why should we have been indignant when they copied the aggressors and attacked them in return? Violence breeds violence, and a lot of it is done in the name of the Lord. I don't think He condones violence or in fact any evil, but how then does He allow it to happen? I hope I shall find some answers during my retreat."

Once again the pastor was waiting for the coach, this time his successor, the young priest was seeing him off on his trip east.

"Father Hennessey" he said, "what happened to the grandpa, is he still at the store?"

"Oh no" answered the pastor, "the poor old fellow had too much to bear. He died of a broken heart a few weeks after he had lost his only relations. They are all buried together up in Beacon Hill cemetery. You will never be able to forget them either. You see, the old man had left his entire estate to the church here. It is ironic that at the time of his death he was also the legal owner of the homestead where the Bakers lived, so the value of that was included in his will. The church council have approved the installation of a carillon in our — no — your church, paid for with the old man's bequest. When you are playing your hymns on the bells an appropriate one would surely be God moves in a mysterious way."

The coach rolled in, he got aboard.

"Goodbye young man, peace be with you" he said.

"Goodbye Father. I hope you find answers to your problems. Come back one day and tell us. God be with you."

Where or When

Pete Ballard put another pair of socks into his suitcase. He was packing for a short holiday in Skegness. He liked to do his own packing, it was a habit formed in his time in the Royal Air Force during World War Two, over forty years ago.

Downstairs his wife Kate was getting the tea. Her packing was complete down to the last curler and nailfile. She had always been efficient and self-sufficient, also very independent. She had organised this holiday trip without any help or suggestions from Pete. It had been that way ever since — when was it exactly? She thought back to the last year of the war.

Pete had almost completed his second tour of 'ops' and was looking forward to getting a bar to his DFC, when he had flown two more trips. Then came that disastrous night when Pete and his crew in the Lancaster crashed by the runway at the end of their twenty-ninth trip. Pete had never been quite the same after that.

Kate remembered going over to Lincolnshire the weekend after the crash. Pete had had a severe thump on his head, but no lasting damage except that his right foot seemed to be a bit wobbly. In his mind he had felt the effects of the crash very deeply, but he managed to complete his tour of 'ops' by going as copilot on a night bombing sortie over the Ruhr. After that he was grounded. The war ended before he was likely to be considered for further bombing missions.

Soon after that Pete began to become morose. It was noticeable to anyone who had known him when he and Kate were married. They had met when Pete was doing his elementary flying at a field near Reading. They went dancing or to the cinema whenever they could fix a date. As they both lived in Berkshire it was fairly easy for them to meet often, but when Pete went on to the service flying training he was too far away for frequent dates.

Then Pete had to spend eight weeks at an operational training unit near Oxford, so they resumed their weekend dates, and it was on one of those weekends that Pete asked Kate to marry him. As Pete would have fourteen days' leave at the end of his course they planned to marry then, and so they did.

Their families pooled their rations to provide a spread. Kate bought a second-hand wedding dress, and all-in-all it was a wonderful wartime wedding.

On returning from their honeymoon Pete had to report to a squadron equipped with Lancaster four-engined bombers. Kate stayed at home with her parents, sometimes managing to spend a few days near Pete's station. She met several of his friends when they went to the pub nearby, and she noted that Pete was a popular member of the squadron.

Pete completed his first tour of operations without any real problems and then had a three-month rest period. At the end of that time he was posted back to the same squadron and was allocated a new crew. They soon settled down together and operated as a good close team.

Opposition from the Germans had increased tremendously since the time when Pete's first tour had ended. Now they had night-fighters to contend with, as well as all the anti-aircraft flak and cluster searchlights. But Pete and his crew survived with only the occasional damage to their aircraft — until their twenty-ninth trip.

On that night the outward journey and the bombing run went off successfully, and as soon as he heard "Bombs gone!" Pete turned for home and changed to his proper height for the return journey. He cautioned the rear gunner to be vigilant looking out for night fighters then settled down to the three and a half hours' flight to base.

They were somewhere near the Dutch coast when the rear gunner's voice came urgently through the intercom "Bandit! Port quarter. Weave!"

Pete threw the aircraft about almost like a fighter plane. He alternatively dived and climbed, weaved to port and starboard, desperately trying to evade the persistent German.

A sharp thump and judder indicated a hit somewhere in the fuselage but the Lancaster was still functioning properly. The fighter had disappeared from view, then just as they were all supposing that he had broken off the engagement a terrific bang scared everyone, and that fear turned to horror as flames were seen in the port outer engine. The flight engineer pressed the fire extinguisher button for the number four engine and prepared to feather the propeller.

A shout from Pete "Number three's on fire too!" put further fear in to everyone's heart.

The number three engine was throttled back and the propeller feathered. This meant that the blades were rotated electrically so that the edges were facing forwards, thus permitting the engine to be stopped and drag reduced. The fires went out on both engines.

To compensate for the loss of all power on the port side Pete opened up the engines on the starboard side to almost full power. The effect of this was to cause the aircraft to want to swing to port, so Pete had to push hard on the right-hand rudder pedal and adjust the trimmer to help hold it there. Even with the assistance of the trimmer the strain on Pete's right leg was extremely tiring. He called up the navigator and asked how long to base.

"About two hours Skip. The wireless operator is sending a message to base with our position and course."

Pete did some rapid mental arithmetic. They were losing height at about 200 feet per minute. That meant that by the time they reached base they would be down to 1,000 feet.

Unless of course either of the two starboard engines packed up, then they would be in real trouble. He called them up on the intercom.

"Skipper to crew, we are over the North Sea. If we can maintain our steady descent and speed we shall make base OK. If anything else goes wrong we may have to ditch, so all crew do pre-ditching arrangements now. Nothing to be jettisoned until then."

Pete's right leg was beginning to go numb with having to keep pressure on the rudder pedal. He motioned to the engineer to help. The engineer crouched by the pilot's seat and stretched out his left leg to push the pedal. He was able to do this for about twenty minutes then he became cramped and had to move. One of the gunners also had a turn but in the end it was left to Pete to struggle on.

When they were about fifteen minutes from their estimated time of arrival at base the navigator called the station flying control and requested permission to come straight in to the runway to avoid having to do a circuit. This was granted.

Dawn was beginning to break so the job of landing would be that much easier, except that it would have to be a wheels up landing. The navigator called the airfield again and notified them that the pilot would be doing a wheels up landing. On hearing this the controller said it would be better to use the grass on the port side of the runway and that all emergency units would be standing by. While they had been talking on the R/T the signals officer had taken a bearing on the transmission, and so he called up the Lancaster and gave them a course to steer that should bring them to the runway.

The morning had become lighter now and soon the bomb aimer called on the intercom to say the runway was in sight. The navigator relayed this information to the controller and almost immediately the runway lights came on.

By this time Pete was almost exhausted having wrestled with the controls for so long, and by now his right leg was becoming numb. He switched on his microphone. "Skipper to crew, take up crash positions and don't move until the kite stops rolling." They acknowledged in turn.

Pete was on his own now; he tried a little flap — no problem there. He reduced the throttles slightly and regulated his approach at ninety-five knots. He dare not go at a slower speed as the risk of stalling was greater having only two engines instead of four.

All was going well, he crossed the airfield boundary at about fifty feet and was all set to slither along the grass when suddenly his foot slipped from the rudder. He jabbed his foot on to the rudder pedal but there was no resistance to his jabbing. Already the Lancaster was yawing to port. He quickly cut both throttles and reached up and switched off both engines. He pushed the stick forward to try to keep the speed up, but it was too late. The port wing dropped. Without that rudder control it was impossible to bring the wing up, so all he could do now was to just sit there. The dropped port wing hit the ground, the aircraft spun horizontally, the starboard wing broke, and as the Lancaster scored the grass verge the fuselage was whipped round by the centrifugal force, the tail plane dug into the ground, the whole fuselage then slithered forward until all force was spent. Everything went deadly quiet.

Pete had received a bang on the side of his helmet and for a few moments sat in his cockpit dazed. As the realisation came to him that they were down and at a standstill his reactions were automatic. He yelled "Everybody out! Watch out for fire!"

He disconnected his intercom plug, stood on his seat and started to clamber out. He looked down, the ground was only about six feet below him so he scrambled down the side to the ground and started to run away from the aircraft. Suddenly he stopped. There was no one else getting out of the Lancaster, there was no sound but that of the approaching emergency vehicles. In fact the fire tender had reached the remains of the port wing and two engines and was dousing them with foam.

An ambulance swung round the wreckage and stopped near him. "Sir, are you all right?"

"Yes, but I can't see any of the others, they should be out by now."

The medics went to the aircraft and one of them found a way in. The other went to the front of the fuselage where the nose had been. He looked in through the shattered Perspex and was horrified at what he saw. The engineer had been thrown forward and his head had smashed in to the Perspex and had been crushed by the impact. There was no movement.

Another ambulance arrived and a medic took Pete and put him in the back. The MO was there and he said "Come on, let's have a look at you. My God you were lucky, look at that wreckage, it's a wonder anyone survived."

He spent a few more minutes giving Pete a quick check and was about to announce to him that he seemed to have nothing seriously wrong when one of the medics appeared at the back of the ambulance. "Could you come with me sir." They moved off together towards the wreckage.

"Sir, we haven't found anyone alive, they're all dead."

"Right. Take Flight Lieutenant Ballard back to sick quarters. I'll see the others got out and brought in."

As the ambulance with Pete aboard sped away to the sick quarters, the MO turned back towards the aircraft where the first of the bodies was being lowered on to the grass. When all the bodies were laid side by side the MO went to each one, checked the identity discs then signalled that all were dead and for the ambulances to take them away.

At sick quarters Pete was put to bed and told to rest until the MO returned to carry out a more thorough examination.

Pete telephoned Kate the next day, said he had had a bumpy landing and had only one more trip to do. She thought he sounded subdued, not his usual bantering self. He told her he thought he would be getting some leave after his next trip.

The MO discharged Pete and so he resumed his place in the mess. His flight commander had told him that he would be allowed to fly his final 'op' as a supernumerary only, and if he wanted to put it off for a few days it would be all right. But Pete was past caring about how or what the flight would be, he just wanted to finish his tour and get away from the station where he and his crew had so many happy times as well as hair-raising moments in the air.

The squadron CO had called him in to have a few sympathetic words with him about his crew and to ask Pete again how did he lose control when he was so near to landing successfully. Pete's reply was always the same — his foot must have slipped, through having been under such a prolonged strain.

When peace came Pete had no trade or profession to go back to, like most of the young men who had enlisted in 1939. He tried several openings, car salesman, estate agent's assistant and local government office, but he was completely unsuited, until one day he saw a government advertisement offering one year training in various trades tor ex-service men of any rank. He took the bricklaying course and found that he had a talent for the work, so that became his job for life.

He never spoke of his time in the Royal Air Force, and if anyone mentioned his slight limp he said it was probably rheumatism. He was never unemployed, he earned good money with subcontracting gangs, and when he retired he was comfortably off. He and Kate had their own house and a small car but no children. Now, in their retirement, they were off on a holiday.

"Come on Pete, I'm ready. Don't forget — I'm driving, you can hold the map."

Very masterful she was, but that did not spoil their relationship. They still adored each other, not with the passion of forty years ago, but with the tolerance of approaching old age.

Their home in Northamptonshire was about two hours' driving from Skegness. They stopped in Lincoln for a break and a look at the cathedral.

"We could see that when we flew in daylight" said Pete, looking up at the towers. "It stands out for miles."

"Yes, I know, you told me that years ago. It never got a scratch on it, yet it was almost surrounded by aerodromes."

On the second half of their journey they were about ten miles from their destination when Kate pointed out a turn to the right. "Know where that is, Pete?"

"Where what is?"

"Over there — the signpost — quick, or we'll be past."

Pete read, "West Larkby four miles. Well I'm damned, it wasn't like this in forty-five."

"No, you're right. We're going there tomorrow, but I'll tell you all about it when we get to our hotel."

Half an hour later they pulled in to the hotel forecourt and were soon installed in their room.

"Now, what was it you were going to tell me?" asked Pete.

Kate went to her case and brought out a newspaper, unfolded it and showed Pete the advertisement. While Pete was reading it Kate started to tell him what she had found out. "Apparently, when the war ended most of the aerodromes were returned to the owners — or rather the land was. The owners of West Larkby decided to leave a piece of it just as it was as an RAF airfield. They've got a piece of runway, a hangar, some crew and accommodation huts and a real live Lancaster. Not only that, they start the Lancaster engines and taxi it up and down the bit of runway, and they have all sorts of memorabilia as well. So that's where we go tomorrow afternoon."

After lunch the following day they prepared to go to West Larkby. Pete had been feeling apprehensive ever since Kate had told him about the visit they would be making to his old airfield. The memories came flooding back, and his mind became a kaleidoscope of images of the people he had lived and flown with. He was glad Kate was driving, he believed that he could not concentrate enough to be safe, not today, anyway.

They set off along the same road that they had come by and soon reached the left turn to West Larkby. After going for four miles they saw the car park sign and pulled in. When they had parked they stood a moment to get their bearings.

"There's the entrance" said Kate, "and look! There's a hangar."

Pete could see the top of a hangar. He thought how near the road it seemed.

They moved to a wooden building that formed the entrance, paid the fee and went in to the foyer. There were pictures of aircraft and of people in flying kit covering most of the walls.

Off the entrance foyer was what looked like an old Nissen hut full of tables and chairs and all sorts of memorabilia.

Kate turned to Pete. "I'll have to go to the 'Ladies' room, I won't be long."

"All right, I'll mooch around here" said Pete.

He noticed a side door opening out to the area that led to the hangar and runway. He went through the door to the outside and saw a concrete path that led to a wooden hut. He turned away and then quickly turned back to look again. "I do believe that's the old crew room" he said to himself and started to walk slowly towards the hut.

As he did so, the door of the hut opened and a young airman in a smart Royal Air Force uniform came out and walked directly towards Pete. He stopped in front of Pete and saluted. "Excuse me sir, you are Flight Lieutenant Ballard?"

"Yes, that's me." 'How the devil did he know that,' he thought.

"Would you follow me please sir." The airman turned and marched back towards the hut door. He held the door open and motioned to Pete. "You may go in sir, they're waiting for you." Pete went in to the hut, the airman left and closed the door behind him.

"Hey Pete! Where've you been?"

"Hi-ya Pete!"

The crew room was filled with aircrew. Some were standing around, some were sitting in the green leather chairs, some were playing cards and someone put a record on the radiogram. Pete recognised the tune, it was called 'Where or when'.

He moved toward them tentatively. "Bill! It's good to see you, and old Dick!"

The one called Dick said, "We'd given you up Pete. Why haven't you been to see us?"

Several others came over and greeted Pete. He knew all of them. It was as though he had never left.

From the radiogram the voice of the singer began, 'It seems we stood and looked like this before, we looked at each other in the same old way, but I can't remember where or when'.

Pete found himself humming along to the music as he met and chatted with more old friends. When the hubbub had died down a bit

Pete went over to Bill and asked, "What's going on? Why are you all here?"

"We're on tonight," said Bill. "Briefing's in about ten minutes. I'm glad it all turned out all right for you. Sorry about your crew." He turned and called to one of his crew "Time we weren't here. Let's go!"

Within a few seconds all had gone out of the back door. As the last one left, someone came in to the hut and closed the door. It was the young airman. "Sir, Chiefy — I mean the flight sergeant — said be sure to sign the 700."

Pete knew what the 700 was. Every time they went on a flight the captain of the aircraft had to sign that he had noted the condition of the plane. "The 700" said Pete. "Where is it?"

"Over here sir." He walked over to a small table at the end of the hut near the door that Pete had entered by. The airman pointed to the table and said, "It's all there sir, you may leave when you've finished." He turned about, opened the door and quickly exited, closing the door behind him.

Pete looked down at the table. There was only one thing on it — the 700. At the top of the thin book was the number F700, the RAF designated number for the mechanical record of an aircraft. Also on the front was the type and serial number of that aircraft. This one read *NB 706 Lancaster Mk VI* — his old kite.

Pete flicked over the pages until he came to the Inspections page. After several entries there appeared in capital letters *AIRCRAFT WRITTEN OFF. ENEMY ACTION.* Underneath this a thick line had been drawn, and on the next line was an entry that, as he read it, caused Pete to tremble. It read, *Before the wreckage of NB 706 was removed I made a thorough re-examination of the rudder system. The cable controlling the starboard movement of the rudders was severed. It appeared that a cannon shell had penetrated the fuselage and partially severed the cable. The remaining few strands had been stretched until they broke from fatigue. This would have resulted in loss of control over the rudder. Signed Flt.Sgt. McVie.*

It took a few moments for this to sink in, but when it did Pete shouted "It was that damned cable! My foot didn't slip. I couldn't have stopped the Lanc from spinning in!" He took out his pen and signed his name under the 'Chiefy's'. He took a deep breath and strode towards the door where he stopped and turned to have a final look at the old hut. It looked as though it had been in a time warp. A few scrappy bits of paper pinned to the noticeboard, dust and dirt everywhere, a few rickety chairs. He passed his hand over his eyes and went out in to the sunlight.

When he reached the door of the entrance block Kate was just pushing the door open. "Oh there you are Pete. I hope I wasn't too long."

"No. No time at all." Just then they heard the roar of a Merlin engine starting up. "Come on old girl," said Pete, "let's go and look at the old Lanc." With that Pete took Kate's arm and started off at a brisk pace towards where they could hear the engines going.

"Here, steady on Pete, what about your knee!" Kate was looking down at his legs, curiously.

"What about my knee? I'm all right, come on!" That reminder about his knee made him conscious of the fact that since leaving that hut he had not felt any discomfort at all in his knee. He hesitated, fingered his knee and considered telling Kate of his experience of the preceding few minutes. He thought better of it, straightened up and strode off, saying to himself "She wouldn't believe me anyway."

The roar of the four Merlin engines increased, Pete felt a warm glow of nostalgia creeping over him. He gave Kate's arm a squeeze. "Come on, let's go and see the old crate that us lads used to go dicing in."

Skin Deep

Ralph put down the letter he had been reading and sat back in his chair musing over its contents. 'So they are coming over again this year,' he thought. 'How do they do it? It must cost hundreds of pounds for fares alone, then there's the accommodation for two or more weeks, and that's not cheap. Steve doesn't appear to have any business connections here so why come over every year?'

He had first met Steve during the war. They were on the same RAF station completing their aircrew training. Steve was one of numerous Australians who had volunteered for the Royal Australian Air Force and in 1943 he was finishing his final course before becoming operational.

Ralph and Steve hit it off from the start, so when at the end of the course they were given ten days' leave it seemed only natural that Ralph should invite Steve to stay for a few days at his parent's home, a small farmhouse in Oxfordshire.

The family consisted of Ralph, his parents, one brother and three sisters who were in the Women's Land Army and worked as hard as any of the men. All his sisters and brother were under twenty but Ralph was the eldest at twenty-four. A working family with no pretentiousness, they lived simply and without extravagance.

Of his three sisters Madge was the most lively and it was no wonder that within a few hours Steve was captivated by her, and by the end of Steve's stay they were engaged. A week later they were married by special licence. Ralph and Steve received their postings to different squadrons and they never met again during the war.

After the war Madge with her two-year-old son was one of hundreds of war brides who travelled to Australia to join their husbands. Steve, who had also returned to Australia, took up his former job with a large company but what his function was Ralph never knew.

Some thirteen years after they had settled in Melbourne, Steve, Madge and their two children — a girl had been born in Australia — made their first visit back to England by sea and spent most of their three-months stay at the farmhouse except for one week when Steve took his family off to St Albans where he was to recruit an agent for his company.

Two years later Madge and Steve came over to England again, and after visiting relatives they spent a week in London before returning home.

They followed this pattern almost every year, coming by air now instead of by sea, first spending some of the time with Ralph's brother Derek and his wife, and then a spell in London. On some visits they rented a cottage and spent most of the time by themselves except for having one or other of Ralph's sisters visit them.

On one trip to England Ralph learned that Steve's company was having some changes at the top. Steve was apparently the company secretary at this time and he was not happy with the changes. The company's share prices started to fall and had soon reached a level that could only be described as worthless. Steve said he was now semi-retired.

Now they were coming over again Ralph wondered how any company that had deteriorated so much could finance a visit to Britain by an executive who was semi-retired, and also what business activity had they still going on in London?

He read the letter again. Steve and Madge were arriving at the end of May, staying with Ralph's brother Derek for two weeks then a week in London.

Ralph's job as a schoolteacher kept him busy all the week and some weekends, but being a bachelor his spare time was his own. An idea was forming in his mind. He had the Whitsun break and probably two weekends before the visitors from Australia arrived, so he thought he would do a bit of investigating, but where to start? He reasoned that Australia House in London would be a good place to begin so he began by calling directory enquiries. He telephoned the number he had been given during his lunch hour.

The receptionist put his call through to the right department. "Good morning, can I help you?"

"I hope so" said Ralph. "A relative of mine is connected with the Melex Trading Company and I wonder if you have the company office address or telephone number here in England?"

"Just one moment sir." Ralph waited, then "Hello sir, yes we have a telephone number for the company secretary at St Albans 079384. No, I can't give you the address, you must phone them at St Albans for that."

"Thank you very much." Ralph replaced the phone. 'No time like the present,' he thought, 'so here goes.' He dialled the number.

Seven rings, eight, nine — "Melex Trading Company, who's

calling?" It was a lady's voice.

"Er, oh, hello, can I speak to the secretary please?"

"I am the secretary, how can I help you?"

"I was wondering if Mr Steve Wessell was there?"

"I'm afraid not, who wishes to know?"

"I'm a sort of relative and I thought he might be there, or coming there soon."

"He's in Australia at present but should be returning here in the near future."

"Do you know the exact date please?"

"I believe it will be early in June, that's all I know."

"I see. Well how do I get there?" Ralph was thinking furiously. "I mean, where exactly is Edinburgh Road?"

"You mean Acton Road don't you? Ring me nearer the time and I'll see if he will be available. Goodbye." She hung up.

As soon as he had put the phone down Ralph knew that he had made a mistake. True, he now knew more or less where the office was, but Steve would be curious as to what relative was enquiring for him, if the secretary told him of the phone call. Ralph decided not to pursue it for the time being but to see what transpired.

At the end of May Steve and Madge arrived from Australia and stayed for a few days with brother Derek and his wife Esme.

The day before they were due to go to London Madge was in the dining room of Derek's house waiting for Steve to come down to breakfast. Steve always took a long time over his ablutions so she never worried. This morning was no exception until she heard a terrific thump from upstairs. As Steve was the only person up there Madge ran to the stairs and called "Steve, Steve, are you all right?" There was no answer, so with her heart pounding Madge ran upstairs and rushed into the bedroom. Steve was lying in a heap by the dressing table. He was unconscious and looking very pale. Madge ran to the stairs and shouted "Derek! Derek! Come quickly!" Derek ran out of the kitchen, Madge shouted again "It's Steve. He's collapsed!"

Taking the stairs two at a time Derek reached the bedroom very rapidly and stooped down over Steve's inert form. "Pass me a hand mirror Madge" he said. Madge took the mirror from the dressing table and handed it to Derek who then held it in front of Steve's mouth. He peered at the mirror closely then said "He's breathing. Loosen his clothes and I'll get the doctor."

Half an hour later Steve was on his way to hospital in the ambulance accompanied by Madge and Derek.

After three hours there they returned. They could do no more by being there. Steve had had a heart attack and was in intensive care on a life-support machine. Derek took up the phone and started to call the other members of the family to tell them of Steve's condition.

It had been three days since Steve's heart attack, his condition was unchanged. Ralph had been saddened on hearing of Steve's illness, and also a little guilty at his suspicion of his brother-in-law.

So it was a complete surprise when he received a phone call from Madge. "I want to talk to someone, Ralph. Can you take me to see Steve then we can talk."

Ralph picked her up at Derek's house and they drove into town and to the hospital. In the single ward Steve lay motionless, his life held on the machine. All they could do was stand and look, so they soon left.

Once clear of the town Madge turned to her brother and said "Can you stop somewhere?"

Ralph pulled into the next lay-by and stopped. "Well, old thing, what's it all about?"

"I don't really know" answered Madge, "but I feel that there is something I ought to do. You see, every time we come over here we go to London for a few days. Once there, Steve leaves me for the first day and goes off somewhere. I don't know where he goes. Once, many years ago he took me to St Albans when he was to see an agent there, but I haven't been since." She paused.

"Well, what's worrying you?" asked Ralph.

"I feel there is something important he does each year and I worry about what will happen if he doesn't do it this year."

Ralph thought a moment then said, "Where do you suggest we begin?"

Madge had obviously been thinking about this for she answered quickly, "He has a briefcase in his luggage, so I think we should look in there, and I think we should check the agent in St Albans."

"Right" said Ralph, and started the car.

Back at Derek's they went up to Madge's room where she quickly unearthed the briefcase. There was a set of keys labelled *Melex Co. E.C.*, a cheque book for a bank in London, a passport, some credit cards, a small address book and a large key labelled *safe*. The only significant address to emerge from the address book was that of a Mrs Sutherland, 147 Acton Road, St Albans and the telephone number.

"I think we should see this Mrs Sutherland first, and then maybe the bank will be able to help with some information."

That afternoon Madge telephoned Mrs Sutherland to tell of Steve's illness and to arrange a visit next day. As it was a Sunday Ralph would be able to take her, but the visit to the bank would have to be Madge's responsibility.

They set off early on Sunday for the two-hour journey to St Albans. With the aid of Mrs Sutherland's directions they soon found the road and eventually knocked on the door of 147.

Mrs Sutherland was a neat motherly woman of about sixty years of age. She welcomed them into her sitting room and expressed her sorrow about poor Mr Wessell.

"Mrs Sutherland." Madge was starting the inquiry. "Can you tell us what Mr Wessell came to St Albans and London for? I was under the impression that Melex had all but finished trading in Britain."

Mrs Sutherland seemed perplexed. "I would have thought that as his wife you would know everything, but as you don't I suppose I'd better start at the beginning." She paused, then continued, "Mr Wessell appointed my husband as the Melex agent about fifteen years ago, 1959 or 1960 it was."

"That was when we first came to England," broke in Madge.

"Yes" went on Mrs Sutherland. "Melex also had a big warehouse somewhere in the East End, but I never went there. The first five years my husband John was very busy, then trade seemed to fall off for about two years. Suddenly my husband died. He was only fifty but it was his heart. That year Mr Wessell wrote to me to say please hang on and he would sort it all out when he next came to England, which he did. He told me he wanted me to keep the office going, that's our little dining room really. I was to open any letters and if it was a trading request I just had to type a note to say we were no longer trading. Any letters marked private were to go in the safe. It's an old iron safe with one big key, no combination. He said the salary would be £2,000 a year paid in a lump sum, cash. When I asked what about the warehouse he said he'd got rid of that and that to all intents and purposes this was the only Melex office in the UK."

She stopped, so Madge asked "And did he pay you each year?"

"Oh yes, every time he came over he paid me the £2,000 in £10 notes. I put it straight in the Post Office and drew out what I need."

"And what about the safe, is there anything valuable in there?" Madge asked.

"I don't think so, just a few papers and anything I put in there."

"May we look? We have to check that there is nothing urgent or important just in case."

Mrs Sutherland took them through to the dining room. There was a phone on a small desk, a few items of dining furniture and the safe on the floor in the corner.

Ralph crossed to the phone and looked at the number, it was the number he had been given by Australia House. "Do you have two phones?" Ralph asked.

"Yes, this is a separate line for the office. I have my own private

165

phone in the hall."

Madge opened the briefcase. "We have a key here marked *safe*, shall we try it?"

"By all means, it looks rather like the one I've got."

Madge put the key in the lock and opened the door. She motioned to Mrs Sutherland, "You take what you have put in and I'll look at what's left."

Mrs Sutherland took out a bundle of papers and envelopes. Madge peered in, then put in her hand and withdrew a package of mixed papers. She laid them on the table and started to sort them. There were three main items, a set of bank statements, some correspondence mainly from India and a bundle of printed matter. The recent statements showed a credit balance of £18,000 in a deposit account and £2,500 in a current account, both in a bank address in London.

The other papers were most interesting and surprising. There were various pamphlets asking for donations to a home for impoverished Indian orphans, plus several newspaper cuttings about the same project, and a full-length article from the *Rawalpindi Gazette*. One of the cuttings contained a photograph. It showed a group of about thirty Indian children around an officer wearing the Royal Australian Air Force uniform. It was Steve. The accompanying article described how Steve had discovered the orphanage when exploring Rawalpindi. He had been based at Chaklala quite near to the town, and on days off would go to help with children and take food and chocolates purchased out of his own pay. He did this for the whole of his two years in India, and promised to help them in some way after the war was over. The article was dated 1945. Madge turned the cutting over, there was one more cutting underneath. It was headed *"Return of Wartime Friend"*. It described how Mr Steve Wessell had revisited the orphanage and had engaged a lawyer to administer any funds Steve might raise to improve the conditions at the orphanage and was dated 1961.

She passed the cutting to Ralph and as he read it she said, "That was the year we didn't come to England, but Steve went on his own. He must have broken his journey and gone to Pakistan from Hong Kong."

Ralph frowned. "Didn't you have any ideas about this project of his?" he asked Madge.

"Absolutely nothing. There was no correspondence about it or I would have seen it when the post was delivered. I wonder what if anything, he is still doing for them?"

"Perhaps you will find out more when you see the bank manager" said Ralph. "I think we've got as much as we can from here."

Having replaced all the documents in the safe, they bade Mrs Sutherland goodbye and promised to keep in touch with her.

They drove back and Ralph dropped Madge off at Derek's. He said "You will have to pursue this on your own now as I have to be in school all the week."

"Yes, well it all depends how Steve is."

"Apropos that, if you haven't already done so I think you should phone Melbourne and let the managing director know about Steve."

"I have," she said.

That evening Madge went to the hospital. She managed to find the doctor, and in reply to her question he said, "Mr Wessell is no better, but also he is no worse, so we must all be patient and see if his constitution can overcome this traumatic upset."

Madge left the hospital with a heavy heart. She felt that her whole life had been changed, not only by Steve's illness but also by the discovery that he had another side to him that he had kept secret from her. Steve had always been careful with money almost to the point of meanness, yet here was a man who was blessed with a charitable nature and apparently revered by one group of people at least. This was a man she just did not know, a man though who deserved to be rewarded with a tranquil long life, not the dark unconsciousness of a failing heart.

Ralph too was feeling guilty. He had, he admitted to himself, harboured alien thoughts about what Steve might have been up to on his visits to England, had even thought that Steve might have been up to something illegal, yet in his heart he hadn't really doubted Steve's integrity. But there still remained the real mystery of what Steve was doing to help the orphanage in Rawalpindi. Where was the connection? Mrs Sutherland was not involved in that, she was only a voice on the end of a telephone. There were two possibilities, either the Melex management or the bank in London held the answer. Ralph fancied the bank, and it was with some impatience that he faced the week, unable to assist in the unravelling.

Two more days passed, Steve's condition was unchanged. Madge felt she could not just sit still and do nothing. She phoned the bank at the number on the statements and made an appointment to see the manager the following day.

It was only an hour on the train to Paddington, so by eleven o'clock the next day Madge's taxi had deposited her outside the bank.

She entered and was ushered into the manager's office immediately. Madge explained who she was. She produced Steve's passport to prove her association with him and then told him of Steve's illness.

"Right Mrs Wessell, I'm satisfied you are who you say you are, so how can I help you?"

"I would like to know has he any money other than that shown on the statements, and how does he get money into these accounts?"

"I am limited as to what information about a client I can impart, but I can tell you that what you see in the statements is what is in these accounts, except that —" Madge leaned forward as he paused. "Except that once a year a sum of money is paid into this account from a holding of stocks and shares."

"Stocks and shares?" Madge broke in. "I didn't know he had any at all."

"Well that's all I can tell you really. The odd thing is that almost immediately most of the money was withdrawn, the surplus going into the deposit account."

"Can you give me some idea of how much the income is?"

"I'll just say it is usually over £20,000 each year."

The bank manager seemed to imply that he had gone far enough so Madge made as if to leave. As she stood up she said, "There is a chance that my husband may not survive this heart attack. If that happens what do I do about all this?"

"Ah, I should have remembered" said the manager. "Mr Wessell left a copy of his will with the bank, and on the envelope it says that the original is held by his Melbourne solicitors, and that the managing director of Melex should be present at the reading of the will whether here or in Australia." He then motioned to Madge to sit down again. "I must mention this. In the event of a client's death nothing can be touched until probate is granted. Also, you may not have noticed that the accounts are in the title of Melex (Melbourne) Ltd. As company secretary your husband can deal with this account as he pleases, but if he should die you will not have any right to touch it, whatever the will says."

The full implication of the remark began to sink in. 'He has been using company money all the time,' she thought. 'God, what a mess.' She felt she could no longer cope with all this. How she wished Ralph was there. There was no more she could do, so she left the bank and took the next train back.

When she arrived at Derek's he met her at the door. "Thank God you're back! The hospital phoned, can you go right away." He added "I'll get the car out."

At the hospital the receptionist called a nurse who escorted Madge to the intensive care section.

A doctor was by the half open door. "Ah, Mrs Wessell, I'm afraid that Mr Wessell is showing signs of deterioration. He still has a fighting chance but I am not hopeful. Stay with him as long as you like."

He led her in. Steve lay there, the life-support paraphernalia all round him. Madge noted the pulsator showing Steve's weak heart response. She felt very depressed.

The doctor called to the nurse quietly, "Nurse, bring Mrs Wessell a cup of tea please."

Madge sat and looked.

Madge woke with a start. Where was she? What day is it? She looked at the bedside clock — six o'clock. 'Oh God. This must be a dream.' When had she left the hospital? Who brought her here? Slowly it all started to come back to her. Steve had gone! He'd gone without any movement whatsoever. Just that wretched pulsator going into a straight line. Surely that wasn't the end of it. Steve was just a straight line. That machine knew he was dead before she did. She was in a state of disbelief and getting worked up.

There was a knock at the door. "It's me, Esme." Derek's wife came in. "I thought you might be a bit restless. Here's a nice cup of tea." She put it on the table by the bed. "You just stay in bed, get up when it suits you. Remember what Ralph said last night, he will take care of everything, and if there is anything he's not sure of he'll ask you."

The morning went in a dream, then after lunch which she only picked at, Ralph arrived. "I've got the afternoon off and we'll start getting the arrangements made," he said. "We'll leave phoning Australia until tonight."

That evening he phoned Madge's son and daughter and it was decided that they had no need to come to England for the funeral. After that he phoned the managing director of Melex at his office in Melbourne. Ralph told him briefly why he was being requested to come to London. It concerned the company and Steve had asked it. He promised to be there the day after the funeral and he would go straight to the bank. Now he could phone the London bank manager and make an appointment for reading the will.

The days dragged along to the day of the funeral and Steve was laid to rest in the cemetery where Madge's parents had been buried. Madge's thoughts turned towards the next day when she would be going to the bank in London. 'Let there be no more trouble,' she thought.

At the bank the manager had brought in a solicitor to read the will and offer advice if required. The managing director had already arrived, so when Ralph and Madge went in the others were waiting. The bank manager took the envelope containing the will and handed it to the solicitor who opened it and started to read. The will itself was quite brief. He left everything to Madge apart from two small bequests to old friends of his.

Then the solicitor opened the other letter that was dated one year earlier, and read, *"I was brought up in a comfortable home with a* loving mother and father. I wanted for nothing and I had the promise of a good career. Then the war came. I volunteered for the RAAF and eventually qualified as a navigator. I went to England where I met Ralph and subsequently Madge who became my wife.

Life was blissful until I was posted to India. Whilst I was at Chaklala I went into Rawalpindi, and just by chance I happened upon a dusty compound with a wire fence round it. In this compound was a motley collection of urchins aged from about four years to twelve or so. They were in a pitiful state, rags hung on them, they were all dirty, and some of the younger ones had dried excreta on their legs. There must have been over thirty of them. I went round and found my way into a large shack on the other side of the compound. There was one big room, a small washroom with one tap, a lavatory that was filthy beyond belief and a cooking place where a middle-aged woman was preparing chapattis. The floor of the main room had several heaps of tattered blankets and other bits of material. These were the beds. As I stood there an elderly man came in and salaamed. He was the one in charge, and he spoke a little English. From him I learned that they were granted food and shelter by local government officials and nothing else was provided.

I started to visit them as regularly as I could during my time off. At first I took a few bars of chocolate and two old tennis balls. Then I took some bars of soap, a couple of tin washing bowls and some towelling, all very cheap from the bazaar. I bought rice and got the woman to increase their meal rations. I found the government official and persuaded him to get some palliasses for sleeping on. Not enough for everyone, but they shared anyway.

All the time I was in Chaklala I visited them and tried to improve their conditions, but the time came when the war ended and I was sent home for demobilisation. Madge came out to Melbourne and we started to make a life together. I progressed in my job and eventually became the company secretary. I was sent on a visit to England to set up an agent there and establish a warehouse. Bob Sutherland was the agent and the warehouse was in the East End. There was still a lot of bomb-damaged property about so I got the warehouse cheap, £18,000. Unfortunately the UK side of our business never really prospered so after a few years I was sent to London to get rid of the warehouse but to keep the agent for a while longer.

That year I travelled alone via Hong Kong and Delhi. Whilst on the flight from Hong Kong I suddenly thought I would break my journey and go to Rawalpindi. As Rawalpindi was now in Pakistan I had a few problems but eventually I got there and went round to the place where I had seen the orphaned children. It was still there, but there was a different man in charge. Conditions had not improved much, and it occurred to me that no one could feel any pride living in such a ramshackle hut and compound. What was needed was a new building and some basic equipment, and then after that extra amenities and clothing for the children. I was determined to do something, but how I did not know.

Then I had a stroke of luck. Outside the hotel where I was to stay that night was a young man, English, dressed in the outfit as adopted by the hippies who were beginning to tour India and Pakistan. He spoke to me first and apologised for accosting me, but he said he was in a pickle having used up all his money and had not the means to get to Delhi where there was a friend of his father's who would help him to get home to England. I asked him into the hotel and we went to the bar to get a cool drink. He told me his name was Charlie Southey, his passport was in order, he had a PhD degree, and was trying to get experience of life before getting down to work. An idea was forming in my mind. I asked him whether he would be in a hurry to get back to the UK if he had something to do in Rawalpindi. He supposed not, but what would keep him there? I outlined a plan. I would give him enough money to keep him there for a month. During that month he would get to know all about the orphanage and its administration. He was to sound out the officials to see if it was possible to organise some building work, and if there were any legal complications. To this latter end he would contact a lawyer for his advice. He would contact a local bank to see how funds could be transferred to Pakistan from any other country, but especially the UK and Australia. He would liaise fully with any officials who would be involved in any of the activities connected with the project. He would report to me either through Mrs Sutherland or to my office in Melbourne marked 'Personal'. He asked how long he had to make up his mind and I told him till the following morning. I then took him to the compound and showed him how I thought that a start could be made on the building. By the time I had finished explaining he had become enthusiastic and was ready to take it on there and then.

The next morning he came to the hotel where I gave him a comprehensive list of his programme, addresses and telephone numbers. I gave him some money and left him to it. He turned out to be a winner. I asked him to continue on a monthly basis. I kept him going with money from my salary, but my immediate concern was how to get further finance from other sources.

My second bit of luck was the sale of the warehouse. In Britain the construction industry was booming and land prices rocketing. When I put the warehouse and site on the market at no fixed price I was astounded to get an offer of a quarter of a million pounds. I am not a crook but I did think it would be easy to keep some of that for my *project, but then I thought of a better way. With the money from the sale I purchased stocks and shares to the full value in the name of our company. The dividends were paid into the bank annually, and annually I transferred the bulk of the dividends to the project being supervised by Charlie Southey. The balance was used to maintain the agent's office in St Albans. Every year I have sent an average of £20,000 to Charlie and he has made a tremendous success of the running of the orphanage. It has a wonderful new building with a dormitory and showers.*

Charlie found himself a job with one of the construction firms that were building the new capital city of Islamabad, a few miles from Rawalpindi, so he is independent of me now financially, but he administers the money I send, and there are plans for more buildings and amenities. The number of orphans never decreases.

The fact that you are reading this means that I have gone, so Charlie Southey will need to be given instructions. The capital in stocks and shares is intact. The surplus is in the two accounts at this London bank.

Judge me how you will, but my philosophy on charity is that the poorer people who work for charity do so because that is all they have to offer — themselves. The better off who have no time to give can best serve by giving some of what they have most of — money. Signed: Steve Wessell.

Madge was stunned by the revelations, how little she'd known him. She looked at the managing director. He was motionless, thinking. She looked at the bank manager.

He cleared his throat and looked towards the managing director. "It will be your decision. What do you want me to do?"

The managing director stood up, looked at Madge and said, "Let it stand."

Before he left, the managing director took Madge to one side saying, "Mrs Wessell, I presume you will be returning to Melbourne soon?"

"Yes, in about four days time" replied Madge.

"Well, this young man Charlie Southey. I feel he should be given this information personally. I wonder if you could break your journey at Delhi and go to Rawalpindi to see him and explain what has happened." He went on to say that the funds would continue more or less as before but it would not be direct from London but from the Melbourne office, and that as the dividends had been from shares owned by the company he would have to do it properly and allocate a set sum annually, but it could be less than what Steve had been sending.

Madge understood this and promised to convey the information to Charlie Southey.

At Rawalpindi five days later, Charlie Southey was waiting in the airport lounge. The flight was announced and he went to the barrier where the passengers would be coming. He had a large piece of white card with *MRS WESSELL* on it in block letters.

Very soon he spotted a fifty-year-old motherly woman walking straight towards him. "Mr Southey?" she queried

"Yes, Mrs Wessell, but please call me Charlie."

They were soon chatting warmly, and then took a taxi to the hotel where Madge would be staying overnight. Once there, they called for some tea and settled down to talk.

Madge learned that Steve had visited Charlie twice a year, so she supposed that he must have worked the trips in with the other business trips he frequently made.

When they had finally exhausted all the topics that concerned them, Charlie said, "Now, you must come to the orphanage and see what Steve started. You will not need to take gifts."

They went by taxi, and when they arrived Charlie took Madge through an imposing pair of gates into a large playground. They walked across to a group of white, cool-looking buildings. There they met the warden who conducted them round, finally ending up in the schoolroom.

As they entered, about twenty boys, all in white clothes stood up. The warden spoke to the boys and told them that this was the memsahib of the Wessell sahib who had been their benefactor. Their teacher had been notified of the visitors beforehand and this was his moment. He blew a note on a small pipe and the boys sang a song of friendship. They were obviously proud to be doing this and when they had finished Madge thanked the teacher and the boys.

Outside, Madge said "What a well organised place this is. You must have worked hard to achieve all this."

"Oh no. I organised it, that's true, but the only way this sort of thing can be achieved is with funds, lots of them, and we were lucky in having Steve find a way to provide most of it." He strolled a few more paces then said, "I did manage to interest several local organisations and I have now got a regular income from them for the orphanage, so the time is near when I shall not be needed any more, and neither will Steve's money."

"Well" said Madge, "when you think that time is due, why don't you come to Melbourne and tell Henry Morgan, the managing director, that he has no further obligations here. You can stay with us and have a nice holiday."

"I just might take you up on that" laughed Charlie.

The next afternoon Charlie took Madge to the airport and saw her off on her journey home.

On the flight Madge was going over the previous day in her mind. 'What a nice young man Charlie is. He would be an asset to any business, he's so likeable.'

Three months later Madge received a letter from Charlie saying that he would be coming to Melbourne the following month and would be able to stay for two weeks' vacation. He had wound-up the financial side of the charity and would be reporting to Melex Company when he came.

Madge wrote back immediately to say that he could stay the whole time with them, but he would be free to pursue his own interests.

Charlie duly arrived and Madge met him at the airport and took him straight to her home.

Charlie expressed amazement at the size of the house, and Madge said that now there were only two of them it would seem a bit large.

"Two of you?" queried Charlie. "Who else lives here then?"

"Why, my daughter Ellen of course, didn't you know?"

"No" said Charlie. "Well that is I thought you had two grown-up children, but I assumed they had left home."

"Dick has," said Madge, "but Ellen finds it convenient to work from here. She's twenty-four and quite independent."

That evening Charlie and Madge were sitting in the lounge having a cool drink. There was the sound of a car pulling up in the driveway and a moment later in rushed Ellen. She hardly stopped moving, breezed up to Charlie saying "Good day to you Charlie, how was the trip?"

Charlie, after several years in Pakistan was a bit overwhelmed by this boisterous approach. "Oh, it was fine thanks."

Madge broke in with "This is Ellen, my only daughter."

"What's for dinner Mum?" asked Ellen.

"Only a light meal, fish, salad and things. I'm just going to see to it."

"Want any help?"

"No. Stay and talk to Charlie. There was a dearth of young women where he's come from."

Left alone they soon got better acquainted, with Ellen doing most of the talking. It was noticeable though that she gradually began to listen instead of chattering, and she showed genuine interest in Charlie's tales.

The next day Charlie saw Mr Morgan at the Melex offices and gave him the full facts of the wind-down of the finances, and at the end of the recital Mr Morgan thanked him for his thoroughness and said that perhaps Charlie should think about staying in Australia where the outlook was promising. Charlie was non-committal, saying he hadn't had time to assess the prospects yet, but he liked what he had seen so far.

About ten days later Charlie and Madge were at home waiting for Ellen to arrive. When she came in, Charlie got her a drink, then he said, "You two ladies have been very kind to me during my short stay, and I really appreciate it. Now I have some news. Mr Morgan called me to his office today, and he has offered me a job here in Melbourne. The job will later involve going to the UK now and then because of the upturn in market trends in Europe. I have accepted."

The two women both jumped up and gave Charlie a hug. Ellen was ecstatic, "This calls for a celebration! I suggest we —"

"Here! Hold on a minute!" cried Charlie, "I'm the man about the house and I do know how to organise. So if you'll just settle down I'll tell you that I've booked a table for the three of us at the Trocadero for 9 p.m. There's a cabaret and dancing afterwards, so get out your glad rags and let's celebrate!"

The dinner was a great success as was the cabaret that followed. All the fun and the champagne made them all sparkle with enjoyment.

When the dancing started Madge said, "Now, I don't want you to think I'm a spoilsport, but I'm not one for doing much dancing, so I'm going to leave you two to have a bit more fun here. So, Charlie, if you'll get me a taxi I'll get on home."

They didn't argue with her. Ellen looked coyly at Charlie and said, "Go on Charlie, do what Mum asks."

In the taxi, Madge lay back in the seat, pulled her wrap round her and sighed, 'I think I've just got a son' she thought.